Cinderella's Secret Agent

INGRID WEAVER

SILHOUETTE® SENSATION™

First published in Great Britain 2002
Large Print edition 2006.
Silhouette Books Limited, Eton House,
18-24 Paradise Road, Richmond, Surrey, TW9 1SR

© Harlequin Books S.A. 2001

Special thanks and acknowledgement are given
to Ingrid Weaver for her contribution to
A Year of Loving Dangerously series.

ISBN 0 373 60339 8

Set in Times Roman 15¾ on 17 pt.
34-0206-73287

Printed and bound in Great Britain
by Antony Rowe Ltd, Chippenham, Wiltshire

Dear Reader,

I was eight years old when I fell in love with the dashing spies in The Man From UNCLE. That summer, I transformed our back porch into my own top-secret spy headquarters using cardboard, old curtains and plenty of imagination...but instead of an international terrorist, I only caught the milkman. My hopes of a career in espionage ended, yet I'm still a die-hard fan of every action hero, from James Bond to Dirk Pitt. I enjoy writing novels of romantic suspense, so naturally I was thrilled when Silhouette invited me to participate in Sensation's twelve-book series, A YEAR OF LOVING DANGEROUSLY.

When I began to write Maggie and Del's story in *Cinderella's Secret Agent*, I discovered an unexpected side of the danger and excitement of cloak-and-dagger work. Fantasising about falling in love with a secret agent is one thing, but just imagine the difficulties it would bring in reality. How on earth could a man who deals in deadly skulduggery hope to fit into the life of an ordinary woman? What happens when their two very different worlds collide?

I sincerely hope that you enjoy reading *Cinderella's Secret Agent* as much as I enjoyed writing it!

All the best,

Ingrid Weaver

To Deb and Kate, who know what
this book means to me.
May you live long and prosper.

Chapter 1

Agent Del Rogers was a hunter. For now his prey had eluded him, but a hunter has patience. He has self-control. And above all, a good hunter never takes the hunt personally.

Turning away from the hospital, Del forced his fists to relax. The reddened skin on the back of his hands twinged, and the patches on his arms where the hair had been singed off were beginning to itch, reminders of his last encounter with the man known as Simon. Yet Del had gotten off lightly compared to the agent he had just seen in the intensive care ward. The bomb in the warehouse last week had caught everyone off guard. The next meeting with Simon would be different. Next time, SPEAR would be ready.

He strode along the sidewalk, stretching his

legs to work out the lingering aches in his muscles. Out of habit, he scanned his surroundings,
yet he knew he wouldn't spot his quarry here.
Yellow cabs shouldered through the late afternoon traffic; car horns and sirens mingled with
the background hum of Manhattan. A warm puff
of air scented with yeast and oregano wafted
briefly from the doorway of a pizzeria before it
was swallowed by the pervasive metallic tang of
exhaust.

It was April. The hunt for Simon had been
going on for almost a year, but it was bound to
end soon. SPEAR was gradually closing the net.
The best operatives in the top-secret government
agency had taken their turn at running Simon to
ground. Despite the traitor's uncanny ability to
elude them, his hiding places were dwindling.
Now it was only a matter of time before he
walked into their trap.

On the corner beside the subway entrance, a
splash of color against the iron railing caught
Del's eye. A flower vendor was sitting on an
overturned bucket, hawking bunches of fresh daffodils. Del dug into his pocket and tossed a coin
to the weathered old man.

"Thanks, sport," the man muttered. He turned
the coin over in his grimy hand. "Hey, what is
this?"

"It's a double eagle."

"Ain't got change for that," he said, squinting at Del.

"Didn't think you would. The last time I had one of those coins was three years ago in Juneau."

As soon as Del said the prearranged code words, the flower seller shrugged and picked up a handful of daffodils. "You must have some hot date."

"Uh-huh." Del took the bouquet, running his fingertips over the stems until he felt the small plastic rectangle that was concealed there. He headed down the stairs to the subway, slipping the microcassette tape out of the flowers and into his pocket. He would have to wait until he met his partner, Bill Grimes, at the surveillance site before he could listen to the briefing on this tape. Like all the SPEAR briefing cassettes, it would erase as it played.

He was pulling the graveyard shift with Bill tonight. Del wasn't being given any consideration for his burns and bruises, and he wasn't asking for any. At this stage of the chase, every available operative was needed to insure Simon didn't slip away again.

The subway train squealed to a halt at Del's stop, jarring his swollen knee. He ignored the discomfort and blended into the crowd that spilled onto the street. He walked a block east, crossed Third Avenue, then paused in front of a shoe store, using the reflection in the glass to check out the passersby. Satisfied that he hadn't been followed, he glanced at the daffodils he still held. His lips quirked as he remembered the flower vendor's comment.

Being holed up in an apartment all night with Bill, staring through a sniper's scope, wasn't Del's idea of a hot date. And he was certain Bill wouldn't appreciate the flowers.

But Del knew someone who would. He lifted his head, his gaze going to the coffee shop on the other side of the street. Maggie was the kind of woman who would love flowers. She would be thrilled to get these daffodils. He could picture how she would smile and stick them in a sundae glass and chatter about how yellow is such a happy color....

No. A bouquet of flowers could carry a message in more than one way. And Del couldn't afford to give any woman the wrong message, especially a woman like Maggie. She deserved better than that. Life hadn't dealt her a good hand, yet she was making the best of it, facing her problems with a good-natured determination that he had to admire.

If things had been different, if he had known her eight years ago, he might have considered giving her more than just a bouquet.

Del wavered for an instant, then tossed the daffodils into a trash can and crossed the street.

"Hey, Maggie. Your cowboy's here again."

Maggie Rice stood on her toes to peer through the round window in the swinging door. From here she had a good view of the coffee shop and the patron who had just sat down. Although his back was toward her, she recognized him instantly, doubtless due to the sudden thump of her pulse.

Clearing her throat, Maggie smoothed her apron over the front of her maternity dress. "Wrong on both counts, Joanne," she said. "He's not mine, and he's no cowboy. Do you see boots or a Stetson anywhere? And have you ever heard even a trace of a drawl?"

"Guys like that don't need the props." Joanne Herbert chewed her bubble gum noisily, blew a bubble and popped it against the roof of her mouth. "The cowboy thing is part of his aura."

Maggie knew exactly what Joanne meant. Of average height and average build, in his neatly pressed khakis and his polo shirt, Del sure didn't resemble the Marlboro Man. Yet there was something so essentially, well, male about him. He moved with the easy self-confidence of a lone wolf, his body loose, his gaze always alert, as if he were some legendary gunslinger, scanning the horizon for his next target.

Oh, Lord. The pregnancy must be affecting her brain. Del? A gunslinger? He was a nice guy, probably one of the last ones left in New York.

"And he is, too, yours," Joanne went on.

"Oh, get real," Maggie said, rolling her eyes. "No man's going to give me a second glance, even if I was interested. Which I'm not. Alan cured me of that. And right now it would be absolutely ludicrous to even think about—"

"Why, Maggie, I meant he's your customer, that's all. He's sitting at your table, isn't he? What on earth did you think I meant?" Joanne chuckled. "But come to think of it, it is kind of a karmic coincidence that he always manages to show up on your shifts."

Maggie groaned. "Don't you have a mantra to chant or some coffee to spill?"

"Nah, I already did that. But now that you reminded me, I do have some buns to burn." Joanne pressed her cheek alongside Maggie's to look through the window. "Mmm, speaking of great buns…"

Maggie bumped her friend with her hip.

''Joanne, behave yourself. If you keep drooling like that I'll have to get out the mop. Wet floors can be hazardous.''

''He looks…hungry.''

''Well, duh. Why else would he be here?''

''Besides drumming up business for us by making everyone's mouth water?''

''If you like him so much, why don't *you* serve him?''

''He's sitting at your table,'' Joanne said smugly. ''Besides, I know for a fact it would hurt Laszlo's feelings if I ran off to a rodeo with Mel here.''

''His name's Del, not Mel,'' Maggie said.

''With those looks, anyone could get confused.''

No, Joanne was wrong, Maggie thought. Del's looks couldn't be confused with anyone else's. With his hawklike nose and his striking amber eyes, he was a one of a kind. He wasn't handsome in a classic movie star or magazine model sort of way, but he was…appealing. Yes, that was a good word for it. Yet unlike most attractive men, he seemed oblivious to his appearance. As a matter of fact, his short-clipped hair and casual, nondescript clothes weren't meant to draw attention.

But he drew hers. Oh, yes. No matter what

shape the rest of her was in, her eyes were functioning just fine. She felt a blush rising in her cheeks and sighed. Was this what she had been reduced to? Lurking behind a door in order to ogle a customer?

He was most likely married anyway. She seemed to have a knack for finding the ones who were married. But it didn't make any difference. Considering her condition, ogling anyone was worse than ludicrous, it was downright gross.

"Uh, Maggie?"

"Mmm?"

Joanne squeaked a fingertip across the round windowpane in the door. "You better get to work, girl. You're fogging up the glass."

Maggie sputtered and turned to make a retort, but Joanne was quicker. Grabbing Maggie by the shoulders, she gave her a gentle shove. The door swung open and Maggie stumbled into the coffee shop with all the grace of an elephant in a tutu.

Laszlo looked up from the grill, his broad forehead creasing in a frown. "Maggie, you okay?"

"Sure. Thanks." She made an exaggerated show of grabbing the edge of the lunch counter for balance, then grinned. "It's no wonder I keep tripping over my feet. I haven't seen them for months so sometimes I forget they're there."

He shook his head as he gestured with his

spatula. "You shouldn't be working," he growled in his thick Hungarian accent. "You should be home."

"What? And give up all this? I plan to put the baby through college on the tips I've been getting lately."

The ends of Laszlo's drooping mustache dipped farther. "You're the stubborn woman, Maggie Rice. Five days, that is all. Then I don't want to see more of you until after the kid is born."

"More? Now there's a scary thought. Any more of me and I won't fit through the front door anyway." Maggie gave him a cheeky wink and picked up her order pad.

Five days, and then she would stay home. In spite of what she'd just told her boss, she was looking forward to the time off. As much as she needed the money this job brought, she had a million things still to do to get the apartment ready and less than a month to go.

"Hello, Maggie. How are you and Junior today?"

She pulled her pencil from behind her ear as she stopped in front of Del's table. As always, his rich voice set off an odd reaction deep inside. It was his tone, so steady and calm and masculine—

Get real, she admonished herself. Sure, he was a nice guy, and they had shared many casual conversations over the weeks since he'd started coming in. Yet she didn't know all that much about him, other than he liked his eggs over easy and his coffee black and seemed to have a schedule that coincided with hers. There was no reason for her pulse to flutter whenever she saw him.

Actually, it wasn't only her pulse that felt fluttery now. Her entire body was...restless. Yes, that's how she would describe it. She had been having tremors and tingles all day. She focused on her order pad, hoping the strange feeling in her lower stomach would pass. "We couldn't be better. She had the hiccups this morning, but she settled down when I changed the radio station. She hates rap."

"She?" Del repeated. "So you think the baby's a girl today?"

"It's just a feeling I have. It really doesn't matter one way or the other."

"Have you settled on any names yet, Maggie?"

"Not yet. I want to wait until I see my baby's face before I decide." She touched her fingertips to the bulge that pushed at the front of her dress. "Oh, it's going to be so good to finally hold her in my arms."

A pair of customers squeezed past on their way out. Del shifted his chair. "Tan sandals."

Puzzled at the change in conversation, she glanced up. "Excuse me?"

Tiny laugh lines crinkled the corners of his eyes. "On your feet. You claimed you haven't seen them lately, so I thought I'd bring you up to date."

He had a wonderful smile, she thought. He didn't flash it all that often, but when he did it added a hint of boyish charm to the cowboy toughness of his face. "Thanks," she said.

"How did you manage to paint your toenails pink?"

"Would you believe a mirror and a brush with a very long handle?" She moved her hand from her stomach to the small of her back. The ache that had started building there this morning was getting worse—she must have strained a muscle somehow. "I could have skipped the polish, though. If the fashion police haven't brought me in by now for this tent I'm wearing, I doubt if they'll notice my toes. Heck, I can't even see them." She winced.

His gaze sharpened. "What's wrong?"

"Nothing. I'm fine."

"Maggie…"

"Really, Del. Aches and twinges are perfectly

normal when a person's carrying around this kind of weight. Want your usual?''

''I'll settle for a coffee.'' He glanced around. ''The place isn't that busy yet. Why don't you take a break?''

''Can't. Laszlo will fry me and put me in a burger.''

''I heard that!'' the cook called.

She lowered her voice to a stage whisper. ''He hates it when I give away his secret recipes.''

''How bad is the twinge in your back?'' Del persisted.

''On a scale of pinprick to root canal, it's a stubbed toe. Relax,'' she said, lifting her arm to tuck her pencil behind her ear. ''I'm healthy as a—'' She sucked in her breath. The pencil dropped to the floor. ''Oh!''

''Maggie? What is it?''

''My back,'' she said through her teeth. The pain took her by surprise, clutching at her spine and radiating to her belly.

Del surged to his feet and came around the table. ''You'd better sit down,'' he said, taking her arm.

She ignored the suggestion but she did lean into his support as the wave of agony gradually ebbed. Shaken, she exhaled hard and gave him a wobbly smile. ''No, I'm fine. It's gone now.''

Del looked carefully into her face. He didn't release his hold on her arm. Instead he guided her to the nearest chair and gently helped her to sit. ''What's your doctor's number, Maggie?''

''Please don't make a big deal out of this,'' she said, attempting to get up. ''I shouldn't have painted my toenails, that's all.''

Del stopped her from rising by placing his hands on her shoulders. There was no humor in his amber gaze, only concern. ''If it's only a strained muscle, the pain won't come back if you don't move. We'll just wait here for a few minutes and see what happens, okay?''

''Oh, for heaven's sake,'' she said. ''My due date's weeks away, so I'm not about to give birth or anything.''

Taking the chair across from her, Del directed a look toward Laszlo. ''Maggie's taking a break.'' Although he didn't raise his voice, his tone was that of a man accustomed to giving orders. And unlike Maggie, no one else argued with him.

Joanne bustled forward and plunked a glass of water on the table for Maggie, leaning over to feel her forehead. ''Are you sure you're okay, hon? I can cover for you if you want to leave early.''

The caring in her friend's gaze unexpectedly

brought the heat of tears to Maggie's eyes. She blinked hard. God, the pregnancy hormones were making a mess of her emotions. "Thanks, but I'll be fine. Really."

And she would. Yes, indeed. Things could be so much worse. She had her friends. She had this job, at least for the next few days, and she had a home. And most important, in less than a month, she was going to have a child.

A child. A baby to love. Sometimes the wonder of it took her breath away.

"It won't be long now."

At Del's softly spoken comment, Maggie smiled. He must have guessed the direction of her thoughts. "Spring is such a perfect time to have a baby, don't you think?" she asked.

"What makes you say that?"

"Spring is when nature renews itself after the winter. The tulips are blooming, the cherry trees are blossoming, birds are returning to build their nests."

"I see what you mean. It's like an affirmation of life."

"Exactly." She beamed. "It's my favorite season. Do you have any kids, Del?"

He hesitated. For an instant, a shadow of something dark flickered over his expression.

Oh, God. What was wrong with her? She

shouldn't have asked him such a personal question. Sure, they were on a first-name basis, but that was because she didn't know his last name. Just because he'd been eating here regularly for almost two months didn't mean she had the right to pry into his personal life. "Sorry, I shouldn't—"

"No," he answered finally. "I don't have any kids. I've never been married."

"Oh." She shifted uncomfortably. The ache was building in her back again.

"My sister has half a dozen, though."

She pressed her palm over her breasts. She seemed to have trouble taking a deep breath. "Really?"

"Uh-huh. The last two were twins. They keep her and her husband busy."

"I can imagine. Wow. What a lucky woman your sister is. I'd love to have a whole houseful someday...*oh!*"

Del caught her hands. He might have said something, but Maggie couldn't hear it over the rush of her pulse in her ears. She gripped his fingers, thankful for someone to hang on to as the wave crashed into the small of her back and stretched around to her stomach again.

It was harder than the other one, and it lasted longer. By the time it receded, Maggie could feel beads of sweat dampening her temples. She panted to catch her breath. "Whoa," she muttered. "Did you see anyone behind me? Feels like someone smacked me in the back with a baseball bat. Heck, where's a cop when you need one?"

Del's face was so close she could see flecks of gold in his amber eyes. He looked at her carefully. "Maggie, I don't believe that was a muscle ache from painting your toenails."

"Could have been from moving the furniture. The crib was delivered yesterday, and I had to rearrange some things to make room for—"

"Maggie, I think you're in labor."

She released his hands and grabbed the front of his shirt. "I can't be. I still have three weeks to go. There are too many things I have to do. The apartment's a mess. I haven't even set up the crib and I didn't get to the laundry and—"

"Everything else can wait. I suspect this baby won't."

"But it's too early."

"You need to get to a hospital."

"It's just a false alarm. They talked about that in the prenatal classes. Mild contractions are perfectly normal in the last trimester, so there's no point rushing anywhere until I'm sure—" She felt a distinct pop deep inside. Seconds later, warm fluid gushed between her thighs. She dipped her head, watching in disbelief as the liquid ran down her leg to form a clear puddle around her sandals. "Oh, my," she whispered.

Crockery hit the floor nearby in a teeth-rattling crash. Joanne rushed to her side. "Maggie! Oh, my God! Is that…"

"I think my water just broke."

"Oh, my *God!* Laszlo!" Joanne screamed. "She's having the baby!"

"No. She can't. This is the restaurant. Maggie, you can't have baby here."

The other customers in the coffee shop, alerted by the commotion, turned their heads to get a better look. Conversation halted briefly, then recommenced with an excited babble.

Joanne spun around, wringing her hands. "Oh, my God, oh, my God. What do we do?"

Maggie couldn't reply. Another contraction caught her in a vise, turning her abdomen to steel. She moaned, tightening her hold on Del's shirt. One of his buttons flew off and hit the floor.

"Laszlo, call nine one one," Del ordered. "Now."

It seemed to last forever. The world shrank behind a red haze as her entire body seized. Maggie tasted a moment of panic. This was no false alarm. It was happening. It really was happening.

She was going to have the baby.

The panic retreated as quickly as it had arisen. What was she afraid of? This is what she wanted. The months of waiting were over. Everything she had gone through—the heartache of Alan's desertion, the struggle to stretch her budget, the discomfort of this pregnancy—all of it faded to insignificance at the enormity of what was taking place.

She was going to have the baby.
Now.

Tears were streaming down her cheeks as the contraction retreated. They could have been from the pain, but they also could have been from the joy. A child to love, her own little family of two. It blew her away.

Del wiped her cheeks with his knuckles. "It'll be all right, Maggie. Don't be afraid. Everything will be fine."

"I'm not afraid." She grinned, licking the tears from the corners of her mouth. "How could I be afraid? My God, Del! I'm having a baby. *My* baby. Isn't that the most fabulous thing in the world?"

The room in the back of the diner was crammed with boxes of surplus supplies and a battered metal desk where Laszlo did his book-keeping. It was dim and stuffy, but at least it was private. Del knelt beside Maggie as she lay on the makeshift mattress he'd fashioned out of a flattened cardboard box and layers of towels. Slipping his arm beneath her back, he propped her head and shoulders up on the cushion he'd ripped from Laszlo's chair. "How's this?"

"Better," she said. "Thanks. This is really nice of you, Del. Laszlo and Joanne looked so upset, I'm glad you thought of...bringing me back...here...oh!"

"Maggie?"

She inhaled sharply, her face flushing red. "Uh. Here...comes...another one."

Del caught her hand, breathing with her as she worked her way through the contraction. Where the hell was that ambulance? The pains were coming fast and hard now, three minutes apart and more than a full minute long. Beneath the thin fabric of Maggie's maternity dress, her abdomen was clenching into the shape of a loaf. The standard SPEAR first-aid training didn't include any obstetrics, and this situation was a far cry from the calvings Del had witnessed on his parents' farm, but he was fairly certain the baby's birth was imminent.

He glanced at the clock on the wall as the contraction finally eased. Longer than the last one.

Damn. "The paramedics should be here any minute."

"She's as impatient as I am," Maggie said.

Del rubbed his palm lightly over her taut abdomen and shifted his gaze to her face. "I think you're right about that."

"My baby. She must know how much I want to see her." She exhaled shakily and smiled.

Del barely saw the way Maggie's dark blond hair was plastered to her forehead, or how her features tightened from the agony her body was going through. Her smile was so radiant, it eclipsed everything else.

The smile turned to a bared-teeth grimace as she rode out another pain. Del did what he could to help her through the next contraction, and each one after that, encouraging her to breathe while her body worked and then using conversation to distract her during the brief respites.

Yet he didn't have to do all that much—she was a marvel of courage. He had known seasoned agents who couldn't handle pain as well as Maggie Rice. This woman was refusing to let anything dampen her spirit.

But that didn't really surprise him. He'd been admiring Maggie's spirit since the first time he'd seen her. She always had a warm smile and a pleasant word for everyone. Open, caring and genuinely kind, she was a sharp contrast to the world he inhabited.

That was why he felt so drawn to her. He'd started coming to the coffee shop because it was convenient, situated only a few blocks from the surveillance site he and Bill were working. It hadn't taken him long to learn the details of the pregnant waitress's predicament. She'd been seduced and abandoned by a married man. Hers was a hard luck story that could have turned any other woman bitter.

Yet there was nothing bitter about Maggie. She never failed to make a special fuss over any children who happened to come into the restaurant, and on more than one occasion Del had seen her slip an extra sandwich to a customer who looked down-and-out. The camaraderie she shared with the rest of the staff was more typical of a small town than a big city. And there had even been times when she'd brought in flowers to put in the little juice glasses to brighten up the tables.

She would have liked those daffodils. But he couldn't give her the wrong idea. He couldn't get close to her or get involved in her life. Because of his job…

Oh, hell. It was too late to think about that now. He was already involved up to his elbows.

If the ambulance didn't arrive in the next five minutes—

"Del!" Maggie cried, her eyes widening.

He checked the clock. The last contraction had scarcely finished and already her body was being contorted by another one. "Hang on," he urged. "The paramedics are on their way."

"I can...feel...something..." Her words ended in a groan.

"Maggie?"

She clutched his hand hard enough for her short nails to draw blood. "Something's happening."

Until now, he'd endeavored to let her preserve some modesty, but the distress in her voice told him this wasn't the time to worry about the niceties. He pried her fingers loose from his hand and lifted the hem of her dress past her hips.

One look and he realized the birth wasn't merely imminent, it was already in progress.

There would be no help from that other waitress, Joanne. She had turned green merely at the sight of Maggie's water breaking. The cook was almost as bad. And Del wasn't going to trust Maggie to some stranger in the restaurant. Ignoring the fact that he was essentially a stranger, he positioned himself between her feet.

Maggie felt as if her body were being ripped

open with each successive contraction, but she kept her lips pressed tightly together to keep the scream inside. She didn't want her scream to be the first sound her baby heard. She wanted her child to know she was loved and welcomed and cherished...but oh, *God,* she couldn't endure this much longer....

"I can see the head," Del said. "You're right. Your baby is as impatient as you are."

She felt Del's hands on her thighs, gently easing her legs apart. She didn't care that she barely knew him—it didn't enter her mind. Modesty was irrelevant. She was running on instinct. "You can see her?" she gasped.

"Yes."

"Oh, God. I want to see her, too."

"Just keep on doing what you're doing. You'll get there."

The urge to push was overwhelming. Maggie held her breath, giving in to the command of her body. Time shrank to a bright pinpoint. Dimly she was aware of Del's calm encouragement, the warm touch of his hands, the strength he was giving her just by his presence...but all of her thoughts, her energy, her being, were focused on the task nature had given her.

"That's it, Maggie," Del murmured. "A little more, just a little more."

She didn't know how long it lasted. She lost track of everything outside the intimate connection between her and the man she was trusting to deliver her baby. Gradually, her body no longer seemed to be fighting her. Every muscle was working, straining, tightening, pushing...until suddenly, just when she thought she would tear in half, the pressure eased.

And the room was filled with the most glorious sound Maggie had heard in her life. It was the tiny, tremulous wail of her newborn child.

Exhausted, drenched in sweat, Maggie somehow found the strength to lift her head.

Del was kneeling between her legs, his large hands carefully cradling a beautiful, wrinkled, red-faced, squirming miracle. "It's a girl," he said, his voice hushed. His gaze met hers, his amber eyes unabashedly moist. "Congratulations, Maggie. You have a daughter."

Chapter 2

" 'They also serve who only stand and wait,' " Bill Grimes intoned. With his bald head and habitually benign expression, he could have passed for an absentminded English professor, an image Bill deliberately played on with the pipe he held between his teeth and his penchant for issuing quotations.

Del shut off the tape player and ejected the cassette. It was barely past midnight and Bill was already into Milton. This was going to be a long night. "I hate to admit it, but that about sums things up."

Bill grunted and adjusted the focus on the telescope he was using. The adjustment wasn't really necessary—the instrument was already carefully positioned on a tripod and calibrated for the optimum range—but it gave him the impression that he was doing something.

Del understood his partner's state of mind all too well. Still, good hunters had patience, and they were going to need a lot of it. The briefing tape he and Bill had just listened to had come directly from Jonah, the head of SPEAR, so they knew it was the best information possible. The situation was essentially the way Del had figured it: Simon had gone underground, but he was running out of places to hide. That's why Del, Bill and the rest of the surveillance team would have to stay where they were. Stand and wait.

Del looked around at the forest of equipment that crammed the small apartment. Bill's telescope was about the lowest-tech piece here. The steel shelf by the back wall held night vision binoculars, infrared detectors, cameras, weapons and body armor. Two video cameras and a parabolic microphone were hooked up to a bank of recording equipment, all of it focused on the window of the apartment across the courtyard.

A studio apartment identical in design to this one, the place hadn't undergone any major renovations in years. Apart from a countertop fridge and a range in the tiny kitchen, and half a dozen folding chairs, it was unfurnished. There was little to recommend it to a potential tenant...other than the location. Situated in midtown Manhattan near the East River, it happened to have an excellent view of one of New York's most famous landmarks: the shimmering glass cereal-box-shaped structure that housed the headquarters of the United Nations.

Weeks ago SPEAR intelligence had learned that particular apartment across the courtyard had been rented for Simon's use. What they didn't yet know was why.

It had to have something to do with the proximity to the UN, that much was obvious. But why? Was Simon's next target some diplomat or politician? Was he going to use the apartment's vantage point to coordinate an assault or hide a sniper? Until now, all Simon's schemes had been aimed at destroying SPEAR itself. Had he changed his tactics?

Del rubbed his face wearily. There were too many questions. With luck, this surveillance would bring them some of the answers.

"By the way, what happened to your hands?" Bill asked without lifting his head. "I hadn't thought those burns were so deep."

Del focused on his hands. To his surprise, he noticed the healing pink skin behind his knuckles was marred by crescent-shaped gouges in several places, deep enough to be noticeable even in the dim light that filtered through the window.

He felt a moment's confusion before understanding dawned. The marks were from Maggie's fingernails. She must have done it when she'd been holding on to him during those contractions.

Immediately, the simmering frustration of his hunt for Simon faded. Despite the state-of-the-art equipment that surrounded him and the grim reality of his job here, Del felt an echo of Maggie's presence. Her warmth, her twinkling good nature seemed to brighten the stark apartment.

It was such an unlikely juxtaposition. Only a few hours ago he had shared in the most basic event in life, the birth of a child. Now here he was immersed in the complex business of international terrorism. His world and Maggie's world couldn't get much further apart than that.

"Those cuts aren't from the explosion," he said. One corner of his mouth quirked upward in a half smile. "They have nothing to do with Simon. They're from something else entirely."

"Something else? Like what?"

"Do you remember that short blond waitress who works in the diner on the next block?"

"The diner that Polish guy runs?"

"Hungarian. Laszlo's place."

"Blond waitress," Bill said, frowning into the

eyepiece. "You don't mean the one that's pregnant, do you?"

"Yeah. Maggie."

"I didn't know you went in for pregnant women."

"It's not like that."

"Isn't it? You've been eating there practically every day since we started this gig. What happened? Didn't she like the tip you left her?"

"She had her baby tonight."

Now Bill did lift his head, peering at Del over the telescope. "You're kidding."

"She went into labor right there at the coffee shop. She held my hand during the contractions. I doubt if she realized how hard she was gripping."

"So you were there?"

"That's right."

"Geez, what a place to have that happen. The ambulance would have needed to use the sidewalk to get through the traffic."

"The ambulance got there too late. I delivered the baby."

"Holy—" Bill removed his pipe and pointed the stem toward Del. "*You* delivered a baby?"

"Yes. It was a girl." He paused. "She has blond hair and blue eyes just like her mother."

"Are they all right?"

"They're both doing fine."

"Good God, what do you know about delivering babies?"

"There wasn't that much I needed to know. It was Maggie who did the work. All I really did was catch." He thought about the look of sheer wonder that had lit up Maggie's face when she'd gazed at her daughter for the first time. He cleared his throat, surprised at the sudden thickness he felt there. "Bill, it was incredible."

"If you say so."

"I was the first person to touch that child. She took her first breath while I held her in my hands." He turned his palms upward. "I actually saw the exact moment when she filled her lungs with air."

"And you said she's all right? She's healthy?"

"That's what the paramedics said. She has all her fingers and toes. And she's not too small, either. She felt like she weighs about the same as a nine-millimeter Colt submachine gun with a thirty-two round clip." He smiled with satisfaction. "That would put her at over six pounds. Not bad for a few weeks early."

Bill shook his head. "I just can't believe this."

"Did I mention her eyes were blue? She looked right at me, and her eyes hardly crossed at all."

"Maggie?"

"The baby. That's pretty smart for a newborn. She's going to be a bright kid."

"Listen to yourself," Bill said, chuckling. "This really got to you, didn't it?"

"It was an experience I'll never forget. I felt...privileged to be there."

"Privileged? I would have been scared spitless."

That made Del laugh. Bill might look like a harmless middle-aged professor, but he was as stolidly fearless as a bulletproof vest. Del couldn't think of anyone else he'd rather have covering his back in a tight situation. "Yeah, right."

"You think I jest?" Bill asked. "I'd rather juggle six pounds of Semtex with a nitro fuse than take on an infant."

"You'd like this infant," Del said. "She's a feisty little thing, just like her mother."

"Spoken just like a proud papa." Still chuckling, Bill put his pipe in his mouth and returned to the telescope.

The shaft of pain took Del off guard. Papa? No, not him. Holding Maggie's child would be as close as he would ever get to that. His grin faded.

"And speaking of the papa, where is the bastard?" Bill asked.

"From what I heard around the coffee shop, Maggie hasn't seen him since last Christmas."

"She's going after him for child support, isn't she?"

"Not that I know of. She seems determined to manage on her own."

"Poor kid. She's going to have a rough time, raising that baby by herself."

That was true. Maggie had been working double shifts in order to save up money for the baby. It was going to be a struggle for her to cope. Ideally, a child should have two parents, a mother and a father, a team.

Maggie was intelligent enough to be aware of the problems she faced. Her persistent good humor wasn't from ignorance of what lay ahead, it was from determination to make the best of it. She was a remarkable woman.

Scowling, Del went over to pick up the metal case he'd left on the equipment shelf. There was no point dwelling on Maggie. He had already gotten more involved in her life than he should have. And he shouldn't let himself get carried away by those feelings her baby had stirred. He'd left all that behind when he'd joined SPEAR.

He opened the case and gazed at the gleaming

pieces of wood and metal that were nestled in the pockets of foam rubber. With an ease of motion that was as practiced as breathing, Del assembled the components into his custom-made sniper's rifle. When it was done, he held the weapon in his hands, his fingers fitting themselves around the familiar shape.

Like all the other operatives in the top-secret government agency of SPEAR, he accepted whatever assignment he was given and went wherever he was posted. It made no difference whether it was deep infiltration or simple surveillance, he did his job. But his specialty, the real talent that had brought him to the attention of SPEAR in the first place, was his uncanny ability with a rifle. He was the agency's best sharpshooter, the one they called in for the impossible shot.

This was who he was, Del thought. This was what he did. He was proud of his skill. With this rifle and the right setup, he could shoot the weapon out of a terrorist's hand or disable any getaway vehicle. He knew all the vulnerable spots on everything from a Learjet to a so-called bulletproof limo, and for those special occasions when no other option was open to him, he knew, too, within a millimeter how closely a bullet had to graze a man's skull in order to knock him out.

He had a perfect record—in his eight years with the agency, he hadn't taken a single life.

Yet even as he felt the familiar weight of the rifle in his hands, he remembered how these same hands had cradled Maggie's baby. Instead of smooth wood and cold metal, he felt the slippery, shaved-velvet softness of the newborn's skin. And as he settled himself at his post to one side of the window, his mind kept returning to the back room of the diner and the sight of Maggie's tears as he'd placed her daughter in her arms.

His presence at the birth had been nothing but a fluke. He shouldn't want to see them again, or worry about how they were doing, or wonder how Maggie was going to manage on her own. He had no business thinking about either Maggie or her baby.

That's what he told himself, anyway. Yet over the next few hours, he failed to get his thoughts of her out of his head.

After what he and Maggie had shared, how could he shrug the whole thing off and go on as if nothing had happened? That's what the baby's father had done, turning his back on Maggie at the time she needed him most. Granted, it wouldn't be wise for Del to get further involved, but it was only natural for him to feel a certain amount of responsibility for Maggie and her baby's welfare.

It wouldn't do any harm to check on them. That would be the decent thing to do, wouldn't it?

"'Tomorrow and tomorrow and tomorrow, creeps in this petty pace.'"

At Bill's murmured comment, Del swallowed a sigh.

From Milton to Shakespeare's *Macbeth*? It was going to be a long night.

Maggie ran her index finger over the back of her baby's hand, marveling yet again at the tiny perfection of her daughter. Perfect little nails, perfect pink dimpled knuckles, absolutely perfect. Not even one day old, yet already her presence filled the room. Heck, more than the room, it filled Maggie's entire life.

"I love you, sweetheart," she whispered, moving her hand to the baby's head. She ran her fingertips over the wispy blond curls, inhaling deeply as she absorbed the warm, fresh baby scent that rose from her scalp. "I love you so much. Every day, for the rest of my life, I want you to know that."

The baby's mouth pursed in her sleep. Maggie didn't even consider putting her down in the plastic-sided bassinet that rested beside the hospital bed. After those long months of anticipation, she didn't want to squander one minute of the chance to hold her baby in her arms.

For what had to be the hundredth time that day, Maggie felt her eyes brim with tears. Had she thought the mood swings of pregnancy were bad? Now her body was bubbling with postpartum hormones. All she had to do was look at her child and the happiness simply overflowed.

"My child," she said, marveling at the way the word tasted on her tongue. She'd had months to prepare for this, but she was still trying to wrap her mind around the concept. Nothing she had read or heard could possibly have prepared her for this feeling that was growing in her heart.

Maternal love was no myth. Her child was no longer connected physically to her, but another, far stronger bond had already formed. It was an emotional tie that no doctor's shears could cut.

Loving Alan had been a mistake. She had been seduced by his smooth talk and clever hands and her own dreams of a husband and family. When she had discovered she was pregnant, she'd been overjoyed. He hadn't. That's when she discovered he already had children...and a wife.

Yes, Alan had been a mistake, but Maggie

could never regard her baby as one. This child was a gift.

Sniffing hard, Maggie turned her head to wipe her eyes against the pillowcase, stirring up the boiled cotton smell of the bedding. Normally, she hated hospitals. She did her best to avoid them after spending so much time in them as a young girl. Strangely enough, though, she didn't feel a breath of uneasiness now. The bad memories had been swept away by a tidal wave of good ones.

The other bed in the double room was empty. The woman who had occupied it had gone home this morning, along with her new son. Her husband and their other two children had come to fetch them—it had been a giddy, noisy celebration as they'd needed to take two trips to carry all the flowers and gifts to their car. They had all waved to Maggie and wished her well, then disappeared into the corridor, a cloud of bright foil balloons bobbing behind them.

Someday, it would be nice to belong to a family like that. A houseful of children to lavish with love, a husband to share her hopes and dreams…deep in her heart, that's what Maggie really wanted.

Someday. But not today. Today—right now—was what mattered. That was Maggie's approach to life. It was how she had learned to cope. As the old proverb went, the longest journey begins with a single step. And at this moment, Maggie had never been happier.

"You and me, sweetheart," she murmured. "We'll have more love between the two of us than a family of ten, you'll see." She dried her cheek against the pillow again, then focused on her baby's features one by one. Sweetheart. Pumpkin. Darling. Her daughter was almost a day old. She really should settle on a name.

"Who do you look like?" she mused. "You have a mouth like a rosebud. Shall I call you Rose? Rose Rice?"

The baby waved her fist in a jerky movement, bumping herself in the nose. Her forehead wrinkled briefly.

"Okay, not Rose," Maggie said. "Maybe I should call you Buttercup, because of your hair. It's a beautiful color." She tilted her head and smiled. "No, don't worry, I wouldn't saddle you with a name like that. How about…Angel. My little gift from heaven. Angel. Angela." She sighed. "No, that makes me think of the Angela who lived next door when I was six. She used to trap cats in the garbage cans."

Yawning widely, the baby relaxed into the crook of Maggie's arm.

"Maybe I should call you Jewel," she said. "Because you're so precious."

There was a quiet rap on the door. Maggie glanced up. When she saw who it was, she felt another spurt of tears.

This was crazy. It didn't seem to take much to set her off, but the mere glimpse of the man in the doorway made her heart turn over.

But maybe it wasn't that crazy. After all, he'd been the one who had shared the most incredible experience of her life. He'd held her daughter even before she had. Until yesterday, when he'd been nothing more than an attractive face and a good tipper, she had been uncomfortable with her reaction to him. Today she couldn't think of anyone she'd rather see.

Smiling, Maggie motioned him into the room with a nod. "Hi, Del."

"Hello, Maggie." He paused in the doorway, pushing his hands into the pockets of his navy windbreaker. "I hope I'm not disturbing you."

"No, not at all."

"I was in the neighborhood and I just wanted to check on how you were doing."

"I'm fine. Great, in fact."

His gaze went over her features, missing nothing. Apparently satisfied, he moved his gaze to the baby. "How is your daughter?"

"Wonderful. Perfect. Amazing." She tipped her head again. "Come and see."

He wavered. For a man who normally appeared so sure of himself, his hesitancy was... appealing. "She's asleep," he said.

"She's beautiful when she's asleep, isn't she?"

"I wouldn't want to wake her up."

"I wish you would. Then you'd be able to see how beautiful she is when she's awake."

The skin around his eyes crinkled into the beginnings of a smile. "And that's a completely objective opinion, right?"

"Of course. Anyone can see that she's the most beautiful baby ever born."

He moved to the side of the bed. He hesitated again, then looked at the child in her arms. "You're right," he said softly. "She's something else."

"She has lots of hair for a newborn, too. Isn't it a gorgeous color?"

"Outstanding. Definitely outstanding."

"She's six pounds, seven ounces. That's a good weight for being early. She doesn't need to stay in an incubator or anything."

"That's great."

"Actually, she might not have been all that

early. My doctor suspects I might have miscalculated my dates.''

''Oh.''

''Yeah. Laszlo was right. I should have quit working earlier. It would have saved everyone a lot of trouble.''

''You had no control over that, Maggie. Your baby decided it was time to be born.''

''Del?''

He glanced up. ''Yes?''

She swallowed hard, determined not to be a watering pot. ''Thank you. For helping me. I know we're practically strangers, and it must have been an awful shock for you, and I'm sorry for putting you through all of that, but...'' She took a deep breath, knowing no words were adequate but needing to express her gratitude anyway. ''Del, I want you to know I appreciate everything you did. The way you delivered my baby, the way you stayed with me until the ambulance came. You went way past being a Good Samaritan. Thank you. From the bottom of my heart.''

He regarded her in silence. Gradually, the lean lines of his face relaxed. The smile that played around the corners of his eyes spread to his lips. ''Maggie, I should be the one thanking you. It was a privilege to share in your daughter's birth. I'll never forget it.''

"Oh, Del," she said, her chin trembling.

"What is it? What's wrong?"

"Nothing. That was such a lovely thing to say."

"You're crying."

"It's the hormones. I can't seem to stop."

He took his hands from his pockets and grabbed a fistful of tissues from the box on the tray table. As matter-of-factly as he helped her the day before, he dabbed the tears from her cheeks. "The tears are nothing to worry about. I heard that every time my sister went through this, my brother-in-law ordered tissues by the case."

"I'm just so—" Her voice caught on a sob. "So happy."

"I have to confess the whole business left me a little choked up myself."

"Crazy, isn't it?"

"Yeah." They smiled at each other for a moment. Then he pushed his hand into his windbreaker pocket and withdrew a black and white object. "Here. I brought this for the baby."

"What..." She looked at the toy on his palm, then picked it up with her free hand. It was a velveteen panda bear with big blue embroidered eyes, a black velvet nose and a pink satin bow tied around its neck. "Oh, it's adorable!"

"The lady in the store said it would be safe for an infant if you removed the bow. There aren't any other parts that could come off, and the bear's washable, too."

"She'll love it. I love it. Thank you, Del. That was so sweet." Her chin trembled again.

Before the tears could fall, he had a tissue poised and waiting.

Sniffing, she set the toy on the tray table and took the tissue from Del. "Thanks again. You must think I'm an idiot."

"No, I think you're a mother who loves her daughter very much."

Shaking her head, she gave a watery laugh. "If you keep saying things like that, I'll never stop crying."

"Sorry."

"No, no. I don't mind. I'm savoring every second of this. Honest." She wadded up the tissue and tossed it toward the wastebasket. "But you really didn't have to bring anything—"

She drew in her breath as she caught sight of the back of his hand. The skin from his knuckles to his wrist was an angry, shiny red scattered with painful-looking gouges. "Oh, my gosh. What happened? Oh, no. Did I do that?"

"It's nothing. I burned myself last week, that's all."

"How?"

He waited half a beat before he answered. "An accident at work."

"An accident?"

He lifted one shoulder in a dismissive shrug. "A coffeepot broke."

"I'm sorry, I hadn't noticed yesterday," she said, her gaze on the injured skin. "And you let me hold your hand. I'm so sorry, Del. That must have hurt."

"Maggie, compared to what you went through, I barely noticed," he said easily.

She had a strong urge to reach out and stroke his hand. She didn't, of course. She might have held on to him yesterday, but those were special circumstances. "I don't know what I would have done if you hadn't been there, Del," she said. "I mean, I took all the prenatal classes, but reading books and seeing videos can't come close to the real thing. It's a good thing you were so calm."

"I'm glad I could help, although you were the one who deserves all the praise. You never let out so much as a whimper."

"I couldn't have. It would have driven away all of Laszlo's customers." Taking a steadying breath, she turned her gaze to the baby. "I was right about having a girl."

"Yes, you were."

"Did you say that your sister has six children?"

"Uh-huh."

"How did she come up with six names? I can't even settle on one."

"She chose names from our family. Altogether we have thirteen aunts and uncles."

"Wow. Big families must run in—" She chuckled. "I was going to say they run in the family."

"It's an old Missouri homesteader tradition, raising your own farmhands," Del said dryly.

"You're from a farm?" Maggie asked, intrigued.

"A long time ago," he answered.

So he wasn't a cowboy after all, she thought. He was a farmer. Well, both professions involved dealing with animals and squinting at the horizon, so it was close enough. Before she could pursue the topic, she sensed a flutter of movement against her arm. She looked at her daughter. The baby's eyelids were flickering. "Oh, Del," she murmured. "She's waking up."

"Sorry," he whispered. "I didn't mean to disturb her."

"She's been asleep for an hour—that's a long time for a newborn. She's such a clever girl. I told you she's a genius, didn't I?"

"No, not yet."

"Well, she is." As her baby's eyes blinked open, Maggie felt a rush of warmth. Would she ever tire of looking at this little miracle? She shifted on the bed to sit up straighter, smiling gratefully as Del rearranged the pillows behind her back. "Hello, precious," she cooed. "How's my little sweetie pie?"

Del leaned closer. Just as he had earlier, he hesitated for a moment, as if debating what to do next. Then he extended his index finger and gently stroked the baby's cheek with his fingertip.

It must be the hormones, she thought, watching Del watch her baby. But the special warmth she felt flowing between her and her daughter expanded to envelop him, as well.

Simply saying thank-you hadn't been anywhere near enough. He had delivered her baby, for God's sake. Even the greeting-card companies didn't have anything that covered that situation.

Would she have felt this way about the paramedics if they'd gotten there five minutes earlier and been the ones to deliver the baby? Or about her doctor if she'd given birth in the hospital? Somehow, she doubted it.

"Del," she said.

He glanced up. His face wore a smile that on anyone else would be called sappy, yet on his starkly masculine features it could only be called…endearing. "You're right, Maggie," he said. "She's beautiful when she's awake, too."

"Del, I—" She stopped suddenly, struck by a thought. "Delilah! That's it."

"What?"

"It feels right. More than right. It's perfect." She grinned. "Delilah Rice."

"Delilah?" he repeated. "You mean as a name for your daughter?"

"Yes. What do you think?"

He stared at her. "Maggie…"

"It's sounds great, doesn't it? She doesn't have any real aunts or uncles for me to name her after, so I can't think of a better choice. You're kind of an honorary uncle. When she grows up and asks me whose name she has, I'll have a terrific story to tell her, won't I?"

A muscle jumped in his cheek. He looked at the baby, then at her. "Maggie, I don't know what to say. Thank you."

"Delilah Rice," she said, catching her daughter's fist in her hand. "Hello, Delilah Rice. I'd like to introduce you to Del..."

Her words trailed off. It seemed absurd, but after everything that had happened, she still didn't know Del's last name.

"Rogers," he said, smoothing over the moment before it could get awkward. "Del Rogers."

"Del Rogers, meet the smartest, prettiest, sweetest, most lovable baby in the entire universe, Delilah Rice."

His throat worked as he swallowed. Tentatively, he reached out and closed his hand over hers and Delilah's. "Hello, Delilah."

It was his voice, Maggie thought, so deep and utterly masculine. Or it could have been the gentleness of his touch. Or maybe it was the postpartum hormones. But for a moment she found herself wishing...

Wishing what? That things could be different? That she could have fallen in love with a nice man like Del instead of a rat like Alan? That Delilah wouldn't have to grow up without a father?

Her emotions were scrambled from the trauma of childbirth, that's all. She still knew next to nothing about Del. She wasn't looking for a knight in shining armor—no matter how nice he might be—to ride in on a white horse and rescue her. Alan had taught her that much. She and her daughter would be fine, a family of two, with enough love to fill a lifetime.

Letting herself long for anything else was only asking for trouble.

Chapter 3

The whiskey bottle clinked as Del splashed more of the liquid into his glass. He'd finished his shift forty minutes ago. The drizzle that had been falling when he'd returned to his hotel room had strengthened to pattering rain, cloaking the dawn in gloom and guaranteeing another few hours of darkness. The routine of the Monarch Hotel was the same in New York as it was in the rest of the chain SPEAR owned—Del knew this because in the course of his assignments, he had stayed in practically every one of them. It would be after nine before the building came fully awake with the muffled thumps of closing doors and the squeaking rattle of the cleaning crew's cart. That left him plenty of time to get good and drunk.

He returned the bottle to the bedside table,

then leaned back against the headboard and cradled the glass in his hand. He hadn't gotten drunk in years. In eight years, to be exact. But the Rogers clan was big on tradition, so maybe he would start one of his own.

Yes, maybe he should make it a tradition. Get blind drunk at least once a year, whether he needed it or not. It might do him good. Maybe if he loosened up more, took some time off from his job occasionally, he wouldn't be hit so hard when something broke through to his emotions.

No, that wasn't right. He was as human as the next guy. There was nothing wrong with his emotions. He had a full complement of them, he just didn't need them for his job. When he was on the hunt, his success required the proverbial nerves of steel. Nothing bothered him, nothing distracted him when his survival and everyone else's depended on his ability to keep calm in a crisis.

Cool as ice, he thought, taking a burning swallow. That's the reputation he had built during his time with SPEAR. Evidently it spilled over into his off-duty hours, as well. After all, he'd kept his head in the back room of Laszlo's diner, hadn't he? Maggie had thanked him over and over for helping her through the baby's birth. As a matter of fact, she'd been so grateful, she'd named her baby after him.

The baby.

Delilah.

The reason Del was getting drunk.

He took another swallow, grimacing at the taste of the liquor. This glassful was going down more easily than the last. Too bad it wasn't working any faster.

He should have left well enough alone. He shouldn't have gone to the hospital to see Maggie yesterday. He'd been around enough hospitals lately. He'd been at a different one the day before, visiting his colleague in intensive care. Until now, he'd never visited a maternity ward—he was more accustomed to dealing with how life ended than to seeing life begin.

No matter what he felt, he wasn't responsible for Maggie or her baby. And as far as they were concerned, he was nothing but a bystander, so he had no right to accept the honor Maggie was giving him.

Maggie had named her baby Delilah out of gratitude. He had understood that. She had meant it as a favor. She couldn't possibly have known about the sore spot she was probing with her innocent gesture.

It shouldn't have bothered him. He had come

to terms with his limitations almost a decade ago. He had a good life now. He was proud of his work. He enjoyed the loyalty he found among his fellow SPEAR agents and he relished the challenge of each new assignment. He didn't need a namesake in order to feel fulfilled.

He shouldn't have told Bill about the baby. It would have been wiser to keep his off-duty life completely separate from his work. Maggie's world had nothing to do with the world of SPEAR. Yet Del had been so moved by his part in the child's birth, he would have had to have mentioned it eventually. Too bad he hadn't left it at that. But when he'd arrived for his shift tonight and Bill had asked about Maggie and the baby, Del had not only told him all about his visit to their hospital room, he'd let slip the name Maggie had chosen.

"Well, well, well," Bill had said, drawing contemplatively on his pipe. "Delilah, huh? Congratulations, Papa."

Del had tried to ignore the twinge of pain Bill's ribbing had caused. "More like an uncle," he'd said. "An honorary one."

"That kid doesn't need an uncle, she needs a daddy."

"Maggie's a strong woman. She'll manage

just fine. Anyone can see she loves her daughter to distraction.''

''Oh? How can you tell?''

''It's all over her face whenever she talks about her.''

''Ah. You mean she gets a syrupy smile and her eyes go soft and unfocused?''

''Something like that.''

Bill let out a puff of aromatic smoke, watching it waft toward the ceiling. ''The description fits you, as well.''

''What are you talking about?''

''Next thing you know you'll be carrying baby pictures around in your wallet and looking for a house with a white picket fence.''

''Bill…''

''Admit it, Del. You're smitten with both of them.''

''Don't be stupid.''

''June's a good time for a wedding, I hear. That's only two months away.''

''I'm not marrying anyone.''

''Then why all the interest in the young *single* mother?''

''I'm not interested in her that way. I'm just trying to do the right thing. After the way she was seduced and abandoned by Delilah's father, she could use a friend.''

"Aha! Methinks you doth protest too much."

Del rolled his eyes at the mangled Shakespeare.

"Maggie's going to look pretty good once she gets back into shape," Bill continued. "Even when she was pregnant she was a cute little thing. You like blondes, don't you?"

"I never really thought about it."

"Why not? You've already seen what she has to offer when she—"

"That's enough, Bill," Del said, cutting him off. He was surprised by the anger he felt at his friend's tasteless remark. "It wasn't some voyeuristic fantasy, Bill. It was the birth of a child."

"Lighten up, Del. No offense meant."

"Anyone who would be thinking of sex under those circumstances would be sick. Perverted. I have too much respect for Maggie to even consider regarding her—"

"Hey, I said lighten up." Bill eyed him warily. "I was only joking."

Del glanced down and saw that he'd curled his hands into fists. It had been an instinctive, protective reaction. He made an effort to relax, taking a deep breath and wiping his palms on his pants legs. "Right."

"You're awfully touchy about it."

"Maggie doesn't deserve to be mocked that way."

"Sorry." Bill continued to scrutinize him. "This whole childbirth thing really did get to you, didn't it?"

"It would get to anyone."

"Ever thought about having kids of your own, Del?"

This time he was ready—the comment didn't cause more than a twinge. Del looked straight at his partner and lied. "No."

Bill shifted his pipe to the corner of his mouth and smiled enigmatically. "Then you must be pleased that Maggie named her baby after you."

Yes, he was pleased, Del thought, tipping his head back to drain his glass. That was why he was getting drunk, because Maggie had made him so doggone happy. He squinted at the bottle beside him and reached out to pour more whiskey.

The last time he'd done this, he'd gotten drunk because he'd been angry. More than angry—furious. Eight years had passed, but he still hadn't forgotten the feeling of helpless rage that he'd tried to drown in the bottom of a bottle. He had just seen the carefully laid plans for his life crumble to nothing.

That's what love did to a person. He'd been

around the same age then that Maggie was now, and he'd been just as wrong about the person he'd fallen in love with.

Only in Del's case, it hadn't been a whirlwind romance with someone who was already married. He had loved Elizabeth Johanson since they had made a papier-mâché model of Mount Saint Helens together for a fifth grade geography project. The finished model had looked more like a crumpled soda can than a volcanic crater, but he had fallen head over heels for Elizabeth nevertheless.

They had gone steady all through high school. No one in the county had been surprised when Del and Elizabeth had become engaged after graduation. While she had gone away to teachers' college, he had stayed behind to help work his parents' farm, counting the days until they would be married. Their love had seemed stronger than ever each time Elizabeth had come home. By the time he was twenty-one, his parents had deeded him a plot of land, and he had already started to build the house he and Elizabeth had designed together. It would have plenty of bedrooms. They wanted a houseful of children.

Oh, yeah, Elizabeth had wanted children. She was wild about them. She came from a family almost as large as Del's and she was devoted to her younger siblings. So when her youngest brother came down with the mumps the Christmas before her wedding, she hadn't hesitated to take care of him. She hadn't realized she would pass on the illness to Del.

Having the mumps at seven wasn't usually serious. It was just another one of those childhood diseases that was more of a nuisance than a danger. But the consequences were different for a man of twenty-one.

Del hadn't wanted to believe the results of the lab test his doctor had ordered. He'd had a second, and then a third, but they only verified the first. The mumps had left Del unable to father children. He was completely sterile.

It had been difficult to grasp. Del hadn't felt any different physically. He still had the same sexual urges of any normal, red-blooded male his age. As far as he knew, his capabilities when it came to lovemaking hadn't suffered. He had thought he was the same man.

Elizabeth had cried when he'd told her. In one breath she vowed she would always love him, but in the next she was telling him their engagement was off. She didn't want to tie herself for life to a man who couldn't give her children.

Del had felt his anger stir then, but he'd had no target to focus the feeling on. He couldn't really blame Elizabeth's brother for coming down with the mumps in the first place. And he tried not to fault Elizabeth for her honesty, either, no matter how hurtful her rejection of him was. If he really loved her, he would want her to be happy, wouldn't he? He would let her go and wish her well.

That's what he'd tried to do. He'd been damn noble about the whole thing. But the nobility had been submerged by a wave of fury when barely a month had passed before he learned that the woman who had promised to love him forever had eloped with his best friend. Their first child had been born eight months later.

So much for love. So much for loyalty. It hadn't taken the love of his life long to find his replacement.

Getting drunk had seemed like a good idea then. It had helped to blunt the pain. It had diluted the frustrated anger he'd felt at Elizabeth, at fate, at his own physical defect.

But he wasn't angry now, was he?

So why was he determined to get drunk?

It was because of Delilah. The beautiful little baby with Maggie's eyes...and Del's name.

Del let his head fall back against the headboard. He could feel a pleasant numbness starting in his lips. It was only a matter of time before it worked its way to his mind.

Trouble was, once the alcohol wore off, the emotions would still be there.

Maggie really had made him happy. It wasn't just because she had named her child after him. It was her openhearted generosity. Even though they hardly knew each other, she was letting him share the joy of her baby. When was the last time he'd felt such pure, simple pleasure?

She had declared him an honorary uncle. He hadn't been much of a real one. He always made sure to send Christmas and birthday gifts to his sister's kids, but he didn't see them often. He couldn't remember the last time he'd been home. He'd deliberately limited his contact with babies.

Until now, he'd never realized how much he'd been missing.

He fumbled to put his glass on the nightstand. Damn, he was drunk, all right. He was getting downright mushy. He could feel the silly smile working across his face as he thought about how incredibly soft Delilah's cheek had felt, and how perfectly Maggie's hand had fit within his.

He wanted to experience those feelings again.

Yet he would never know the touch of his own child. There would be no blood of his blood, flesh of his flesh. He wouldn't be able to put that glow of happiness on a woman's face that he saw on Maggie's when she held her baby. He couldn't give her the seed that would grow the miracle.

Rubbing his eyes, he shook his head. He was getting downright maudlin.

Maggie wanted more children. She had made that clear even when she'd been in the throes of labor. Del knew better than to get involved with a woman like that. It would only lead to pain and disillusionment. It would be Elizabeth all over again.

The solution to Del's problem was dead simple. All he had to do was keep away from any woman who wanted children. That way, his sterility would never be an issue.

He shouldn't have gone to see Maggie yesterday.

But he would see her today. And tomorrow. And as often as he could until his work here was over and he moved on to the next assignment. At least the whiskey had made him honest enough to admit that much.

Damn it all, he wanted to see her. And he wanted to see the baby. They made him feel good.

Besides, he didn't intend to get *involved* with Maggie. He only wanted to do the decent thing, to be her friend. He still felt a certain amount of responsibility toward her, especially now that she had named her child after him. As long as he limited their association to friendship, there wouldn't be any risk of hurt to either of them.

Yes, he could be her friend, he reasoned. He could be an honorary uncle to his namesake. Just because he couldn't have children of his own didn't mean he had to cut Maggie and Delilah out of his life entirely, did it?

And as he'd already reminded himself, he didn't need to be able to father children to be a success in the life he had now. Having children was damn inconvenient for a SPEAR agent. Hunting international terrorists and keeping the world safe for democracy were dangerous business. On top of that, Del never knew where he'd be from one day to the next. A man like that wouldn't make a good father, even if his plumbing did work.

When he thought about it, there was a certain irony to the situation—the top marksman in SPEAR was only capable of shooting blanks.

Was that one of the reasons he'd become such a crack shot, to compensate for his failure in that other area? Was that why he was so adamant about never taking a life, because he knew he'd never be able to create one?

Del sighed and slid down to stretch out on the bed. He'd definitely had enough to drink. He'd progressed from mushy to maudlin and now he was headed straight for philosophical.

Maybe he should forget about doing this once a year. Every eight years was more than enough.

The rain hit the front window of the diner with the determination of machine-gun bullets. Near the counter there was a crash of breaking crockery. Del winced as echoes of the racket ping-ponged through his skull. He held his breath, waiting until his brain stopped sloshing around, then hunched his shoulders and took another gulp of coffee.

"Broom is in the back room," Laszlo said from his post in front of the grill. He scowled at the teenager who stared at him defiantly.

"I'm not cleaning that up. I didn't do it." The girl pointed a black-tipped fingernail toward the other waitress. The black nail polish matched her lipstick, as well as the studs that marched in an arc along the edge of her right ear. "It was *her* fault."

Joanne blew a large bubble and popped it with a snap. "Taking responsibility for your mistakes is good for your karma, kid. You don't want to come back as a toad, do you?"

"You bumped my elbow."

"I was nowhere near you, hon."

"Yeah, right. What's the matter? Memory failing? Take too many acid trips back in the sixties, Grandma?"

Joanne chewed her gum harder. "Twerp."

"Cow."

The two customers nearest the door evidently decided it was a good time to leave. They stood up, their chairs screeching across the floor with a noise akin to a freight train making an emergency stop.

"Enough," Laszlo growled. "You get broom now, or you look for the other job."

"Hey, fine with me, Fatso." The girl pulled off her apron and tossed it on the counter. "This job sucks. I can make more money with a squeegee." She strode to the door, her six-inch platform shoes pounding across the floor like an artillery barrage.

Del squinted as his left eye began to water.

"Nice going, Laszlo," Joanne muttered. "That's the second one in two days."

"She was the idiot. She look like the witch and scare customers."

"I suppose she couldn't help it. I noticed right off that her aura was unbalanced." Joanne retrieved the broom and swept up the shattered dishes. The shards clinked together with the rat-a-tat sharpness of a tap-dancing troupe practicing on a sheet of aluminum.

Del finished his coffee. Placing a paper napkin across his saucer to muffle the clunk, he carefully set the cup on top of it. The bagel he'd managed to eat was sitting in his stomach like a stone, but at least it had gone down quietly.

"Would you like anything else?"

He stifled a groan at Joanne's perky inquiry. He started to shake his head but thought better of it. "No, thanks."

"Sorry about the commotion," she said. "We're having a hard time finding a replacement for Maggie."

"That's what I figured."

"Poor kid. She was so eager to have that baby, but it took all of us off guard."

"That it did."

"We sure were lucky that you happened to be in here. My gosh, I don't know what we would have done when she went into labor like that." She tilted her head, smiling at Del. "She told me she named the baby after you."

"Yes. Delilah."

"That's just like Maggie. She's such a sweet girl."

"She'll make a good mother."

"That's for sure." She gave her gum a pensive chew. "Do you have any kids, Del?"

Why was everyone asking him that lately? "No, I don't."

"Maggie's just nuts about them. When I called her this morning she was already talking about having more." Joanne gasped and smacked her forehead. "Oh, no. Maggie!"

"What about her?" Del asked immediately. "Is something wrong?"

"No, nothing like that. She's going home today."

"Already?"

"I promised I would take her, and she's anxious to leave. She hates hospitals. Laszlo said he'd lend me his car." She whirled around. "Laszlo! You've got to get her back."

"Who?"

"The kid with the earrings."

"No. She is the witch."

"But I have to pick up Maggie. If you don't get that earring girl back, who's going to cover for me?"

Laszlo scowled. "You can't go. Maggie will wait."

"She can't wait. She has to clear out of the room this afternoon."

"She can take subway."

"The *subway?* Laszlo, you don't understand. She doesn't just need a ride, she needs someone to help her get the baby settled. It would be horrible for her to have to go home all by herself. And taking her child home is such a momentous occasion, she shouldn't be alone—"

"I need you here."

"But I promised. She's expecting me in an hour."

Del listened in silence as the two tried to figure out what to do. Of course, there was an obvious solution to the problem. His shift wouldn't start for another few hours. He could easily get to the hospital, pick up Maggie and Delilah and take them home. That would still leave him plenty of time to get them settled before he had to meet Bill at the surveillance site.

That would be the decent thing to do, wouldn't it? The kind of assistance a friend or an honorary uncle would give? Last night he'd already decided there would be no harm in that, right?

Despite the rain that sheeted down the window and the hangover from hell, the day suddenly seemed brighter. Del's teeth barely ached as he scraped his chair back and stood up. "Maybe I can help," he said.

At least the taxi was yellow instead of white, Maggie thought as the cab splashed its way across the Queensboro Bridge toward her apartment in Astoria. As long as the cab was yellow, there would be less risk of getting Del confused with a knight on a white horse, riding to her rescue.

She turned her head to look at him. His dark brown hair clung wetly to his scalp, molding the contours of his head like a helmet. His navy blue windbreaker appeared black, soaked through from the rain and weighed down against his shoulders like tightly woven chain mail. His usually neatly pressed chinos stuck to his thighs, outlining muscles that could easily control a horse.

He'd brought an umbrella with him, but it had been one of those small, collapsible ones. He'd used it to keep her and the baby dry instead of himself.

Darn chivalrous of him, wasn't it? Like an old-fashioned knight, or maybe a cowboy out of some Gary Cooper western?

Maggie grimaced inwardly. The roller coaster ride she'd been on with her emotions since Delilah's birth was beginning to slow down, but it wasn't over yet. She was pathetically vulnerable right now, so she had good reason to be cautious about her reaction to Del.

He was a nice guy, that's all. A really nice guy. He didn't deserve to be the focus of all this silly fantasizing—she'd already decided that would only lead to trouble.

After all, that was how it had started with Alan: a chance meeting in the diner, an instant attraction to the man with the charming, too-good-to-be-true manner. He had flirted outrageously, then had swept her into a whirlwind romance. He'd topped it all off with an impetuous declaration of love that she'd wanted too badly to believe.

But Del wasn't like Alan. He was tender and honest....

Hormones, she reminded herself, swallowing hard against the sudden lump in her throat. She'd read about this in the baby books, too. That's why she was making such a big deal out of Del's friendly gesture. He wasn't trying to be charming, he was simply being, well, nice.

"How's the baby doing?" he asked.

Maggie lifted the corner of the receiving blanket and peeked at Delilah in the car seat. "She's still asleep."

"Good. I was worried the rain might have woken her."

"Thanks to you, she didn't get a drop."

"Great."

She brushed her thumb across the baby's knuckles. "It seems as if I'm always thanking you, Del."

"You don't have to. I'm glad I could help."

"I'm sorry about the way Joanne roped you into this."

"No need to apologize. I volunteered."

"Thanks, Del."

Thunder rumbled as the taxi pulled up in front of Maggie's apartment building. Del got soaked once more as he held the umbrella over Maggie and Delilah and escorted them to the entrance. When they reached her apartment on the third floor, he took the key from her hand and unlocked the door.

Maggie had always liked this apartment. She'd decorated the place on a shoestring, scouring the neighborhood discount stores for bargains and brightening the walls with paint the color of pale daffodils. She loved the earth-toned fringed rug and the overstuffed couch, the tapestry pillows and the lamp with the stained-glass shade. All the little touches she'd stretched her budget to add made the place cozy and welcoming.

She paused on the threshold. Everything was exactly the same as it had been when she'd left for work the day her baby had been born.

And that was the problem. It was *exactly* as she'd left it.

In the gray light from the window, she could see the heap of laundry still on the couch and the dishes she'd left in the sink. The high-backed rocking chair she'd found in a thrift shop last week was buried under a layer of newspapers and baby books. Through the doorway that led to her closet-size bedroom, she could see the trailing edge of a crumpled sheet.

She hadn't tidied up before leaving for work that morning—her back had been aching in what she now realized had been the onset of labor. On top of that, she'd been too tired out after taking most of the previous evening to rearrange the bedroom furniture to clear a space for the crib.

Her gaze swung to the far wall and the pieces of what was supposed to be Delilah's crib. She had believed it would be weeks before she would need to assemble it. She wasn't sure where the sheets for it were. She hadn't finished organizing the clothes she'd been acquiring for the baby, either—she had assumed she'd have plenty of time to get the apartment into shape once she stopped working.

As she contemplated the tasks ahead of her, Maggie's emotions did another roller coaster twist and dip, swerving toward despair. But then she glanced at her daughter, and she was swooping upward again.

This was another one of those moments she'd anticipated for months. She had her baby safe and warm in her arms, and she was about to bring her into the home they would share together.

What did it matter if the place wasn't perfect? Who cared if there was more work to be done? Fancy furniture and clean laundry didn't make a home. Love made a home. And she and Delilah would have plenty of that.

She would manage somehow. She always did. One day at a time.

"Are you crying again, Maggie?"

She licked a tear that had trickled to the corner of her mouth, then firmed her chin. "No."

"That's good," he said, patting the pockets of his sodden jacket. "Because I don't think I have anything dry on me."

His stab at humor only made her eyes fill faster. Maggie took a shaky breath and led the way inside. "Take your jacket off, Del. I think we could both use some towels."

He closed the door behind them and looked around briefly, then peeled off his windbreaker and hung it over the doorknob. "Don't worry about me, Maggie."

"It's the least I can do after the way you

brought us home and everything.'' Holding Delilah to her shoulder, she walked to the bathroom and took a large bath towel from the shelf over the tub.

By the time she returned, Del had cleared the newspapers and books off the rocking chair and was stacking them under the window. He grabbed a pillow from the couch and propped it against the chair back.

''Del, you don't have to—''

''Here.'' He took the towel from her hand and draped it around his neck, then cupped her elbow and guided her to the chair. He hovered by her side until she and Delilah were comfortably settled. ''You should be taking it easy.''

The concern in his voice brought a lump to her throat. It was only gratitude she felt, and a good dose of postpartum hormones. Her emotions were as much a mess as her apartment. ''Thanks, Del.''

He used the towel to wipe his face and briskly rubbed his hair dry. ''With Delilah's birth coming so unexpectedly, I realize you likely haven't had a chance to make all the preparations you would have wanted to, so is there anything you need?''

She swallowed hard and forced a smile. ''You

mean like a road map for the apartment or maybe a bulldozer for the mess?''

''I was thinking more in the line of food or diapers, but I'll clean up whatever you want.''

''I appreciate the offer, Del, but I'll be fine. The fridge is full, and there's a carton of diapers around here somewhere. If I can remember where,'' she added under her breath.

''What about formula? Baby bottles?''

''Oh, I don't need any of that. I'm...'' She hesitated, surprised by the sudden self-consciousness she felt. This was the man who had witnessed her baby's birth. They had shared an intimacy that transcended sex, and yet she knew by the heat in her cheeks that she was coloring into a beet.

This was absurd, she told herself. Her modesty was misplaced. As natural functions went, this had to be the most wholesome of all. ''Delilah won't need any formula,'' she answered finally. ''I'm breast-feeding her.''

Beneath the beginnings of Del's five-o'clock shadow, his face appeared to redden. He gripped the towel he held more tightly. ''Oh.''

At his obvious embarrassment, Maggie relaxed. It really was silly to feel awkward, considering what they'd already gone through. She shifted the still sleeping Delilah to the crook of her arm and rested her elbow on the pillow Del had supplied. "Didn't your sister breast-feed?"

"I don't know. I guess I never thought about it."

"It's the best thing for the baby. Mothers' milk is the easiest to digest, so the longer I keep it up, the less likely she is to develop allergies."

"Uh, yes. I can understand that."

"And it will give her immune system a boost, since she'll get all my antibodies through the milk."

"That makes sense."

"It's also a lot easier for me."

He kept his gaze scrupulously on her face. "I suppose so."

"Especially for night feedings, since there's no bottle to warm up and nothing to prepare."

"Uh, right."

"Considering the state of this place, that's a good thing."

"How's that?"

"I'll never lose track of where I left the milk."

He let out a startled laugh. "No, I guess you wouldn't."

She grinned, glad to see she had put him at ease.

Del gave his hair one last rub with the towel, then tossed the towel on top of the laundry pile.

"Okay, it seems as if you have the basics covered. Is there anything else you can think of that you might need?"

"No, thanks, I'll be fine. *We'll* be fine."

"Is there a Laundromat close by?"

"There's a laundry room in the basement, but I'll get to it, Del. Honestly, contrary to how things look here, I'm normally a very competent person."

"I know you are, Maggie. But I realize Delilah's birth being earlier than you expected must have caused you problems." He paused. "If having to quit work so soon is going to leave you in a tight spot..."

"Hey, did I mention the other good thing about breast-feeding? It's cheap."

He didn't smile. "Maggie, I don't mean to pry into your finances, but if you need money, just ask."

Her grin faded. "Del, I appreciate your concern, but I'll get by. I do have some money put aside, and the baby-sitting I'll be doing for my neighbor will help tide me over until I can go back to work."

He nodded. "Okay, but if something comes up, I would be happy to give you a loan, no strings attached."

"Really, you don't have to feel obligated...."

She was struck by a sudden thought. "Is that it? Do you feel you have to help because I said you could be Delilah's honorary uncle?"

"I don't feel obligated to help. I want to."

"Because I didn't name Delilah after you just to manipulate you into feeling responsible, and I sure wasn't looking for money—"

"Maggie, I never thought you were like that," he said. "I feel privileged to be part of Delilah's life. Believe me, what you've given me is far more valuable than anything I could offer you."

How did he always know exactly the right thing to say? she wondered. "Thanks, Del."

"I'm the one who should be thanking you. I do a lot of traveling because of my work, so I don't see much of my nephews and nieces back in Missouri. I'm only in New York temporarily, too, but while I'm here, I'd really like the chance to be Delilah's honorary uncle. And your friend."

The roller coaster did another dip and swirl. A friend? Maggie thought. A friend was safe. And a man friend who was only here temporarily was even safer.

What was she worried about? Why was she fighting him? She wasn't in danger of falling into the same trap with Del that she had with Alan. She wasn't going to start mistaking her dreams for the real thing. This was a different situation altogether. Yes, it was.

"Thanks, Del," she said softly. "I can use all the friends I can get."

The corners of his eyes crinkled as he returned her smile. "All right. Since your hands are full, how about if I put that crib together before I go?"

"Well…"

"Trust me, I'm good at putting things together. Or would you rather have me do the dishes instead?"

"No. Really. They don't matter."

"You're right. I think having someplace for Delilah to sleep tonight is the priority." Before she could voice another objection, he switched on a lamp and crossed the room. After a cursory inspection of the parts of the crib, he laid the pieces out on the floor and opened the small plastic package that contained the necessary hardware. "Do you have a screwdriver?"

"In the drawer beside the stove."

It was probably only a trick of the lighting combined with the pesky moisture that kept filling her eyes, she decided. Yet as Del progressed with his task, Maggie couldn't help noticing how the lingering dampness on his shirt and pants reflected the lamplight with a gleam that was almost metallic, almost like…like armor. Shining armor.

Maggie pressed her cheek against the top of Delilah's wispy curls, unsure whether to laugh or cry.

Chapter 4

''These pictures are great, Del! Oh, look at this one. You caught the way Delilah wrinkles her nose.'' Maggie tilted her head, smiling as she examined the photograph.

''She takes a good picture.''

''Well, so do you. Literally, I mean. You have a real knack with that camera of yours.''

''I'm glad you think so.''

She looked at the next one. ''Ooh, she's blowing a bubble here.''

He folded his arms on the back of the rocking chair and leaned forward to look over her shoulder. ''Yeah. That's a cute one, isn't it?''

''They're all cute,'' she said. ''Each and every one. It's weird, isn't it? If I want to look at her, all I need to do is walk into the bedroom and glance down at the crib, but I can't get enough of these pictures.''

''That's understandable. She's changed a lot since you brought her home.''

''You're not kidding. Two weeks old today, and she's already gained ten ounces,'' she said proudly, shuffling through the stack of photographs. ''Wait a minute. Where's the picture I took?''

''Which one was that?''

She twisted around to look at him. ''The one with you holding Delilah.''

He hesitated a beat, then shrugged. ''I guess it didn't turn out.''

''Darn. That happened on the last two rolls, too.''

''My camera can be temperamental sometimes.''

''That's downright…chivalrous of you to say, Del,'' Maggie said, her lips quirking. ''But I guess photography isn't one of my talents.''

''Well, you're doing a great job with Delilah.''

''That's not a job, that's a joy.'' She turned back to look at the photographs, starting through them again. ''And speaking of joy, can you believe she's still asleep? That's almost two hours.''

''A new record?''

"You bet."

"What about you, Maggie? Did you manage to get any sleep last night?"

"Sure. I think."

He placed his hands on her shoulders, squeezing the muscles above her collarbone in a gentle massage. "You think?"

At the feel of his long fingers working the stiffness from her shoulders, she groaned. "Oh, that feels good."

"Why don't you have a nap while I'm here? I can see to Delilah when she wakes up."

She sighed, dropping her chin to her chest. "I don't think you can, Del."

"You taught me how to change her diaper. I believe I finally got the hang of those little sticky tabs now."

"Mmm."

He found a knot at the side of her neck and pressed firmly with his thumbs. "Is that better?"

"Mmm." She exhaled slowly. He had wonderful hands, large yet gentle, thoroughly masculine. And he'd been adept when it came to manipulating the tiny fastenings of Delilah's clothing—his fingers were remarkably nimble. "You wouldn't have any trouble changing Delilah's diaper, but there are some things you can't do for her."

"I'm a quick study. If you show me how—"

"Del," she interrupted with a smile. She gestured toward her bosom. "You don't have the equipment."

He stilled for a moment, then chuckled and resumed the massage. "You got me there."

"This feels heavenly," she said, rolling her head.

"Part of the trouble with staying up all night is getting overtired. Your brain is too wound up to let your body relax and get the rest it needs."

"You sound as if you've had your share of sleepless nights."

He rubbed the heels of his hands in slow circles at the top of her spine. "A few."

"What do you do to relax?"

"I exercise to work off tension."

"Ugh."

"With me, though, it's coffee rather than a baby that keeps me awake."

"Mmm, coffee," she murmured. She leaned forward in the chair to give him better access to her back. "I have a vague memory of what coffee was like. I haven't had any since last year. When I first got pregnant it made me nauseous. Now I can't have it since the caffeine makes Delilah edgy. I'd be happy to make you some, though, as long as I can stand over the pot and inhale.''

''Don't bother, Maggie. You should be relaxing while you can.''

She couldn't argue with that, and she didn't really want to. This impromptu back rub was bliss. It was because of those surplus hormones in her system, she decided, but she couldn't recall feeling so sensitive to a friendly touch before. Del hadn't touched her often, but each time he did, it had a strange effect. Today it was stronger than ever. Wherever his hands moved, the skin beneath her blouse tingled.

Tingled? As in stimulated? Nah, it definitely had to be hormones.

''Is there anything you can think of that you might need tomorrow?''

Mmm, she thought. What she needed was more of the same. Or maybe a full-length body massage, with scented oil and fluffy towels to lie naked on…and Del could use those long, strong, nimble fingers on other places besides her back…and she could start to feel like a woman again instead of just a mother….

She blinked, chagrined by the wayward image that sprang to her mind. Yes, stimulated was the right word after all, she realized, feeling a twinge of warmth low in her stomach.

Quickly, she forced the image—and the warmth—away. This was nuts. She barely had enough energy to see to Delilah, so how could she even think about anything remotely sexual?

And how could she contemplate getting naked for anyone? She had come a long way in two weeks, but her body still looked and felt like overrisen bread dough.

"Relax," he said, working his thumbs along the side of her neck. "You're tensing up again."

Maggie exhaled hard. Poor Del. He was such a gentleman, and so endearingly considerate of the new mother, he would be horribly embarrassed by the nonmaternal direction of her thoughts.

From beneath her bangs, Maggie looked around the apartment. The place was as tidy as possible, considering the baby's night-owl schedule, but somehow it seemed to get more cluttered every day.

That was due in large part to Del. Since he had brought her and Delilah home from the hospital, he had been dropping by to visit daily. And he never came empty-handed.

She had given up trying to object to his gifts. Pride was one thing, but she was too practical to indulge in it, especially when it would mean depriving her daughter of the little extras she wouldn't have been able to provide herself.

Little extras? Last week Del had shown up with a stroller, not a secondhand one with a loose handle like the one she had been considering, but a brand-new top-of-the-line model complete with a rain shield, a blue polka-dotted sun shade and a five-position quilted and ruffled convertible seat.

Three days ago he had brought a special infant chair made out of fabric suspended from a wire frame that gave the perfect amount of support to Delilah's tiny body. He knew that Maggie seldom wanted to leave her daughter out of her sight, and he was concerned that she would tire herself out by carrying the baby around all the time, so he'd chosen something she could place anywhere.

And good Lord, the baby clothes Del had brought were overflowing Delilah's little dresser, and there were so many stuffed toys, Maggie had resorted to tying them all on ribbons and letting them dangle along the wall.

It wasn't only Delilah who was benefiting from his generosity, either. Two days ago Del had brought groceries, and then proceeded to cook dinner. Yesterday he had taken out the garbage. Today he'd brought a bag full of paperbacks for her along with the photographs of the baby. And of course, he should be registering his hands as lethal weapons, considering how dangerous this massage of his was.

He was a nice man, Maggie thought. A really, *really* nice man. A great guy. A perfect gentleman. A veritable knight.

And it would be oh-so-easy to get used to this, maybe on a more permanent basis....

She drew in her breath quickly, alarmed by the direction of her thoughts. Getting a passionate twinge was bad enough, but entertaining ideas about permanency was out of the question. He'd already made it clear he was only in New York temporarily. And she wasn't in any condition to take a step like that. No, indeed. It had been days since the last time she'd cried, but she wasn't about to trust her judgment when her emotions were still so raw.

He was her friend, she told herself firmly. That was it, that was all, that was plenty.

"Thanks, Del," she said finally, remembering his original question. "Considering what you've brought so far, what else could we possibly need?"

"What about a nursery monitor?"

"Here?" She glanced at the bedroom door. "Thanks, but I really don't think I need one. I can hear Delilah perfectly well the second she wakes up. Actually, I think I have some kind of radar. I'm usually on my way to get her even before she cries.''

''I was just wondering.'' He paused. ''I know someone who can give me a good deal on monitoring equipment.''

''I appreciate the thought, but it really wouldn't be necessary.''

''If you think of something else, let me know, okay?''

''Sure.''

''You have my number at the hotel, right?''

''It's stuck to the fridge.''

''Great. I've got voice mail there and—'' His words were cut off at a sudden ringing sound. He immediately withdrew his hands from her shoulders and straightened. Frowning, he pulled a cell phone from the pocket of his pants.

Maggie watched, surprised. This was the first time she'd seen his cell phone. She hadn't known Del had one. He'd been insistent about giving her his number at his hotel and making sure she could leave a message if he wasn't there, but it would have been a lot simpler if she could call him on his cell phone, wouldn't it?

It had been the other way around with Alan. He had given her the number of his cell phone, but not the number of his home phone. At the time, he had explained she was far more likely to reach him that way, but now she realized he had only been trying to keep her from finding out the truth. After all, if she had called his house, his wife or one of his children might have answered.

Maggie should have known something was wrong then, but she'd been too infatuated with Alan to be suspicious. She had deliberately ignored the warning signals because she had wanted so badly to believe in him.

Of course, there was a logical explanation as to why Del only wanted her to call him at his hotel.

Wasn't there?

Del spoke quickly into the phone, then collapsed the antenna and snapped the set shut. ''I have to go,'' he said, putting the phone in his pocket. He pushed the stroller aside so he could walk to the door.

She rose to see him out. ''Problems?'' she asked.

''No. I just need to get to the office.''

''I see. So that was your office that called?''

''Right. See you tomorrow, Maggie.''

And with that, he was gone.

Maggie closed the door behind him and

turned, slumping against the wood panel. The pleasant tingles his touch had evoked faded quickly, replaced by a niggling sense of unease.

His office? She didn't even know where it was. He never talked about his work.

That was odd, wasn't it? Most men loved to talk about their professions, but whenever she asked Del about his, somehow the conversation always veered to another subject. After two weeks, she still didn't know exactly what he did for a living.

Why was that? she wondered. Could he possibly be…hiding something?

Was she doing it again? Misplacing her trust?

Oh, Lord, she thought, dropping her head against the door. What was wrong with her? Del wasn't Alan. Del was her friend. He was a kind and generous person. He had fixed her dinner and bought a stroller and rubbed her shoulders. Was this how she repaid him? With suspicions?

From the corner of her eye she caught sight of the stack of books and the glossy photographs Del had brought today, and shame flooded through her.

Del was simply a nice guy. He was coming over because of his namesake, that's all. The baby was the only reason they had come together in the first place. That's why the conversation always seemed to get steered away from his personal life. They were too busy talking about Delilah.

She had no right to question where he went or what he did when he left here. It wasn't her business. Besides, what reason would he have to hide anything? He had told her he wasn't married, but even if he'd lied, what did it matter? It was irrelevant. They were *friends,* that's all.

And she wasn't looking for more, no matter how easy it was becoming to get accustomed to Del's presence.

''Hormones,'' she muttered to herself. She raked her fingers through her hair and sighed. ''If you're not thinking straight, you can still blame it on the hormones.''

But how much longer would she be able to use that as an excuse?

''Well, that certainly took you long enough,'' Bill remarked. ''Where were you?''

''In Astoria.''

''At Maggie's, of course.''

''Yes. And it wasn't long, Bill. I timed the subway ride from Queens. It took one minute longer than taking a taxi from my hotel in rush hour, so there's nothing to get worried about.''

"Who's worried? Just as long as you don't make me look at any more baby pictures."

Del decided not to bring out the extra set of prints he'd had made for himself. He put the camera he had borrowed from the equipment pool on the shelf where he kept his rifle. "What's going on?"

"We're not sure," Bill said, falling into step with Del as they crossed the room. "But I thought after all the time you've put in with me staring at an empty room, you might want to see this for yourself."

Del greeted the pair of agents positioned in front of the window. A specially treated screen had been set up between the monitoring equipment and the glass so that enough daylight was reflected outside to make the inside of this apartment essentially invisible to anyone looking in. The view from this side wasn't impeded at all. Del could clearly see a shadow of movement in the apartment they were watching. "It's about time something happened," he said.

"My sentiments exactly," Bill commented, handing him a set of binoculars. "It's not even dark yet and the cockroaches are crawling out of the woodwork."

"Is it Simon?"

"No such luck."

Through the binoculars Del could see a stocky figure moving along one wall of the main room. Using a door frame for scale, he judged the person to be five feet nine, five ten at the most. He felt a stab of disappointment. According to the few witnesses who had met Simon in the flesh— and lived to tell about it—Simon was taller, at least a few inches over six feet.

There was a glint from something metallic. Del adjusted the focus until he could make out a thin, U-shaped wand that was attached to a small box in the man's hand. A blue tattoo snaked from the back of his hand to his wrist. "What's he doing?"

"Scanning for electronics," Bill said. "He's looking for bugs."

Del lowered the binoculars. "Are they on to us?"

The young blond agent who was monitoring the parabolic microphone shook his head as he glanced at Del. "I don't think so. Our visitor seems relaxed. He's whistling."

"I'd guess it's just a routine sweep," said the other agent, a tall woman who appeared to be in her early twenties. "Judging by his body language, he's not expecting trouble."

"It's a good thing Jonah advised against wiring the place,'' Bill commented. ''Otherwise, they would know we're here.''

''I've never met Jonah,'' the blond man said. ''I've heard he's got some kind of disfigurement and that's why he retired from fieldwork to run the agency.''

''No,'' his companion said. ''The way I heard it, Jonah doesn't really exist, he's a committee of retired SPEAR agents. Together they've got the best brains in the country.''

''Someone else told me Jonah's really a woman,'' the blond man said.

Bill took his pipe out of his shirt pocket and tapped the bowl thoughtfully. ''Actually, he's a clone of the last three directors,'' he deadpanned. ''That's why everyone had to give a tissue sample when they were recruited, in case it's needed later. Top-secret, experimental stuff, of course, from the lab in area fifty-one.''

The young agents turned to look at him.

Del struggled to swallow his laughter. To most operatives in SPEAR, Jonah was a voice on a briefing tape or the authority behind an intelligence report. Few people spoke directly to the reclusive head of the organization, and none had met him face-to-face. Del and Bill had been around long enough to know that Jonah was an ordinary man, albeit a man dedicated to the success of the agency he had headed for the past decade, but because Jonah's past was a mystery, speculating about his identity had become something of a tradition among the junior agents.

Bill lifted an eyebrow as he looked at Del. "Come to think of it, the technology behind the cloning was purchased right here in New York."

"Oh?"

"From a gentleman who also sold the Brooklyn Bridge."

The blond agent muttered an oath under his breath and pressed the headset more firmly against his ears.

Clearing her throat, the woman turned to the telescope. "The subject is progressing to the rear wall now," she said briskly.

Del exchanged a grin with Bill, then turned his mind to business. "Since they're doing a sweep, that might mean they're expecting Simon soon," he said.

"Possibly," Bill agreed. "If we're lucky."

Del raised the binoculars once more and turned his attention to the street. First he looked for anyone loitering nearby. When no one caught his eye, he watched the traffic, both vehicular and pedestrian, for any pattern of repetition. "I don't think anything major is going to happen soon," he said. "There's no backup in sight. Our tattooed visitor over there appears to be on his own.''

''Too bad.''

''Maybe not,'' Del said. ''Since he's alone, it would be easy to follow him when he leaves.''

Fifteen minutes later, Del was walking along the sidewalk, a newspaper tucked beneath his arm and his head down. He strode quickly, endeavoring to appear as if he knew exactly where he was going so that he wouldn't attract any attention to himself if his quarry decided to look back. The man did pause once outside a subway entrance, but Del strode right past him and down the stairs without glancing sideways. The maneuver paid off. When the man came down the stairs a few minutes later, Del had no trouble following him onto a train.

Over the next three hours, Del trailed the man to a triple-X-rated movie house near the Port Authority bus terminal, a pool hall in the Bronx and finally a run-down apartment building across from a gas station.

In all likelihood, this man was just a small fish in Simon's organization, but the tighter SPEAR drew its net, the fewer places Simon would be able to hide. Del used his cell phone to relay the information he had gathered, then remained nearby until he saw a SPEAR surveillance van move in. The man in the passenger seat flicked a cigarette lighter, a signal to Del that he was no longer needed. His job done for now, Del turned and headed for his hotel.

There was no message waiting from Maggie when he reached his room. He hadn't expected any, and he understood why. She was still cautious about their friendship, and he couldn't blame her, after the betrayal she had suffered from Delilah's father. Nevertheless, over the past two weeks, Del sensed she was starting to trust him.

How would she feel if she learned how often he had lied to her?

A familiar twinge of guilt tweaked his conscience, but Del forced it aside. He wasn't doing Maggie any harm. He was giving her a hand with the child he had helped bring into the world, and in the process, he was enjoying himself. Why should he feel guilty about that?

He rolled his head, feeling the bones in the back of his neck grind from the tension in his muscles. He kicked off his shoes, then stripped down to his boxers and dropped to the floor. He'd told Maggie that exercise helped him work off tension. Lately it had become a nightly habit. He went through his routine by rote, counting off the sets of push-ups. He rolled to his back on the carpet and propped his feet on the edge of the mattress to prepare for his sit-ups when his gaze was caught by the two photographs he had propped on the nightstand.

One was of Maggie cradling Delilah in her arms. He'd taken it the day after he'd brought them home from the hospital. There were faint circles of exhaustion beneath Maggie's eyes, but her face was filled with such naked love for her child, she looked dazzling.

If ever a woman was born to be a mother, it was Maggie. She hadn't breathed a word of complaint for the sleepless nights she'd been having or for the constant demands of a newborn. Del had done everything he could to help her, short of hiring a housekeeper...or moving in himself. And God help him, the latter option was looking more appealing every day.

Each time he left Maggie's, he noticed the sterile silence of this hotel room more and more. It had never bothered him before. He liked to have his surroundings orderly and uncluttered. Now he was beginning to prefer the cramped chaos of the little apartment in Astoria.

But Maggie was born to be a mother. And Del could never be a father.

He clasped his hands behind his head and curled upward, concentrating on contracting his abdominals. He gradually increased his pace until he could feel sweat beading on his forehead and upper lip. Yet still his gaze returned to the pictures on his nightstand. The second photo was one that Maggie hadn't seen. It was one of the three she had taken, and like all the rest, it had turned out perfectly.

It had been right after she had taught him how to change Delilah's diaper and then had trusted him to do it on his own for the first time. He had just managed to put a fresh sleeper on the baby and had picked her up to hold her against his shoulder the way Maggie had shown him when she had snapped the picture.

Del almost hadn't recognized himself when he'd first seen that photograph. He looked nothing like the man who hunted terrorists as a SPEAR agent. He looked younger. Happier. More relaxed.

That's what Maggie and Delilah were giving him. And what had he given them in return? Friendship, a few baby items…and continuing deceit.

But he'd had no choice. It had been necessary to lie about those pictures she had taken. Like the agents in most clandestine government agencies, he didn't allow himself to be photographed.

He couldn't afford a record of his face to get around.

And he couldn't have given her the number of his cell phone. It might look ordinary, but it was specially modified to route calls through a scrambling system that guaranteed security. Only top SPEAR agents with high enough clearance were issued one. Del had been skirting the line when he'd borrowed one of the agency's cameras to take baby pictures. He couldn't risk compromising himself and everyone else by divulging his contact number.

He didn't like lying to Maggie. That's why he changed the subject whenever she asked about his job. Yet that left him feeling even worse. She was so honest about everything, so down to earth and good-natured, he knew she deserved better.

What kind of man had Delilah's father been? What kind of selfish idiot could have taken Maggie's love and then turned his back on his child?

Judging by the wholehearted way she devoted herself to her daughter, Del would bet that Maggie would have been a passionate lover. She would be earthy, sensual and uninhibited. Del could easily imagine how her eyes would sparkle and her laugh would turn low and sensuous in bed. The pregnancy had left her body with extra weight on her breasts and hips in a way that accentuated her femininity. She wasn't any svelte model-thin waif. No, she was all woman. Beautiful. Ripe. Desirable.

Desirable?

Damn, he shouldn't have touched her today. She had been so tense, he'd only meant to help her relax. Once he'd started that massage, though, he hadn't wanted to stop.

Two weeks ago he had told Bill that thinking about Maggie in a sexual way would be wrong. Del had too much respect for her to take advantage of the intimacy of their situation. He only wanted to be her friend.

And he didn't need to kill another bottle of whiskey to remind himself of all the reasons friendship was all he could offer.

Clenching his jaw, Del rolled to his feet and headed for the shower. "Her friend," he repeated, stepping under the spray. For a man who had a reputation for nerves of steel in life-and-death situations, exercising self-control around Maggie should be simple.

But just to make sure his body got the message, he adjusted the water temperature to its coldest setting.

Chapter 5

"You're toast, mister."

The instant the narrow-bored cylinder pressed into his back, Del's body stiffened. The gun had the diameter of a nine millimeter, thick enough around the rim to have been fitted with a silencer or a muzzle flash suppressor. Del had checked the hall automatically before he had stepped off the elevator and it had been clear, so his assailant must have been concealed behind the stairwell door. They were less than a step away from it now, and Del hadn't heard the door close. That meant if he dived to his right and kicked left he would knock the gunman down the stairs.

All this flashed through Del's head in less time than it took for the surge of adrenaline to hit his muscles. He was a heartbeat away from exploding into action.

Fortunately, before Del's body could follow through, his brain absorbed the wording of the threat…and the lisp in the speaker's high-pitched voice. He turned around.

A red-haired boy with freckles and a striped shirt was standing in the hallway. He brandished a bright orange plastic toy that looked like something out of a science fiction movie. Jumping backward, he made a high-pitched whirring sound, following it with a whooping siren noise. ''Intruder alert! Intruder alert!''

Del exhaled silently, relieved he had held himself back from overreacting. Luckily, he hadn't been on full alert anyway, since this was Maggie's building and he could afford to lower his guard. He lifted his eyebrows at the boy. ''Excuse me?''

In response, the siren increased in volume. ''Die, alien slime!''

A door to an apartment down the hall opened suddenly. ''Robbie?'' a voice called.

More whirring sounds mixed with sharp tongue clicks.

An elderly woman poked her head into the hallway. The white bun on top of her head wobbled like jelly as she looked from side to side.

As soon as she spotted the boy, she jabbed her thumb over her shoulder. "Robbie, you get back here right now."

"Aw, Gramma."

"Now, Robbie. You know better than to talk to strangers," she said to the child. She pushed her glasses up her nose and eyed Del. Despite her small stature, she bristled with all the defensive menace of a mother bear with an errant cub.

"He's not a stranger. I seen him lotsa times going to Aunt Maggie's."

Del felt a start of surprise. He'd never seen the child until now. That meant the boy must have been watching him through the window, or through the peephole in the door, or from the concealment of the stairwell. It was disconcerting—Del had done surveillance often enough but wasn't accustomed to being the target himself.

Good thing he was only the target of a boy armed with a plastic ray gun.

The woman's stance relaxed somewhat. Nevertheless, she grabbed the boy by the shoulder as soon as he came within range and guided him behind her. "You saw him, not seen him."

The boy slipped out the moment she turned to shut the door. "Zap, zap," he said, waving his orange weapon.

Del shifted the shopping bag he was carrying

and clutched his hand over his heart. "Agh! You got me."

Chortling in glee, the boy raced into the apartment.

The woman sighed. "Sorry about that," she said to Del.

"It's okay. I don't mind."

"I hadn't realized you were Maggie's friend. These days, you can't be too careful."

"That's true."

"I keep telling Robbie not to play in the hall, but I can't catch him every time. Are you on your way to Maggie's?"

He started forward. "Yes, as a matter of fact I am."

"I'm Armilda," she said, offering a smile. She didn't let go of her door, though. "You must be Del. I've heard about you. You're the Good Samaritan who delivered her baby."

"That's right."

"Maggie baby-sits Robbie for me now and then."

Del remembered that Maggie had told him she was going to baby-sit for her neighbor as a way to earn extra money. "Yes, she mentioned something about that to me."

"She's so busy with that baby, I don't know where she finds the energy. Raising Robbie alone is sometimes more than I can handle." There was a sudden crash from within her apartment. She turned her head sharply. "Robbie?"

"It's okay, Gramma," he called. "I saved the lid."

"That's the second cookie jar this week," she muttered. With a hurried goodbye to Del, she closed the door.

Del continued along the hall until he reached Maggie's apartment. Even before he knocked, he could hear Delilah's fretful crying through the door. If it hadn't been for Robbie's space siren, the crying would have been audible all the way to the elevator.

"Hi, Del," Maggie said, jiggling Delilah against her shoulder. She pushed her hair off her forehead with her free hand and gave him a weary smile. "You might want to wear hearing protection if you come any further."

"I just survived a ray gun attack, so I can survive this."

"Robbie?"

"Uh-huh. What's wrong with Delilah?"

"Oh, she's fussy today." Maggie rubbed the baby's back and paced past the couch. "I think it's because of the broccoli."

"Broccoli?"

"I ate some for dinner yesterday so she's been

getting my version of cream of broccoli milk today. I think it gave her gas.''

''What can I do to help?''

''Other than find some industrial strength earplugs?''

''Does she need a doctor?''

''No, I don't think so.'' Maggie reversed direction to pace back again. ''She doesn't have a fever, and her appetite is good. I'm sure this will pass.''

As if on cue, Delilah chose that moment to interrupt her wailing long enough to emit a loud burp.

''Clever girl,'' Maggie said, patting her back.

The baby was silent for a moment, then drew up her legs and resumed her sobs.

Maggie sighed and pressed a kiss to the top of her head. ''Oh, you poor thing,'' she murmured. ''I'm so sorry, sweetheart. No more broccoli, I promise. I don't even like it that much. It's nasty, nasty stuff. I just wanted to get our vitamins.''

In spite of her efforts to appear cheerful, Del could hear the fatigue in Maggie's voice. He set the shopping bag on the coffee table and held out his arms. ''Here. Let me take her for a while.''

''It's okay, Del. I can walk with her.''

''How much sleep did you get last night?''

"Sleep? You mean people are supposed to sleep at night? Hey, what a concept."

He stepped in front of her on her next circuit of the room and smoothly plucked the baby from her grasp. "Hi, Delilah," he said, transferring her to his shoulder. "Let your uncle Del have a turn."

At the change of position, Delilah snuffled.

Del cupped the back of her head in his palm and took a few steps. "There you go," he said. "You must be as tired as your mom by now."

Delilah let out a whimper and curled her knees into Del's chest. Her sobs tapered off into a tired sigh.

"That's it," he said, moving his hand to her back and rubbing slowly. "We'll walk around a bit until you're feeling better. Then I'll show you the unicorn mobile I brought you. It fits over your crib and the unicorns will dance for you if your window's open. I think you'll like them."

Maggie stood where she was, her mouth agape. "How did you do that?"

"What?"

"She stopped crying."

"Being held by a different person could have distracted her."

"It's your voice."

"My voice?"

"It's very..." She hesitated. "Nice," she said finally. "And you have, um, nice hands."

"Thank you."

Maggie ran her fingers through her hair and flopped down on the couch. "No, thank *you.*"

Del could feel Delilah's tiny body begin to relax as her breathing steadied. He was struck by the complete helplessness of the infant—and the total trust.

What would she think of the lies he kept telling her mother?

But he wasn't deceiving anyone now, he told himself. This warmth he felt for Delilah was genuine, as was his concern for Maggie.

He eased into the rocking chair. "I think you could use a break."

"Me? No, I'm fine."

"You were practically asleep on your feet."

"Oh, that's one of the perks of motherhood."

"Things are quiet at work for the moment, so it wouldn't be any trouble for me to give you a hand."

She glanced at him. She hesitated, chewing her lip for a while as if uncertain of what to say. "I've been wondering, Del. Would you mind if I asked you something?"

He smiled. Finally, he thought, she was about

to admit she could use his help. "Anything, Maggie. Go ahead and ask."

"What exactly do you do?"

"What do you mean?"

"Your profession. What kind of work are you in?" She laughed nervously. "I'm not trying to pry or anything, I'm just curious, that's all."

There was no way out now, he realized. He couldn't refuse to answer her direct question. So he had to come up with yet another lie.

"I'm a consultant for an import-export business."

"Oh. Um, okay."

"We deal mostly in electronics."

"Ah. That's why you mentioned you could get me a deal on monitoring equipment."

"Right."

"And that explains your hands."

"My hands?"

"Your fingers are very nimble. It must come from handling all those little electronic thingamajiggies."

Actually, his dexterity came from cleaning, assembling and disassembling weapons on a regular basis. "Something like that. My work also involves a lot of traveling and odd hours, depending on when a shipment is due," he said, expanding on the impromptu cover story.

"I see."

"It's all pretty routine stuff. And it isn't any-where near as challenging as the job you're do-ing."

"I told you before, this isn't a job." She yawned. "It's a joy."

"How often do you baby-sit Robbie?" he asked, smoothly changing the subject.

Maggie put her forearm over her eyes and dropped her head against the back of the couch. "Only a few times a week after school."

"He seems like a very active boy."

"That's for sure."

"Armilda's his grandmother, right?"

"That's what he calls her, but she's really his foster mother. He's been with her for about three months. She's very fond of him, but she doesn't have the energy to take him on permanently. They're trying to find him a family."

"Where's his mother?"

"His parents were killed by a drunk driver two years ago when he was four. He doesn't have any other relatives."

"That's terrible."

"The pits," she agreed. "He's doing okay, though. Kids generally are resilient, but Robbie has adapted quite well. He takes each day as it comes and tries to make the best of it. Life threw him some lemons, so he's going to make lemonade.''

''That sounds like you.''

She rolled her head along the couch to look at him. ''Hmm?''

''You have a very positive attitude. I saw that about you even before I knew your name.''

Smiling, she looked at her baby. ''I have a lot of things to be positive about, starting with an absolute angel for a daughter.''

As if in response to her mother's voice, Delilah squirmed briefly and let out another burp.

Maggie laughed softly. ''But I don't think she's going to become a broccoli farmer when she grows up.''

''I think you're right.''

''What kind of farm did you grow up on, Del?''

''Dairy.''

''Really? So you milked cows and all that?''

''Mostly the machines did the milking.''

She gave a mock shudder and crossed her arms over her breasts defensively. ''That must be horrible for the cows. They have my sympathy.''

''They didn't seem to mind. My father used to pipe Mozart into the barn to put them at ease.''

''You're kidding.''

"No, he really did. It increased the milk yield."

She lifted one eyebrow. "Do you think it might work for me?"

Del kept his gaze carefully above her neck. "Uh, Maggie…"

She grinned. "I'm sorry, Del, but it's so much fun to make you blush."

The heat Del felt in his face wasn't from embarrassment. It was from the increase in his heart rate as he pictured the size of Maggie's breasts. "I'm glad I can amuse you."

She settled more comfortably against the couch cushions. "I grew up in Brooklyn. The closest I ever got to a farm was watching reruns of 'Little House on the Prairie.'"

"Well, the Rogers' place is nothing like that."

Her nostrils flared as she attempted to stifle another yawn. "Did you have an old rusty truck and a hound dog named Duke?"

He chuckled. "We weren't the Beverly Hillbillies, either, but we did have a dog. He was a shepherd-Lab cross, and we called him Butch. We even had indoor plumbing."

"Wow. Television, too?"

"Yep."

"Tell me about it, Del. What was it like?"

This was one subject he didn't have to lie

about, Del thought. He shifted Delilah to the crook of his arm and pushed the rocking chair into motion. "Depending on the season, I thought of it as colors. The winter was blue and white, big stretches of it when the sun glinted off the snowdrifts. Spring was green...."

As he talked, he felt Delilah's body grow limp with sleep. A few minutes later, Maggie's eyes drifted shut, and her head lolled to one side.

Del sat where he was for a while, simply absorbing the sense of peace that surrounded him. A door slammed down the hall. Out on the street a dog barked and a jet roared in the distance, yet in this cozy apartment the only sounds were the soft creaking of the rocking chair and Maggie's deep breathing.

How long had it been since he'd talked about his days on the farm? Usually he avoided the memories because they were all tangled up with the pain of his failure with Elizabeth. Odd how it didn't bother him to talk about it with Maggie. Maybe it was because of Maggie's positive attitude. That's just the way she was, always looking on the bright side, making the best of her situation.

Maggie's lips parted on a delicate snore.

Del smiled. On the other hand, a positive attitude only went so far. Right now, exhaustion had the upper hand. He rose and transferred Delilah to her crib, then came back for Maggie. Slipping his arms under her knees and shoulders, he carefully lifted her from the couch.

She was lighter than he had expected—with so much vitality in her frame, he often forgot how small she was. She fit perfectly into his arms, her head nestling snugly against his shoulder as the side of her breast rubbed warmly against his chest.

A tremor moved through him at the feel of that soft contact. He shouldn't have been thinking about her breasts earlier, despite Maggie's teasing. Now he was excruciatingly aware of every cubic inch. Gritting his teeth, Del did his best to ignore his stirring libido as he carried her past Delilah's crib and laid her down on her bed. Maggie was so soundly asleep, she barely stirred as he eased off her shoes and pulled a light blanket over her. She wouldn't even stir if he leaned over and brushed his lips across her cheek…or her mouth.

Del straightened slowly, his gaze going from Maggie's cheek to her parted lips. Her scent teased his nostrils, a combination of baby powder, soap and lemons…and an underlying note of something tangy that had to be pure Maggie. And despite his best intentions, that scent only reinforced the reaction that the contact with her body had started.

His gaze lowered. Beneath the blanket, her chest was rising and falling with her breathing. The light fabric molded to her curves the way his palm itched to do....

His conscience sounded a warning. He shouldn't be standing here like this. She trusted him. He was taking advantage of the situation—

No, he wasn't. He was being damn noble. If he really wanted to take advantage, he'd be leaning over the bed instead of standing beside it. He'd be bracing his hands on either side of her shoulders and lowering his head until he felt her breath on his lips. And then he'd lean closer still, until he could fit his mouth to hers. Her lips were already soft and parted in sleep. It would be so easy to slip his tongue between them.

How would she taste? As good as she smelled? And would her mouth be warm and inviting as his tongue probed deeper? Would her lips surround him and draw him inside as she moaned in her sleep? Would she make room for him on the bed and lift the blanket to welcome him—

Del rubbed a hand roughly over his face, bringing himself back to reality.

This had been worse than the last time, and he had barely touched her. Was this how he repaid

Maggie's trust and her friendship? Standing here entertaining lascivious thoughts while she was unconscious?

This was sick. It was almost as bad as what he'd accused Bill of. What the hell had come over him? What was he thinking?

That was the problem. He wasn't thinking with his brain, he was thinking with his body. How much longer could this go on? Maybe he should call a stop to this friendship of theirs now, before his more-than-friendly feelings got out of hand.

But who else would help her if he didn't? She was exhausted. Just look at how quickly she had fallen asleep when he had taken Delilah off her hands. She needed him. He couldn't turn his back on her now, could he?

The sudden knocking on the apartment door snapped his head around. As long as whoever it was didn't wake up Maggie or Delilah, the interruption couldn't have been timed better. He strode away from the bed and eased the bedroom door shut behind him, then went to answer the knock.

Before he could reach for the doorknob, a key scraped in the lock. The door swung open and a blond, middle-aged man stepped into the apartment.

At the sight of the intruder, adrenaline surged

through Del's muscles for the second time that afternoon. It was similar to his reaction to the feel of Robbie's toy gun against his back. But this time it wasn't any harmless six-year-old who had triggered the automatic response.

The man was tall and dressed in an expensive suit. His face had the pale, soft cast of someone who spent most of his time behind a desk, yet there was a shiftiness to his eyes and a stealth to his movements that set off alarms in Del's brain.

There could be an innocent explanation for this man's presence in Maggie's apartment, but with Maggie and the baby both sound asleep and completely vulnerable in the next room, Del wasn't going to take any chances. He would take charge of the situation first and ask questions later. In one smooth motion, he caught the man's wrist, spun him around and pressed him face first against the wall.

"Hey!" the man exclaimed. "What—"

"First question," Del said, twisting the man's arm up his back to hold him immobile. "Who are you?"

"What's going on? Let go of me."

"Certainly," Del said. "But first you answer my question. Who are you?"

"That's none of your business. I demand that you release me this insta—" His words ended on a grunted exhalation as Del increased the pressure on his arm.

"The way I see it," Del said calmly, "you're not in any position to make demands."

"You want money? Take my wallet. Take my watch. It's a Rolex. Just don't hurt me."

"You have it backward. You're the one trespassing. I could have you arrested if I wanted to."

"I'm not trespassing. I have a key."

"I noticed." Del plucked the ring with the pair of keys the man still held and tossed it to the floor behind him.

"What is this?" The man struggled ineffectually and made a sputtered protest. "Are you the police?"

"Would you like to find out how much farther I need to twist your arm before it breaks?"

The man muttered an expletive.

"Fine. Let's start again. What is your name, and why are you here?"

"I'm here to see Maggie."

"Is she expecting you?"

"That's irrelevant." The man paused for a moment, as if gathering his courage now that the immediate threat of being mugged had passed. "If you're a cop, I hope you have a good lawyer because I'm going to sue your pants off."

Del's lip curled at the show of bravado. First the man was ready to surrender his valuables without a fight, now he was arrogantly threatening to sue. "Uh-huh. I'm quaking in my boots, Mr...?"

"Blackthorn," he said. "Alan Blackthorn."

His name was Alan. He had a key to Maggie's apartment. His hair was blond...like Delilah's.

The pieces clicked into place. Damn. This had to be Maggie's ex-boyfriend. Delilah's father.

Del knew he should let him go.

But what he really wanted was to follow through and break Alan Blackthorn's arm. It would be a token payback for all the pain the bastard had caused Maggie.

Del swore under his breath. As tempting as it was, breaking Alan's arm would lead to too many complications. The creep undoubtedly would get a lawyer. There would be no hiding behind SPEAR immunity, either—Del was on his own time.

Worst of all, doing Alan damage would upset the softhearted Maggie. So in what was rapidly becoming a habit, Del forced himself to let his brain overrule his more primitive urges. He released Alan and stepped back.

"Here's some free advice, Mr. Blackthorn," Del said, his tone one notch above a growl.

"Don't make a habit of letting yourself into other people's apartments. They might get the wrong idea."

Alan turned to face him warily and lifted his arm to rub his wrist. "Who are you?" he asked.

"I'm Maggie's friend."

"Then where is she?"

"What makes you think she's here?"

"She's not at work. They told me she was home because she'd had the baby. Is that true?"

The baby. Not *my baby* or *her baby* but an impersonal *the*. This man didn't deserve to be a father. He had no right to a child as sweet as Delilah. "Why don't you give me your number. I'll have Maggie call you."

Alan shifted his gaze away. "I need to speak with her. I'll wait here."

Del didn't want him here. He didn't want him polluting this cozy home with his presence. Most of all, Del didn't want to think about how many other times Alan had been here. With Maggie.

It wasn't simply concern for Maggie that motivated Del now. It was primitive, male territoriality. "That wouldn't be a good idea," he said.

Alan brushed the front of his suit coat and straightened his tie. He didn't need to smooth his hair—the thinning locks were styled so stiffly not a strand had moved out of place. "I know my rights," he said. "If you don't show me your badge, I'll have you brought up on brutality charges."

"I'm not a cop."

"Then perhaps I'd better call one."

"You do that," Del said. He scooped the set of keys off the floor and dropped them in his pocket. "And while we're on our way to the station, I'll call your wife."

Alan's mouth immediately lost its arrogant tilt. Instead, it curved into a smile as charming—and about as sincere—as a toothpaste ad. "I don't want any trouble. I just wanted to see Maggie, but if that's—"

"Del? Is something wrong?"

At the soft voice, both men turned toward the bedroom.

Maggie was standing in the doorway, her hair tousled, her face still softly flushed from what had been far too short a sleep. The moment she caught sight of her visitor, though, all trace of relaxation fled from her frame. She squared her shoulders and stepped forward, closing the bedroom door firmly. "Hello, Alan."

He turned his smile up a few watts and hurried toward her. "Maggie, how are you doing?" he said, holding out his arms. "I've been so worried."

She sidestepped to avoid his embrace. "I haven't seen you for five months, Alan, and the first thing you say to me is a lie. That figures."

"Maggie, please—"

"What were you worried about? My health? My finances? Oh, I know. You were worried that I was going to show up at your doorstep with my baby. Too bad it doesn't snow at this time of the year. That would have added to the effect beautifully."

Del had been poised to grab Alan and throw him out bodily at the first indication from Maggie, but he should have realized that she would be able to handle this herself. He'd always admired her spunk. Crossing his arms, he leaned one hip against the back of the couch and watched the unfolding confrontation.

Alan dropped his arms to his sides. His smile faded as he tilted his head and put on a cajoling expression. "Oh, sweetheart, I've been concerned about you, of course."

"Were you really?"

"Oh, yes."

Del snorted.

"Do you mind?" Alan said over his shoulder. "We'd like to talk in private."

Del didn't want to leave her alone with this

man, but he knew it was her call. "Maggie?" he asked.

She shook her head. "I'd like you to stay, Del."

Alan managed to look offended and cajoling at once. "He's not your boyfriend, is he, Maggie? I couldn't bear it if you've found someone else already."

"Del is my friend, Alan. That's all. Not that you have any right to ask."

"But, Maggie, sweetheart—"

"Alan, are you still married?"

He jerked. "Well, yes, but—"

"Then we have nothing more to say."

"Wait. Please, Maggie. I love you."

The magic words, Del thought with disgust. When all else fails, trot out the love factor. Elizabeth had done that. And her love had stood up to the test about as well as Alan's. Del was about to snort again when he saw the expression that flitted across Maggie's face.

It wasn't disgust. It wasn't disbelief. It was...longing.

That jarred him. Was she longing for Alan, or for the words?

"I love you," Alan repeated, catching one of her hands. "We were good together, Maggie. I miss you so much. Please, just give me another chance. We can work things out somehow.''

Del held his breath. He wanted to grab Alan by the back of his expensive suit and give him the bum's rush to the sidewalk. He wanted to sweep Maggie into his arms and carry her away from here, away from old boyfriends, from men who could give her children.

But he didn't have the right to do that, did he? He was only her friend, only passing through her life.

And the hell of it was, in his own way, he was as much a liar as Alan.

''Work things out?'' she repeated. ''How, Alan? Are you going to get a divorce and marry me and raise our children and promise me forever?''

''Maggie...''

''Because that's what I want. A family and forever. But you're not the man who can give me that.''

''I can give you other things, Maggie,'' he murmured. ''Remember?''

She yanked her hand from his and wiped it on her skirt. ''Are you really so arrogant, so *stupid,* that you assume we'll pick up where we left off? Is that why you came around?'' Her voice rose. ''You want sex, Alan? Is that it?''

"You have every right to be angry with me, Maggie," Alan said, trying his smile once more. "I was so mixed up before. It took losing you to realize how much I care—"

"My God, I knew I had made a mistake with you, but I hadn't realized just how bad it was." She blinked hard. "It's just as well you reminded me."

At the sight of tears in Maggie's eyes, Del had had enough. He crossed the room and placed himself between Alan and Maggie. "Your visit is over," he said. "Leave now."

Alan hesitated. "You've misunderstood everything, Maggie. I do love you. I'll come back later when we can talk in private, okay?"

She shook her head quickly. "No, Alan. Stay away from me."

"You heard her," Del said, reaching for Alan's wrist.

"Touch me again and I'll have you charged with assault," he said, retreating toward the door.

"It would be worth it," Del muttered. He was almost disappointed when Alan left without any further argument. He would have liked an excuse to land a punch or two. A broken nose might have given the man's smooth face more character.

After turning the lock and sliding the security

chain in place, Del turned back to see that Maggie was leaning against the bedroom door, her faced buried in her hands. He was by her side in an instant, slipping his arms around her back to pull her against him. "I'm sorry," he said.

She dipped her head, pressing her forehead into his chest. "It's not your fault," she said, her voice muffled. "It's mine."

"I should have thrown him out when I realized who he was."

"I had to face him sooner or later. I'm just glad that you were here."

Del felt his shirt grow damp as her shoulders shuddered with a sob. He hesitated to ask the question but knew that he had to. "Do you still have feelings for him?"

There was a brief but agonizing silence. "No," she answered finally. "Whatever I felt, or whatever I *thought* I felt, died months ago when I learned about his lies. I trusted the wrong person, that's what it comes down to. Damn, how could I have been so blind?"

Del had no answer to that one. And he wasn't yet enough of a hypocrite to condemn someone else for lying. "Sometimes we see things in people we love that aren't really there."

"Or maybe we imagine things in the people we *want* to love."

"What do you mean?"

"I was such a fool, Del. I *wanted* to love Alan. He was so charming and so smart. I thought he was my shot at happiness. I was so wrong."

"We all make mistakes."

"Well, this one was a doozy. My God, I can't believe he had the...the nerve to stand here and talk about love and ask me to be his...mistress, as if he were doing me a favor. As if I were even capable...." She drew in an unsteady breath. "I gave birth less than three weeks ago. How could he possibly think I'd be interested in sex?" she mumbled.

Del felt a stab of guilt at his own feelings. "Any man who came on to you now would be an insensitive jerk," he said, as much for his benefit as hers.

"But do you know what the worst thing was? He never once asked about Delilah. Not once. It's as if she never happened."

"You're both better off without him."

"That's for sure. And to think I'd been feeling guilty over not telling him about his daughter."

"It was his choice, Maggie. He made that clear before she was born."

"I know, but I thought it was unfair of me. Selfish. I wanted to have her all to myself."

"And now you do."

She sniffed. "Yes, now I do."

He tightened his hold, pulling her more firmly to the front of his body. "He won't bother you again. I'll call a locksmith and have your locks changed."

"My locks?"

"He used a key to get in."

Maggie lifted her head to look at him. Confusion misted her eyes. "He used a *key?* But he returned the set of keys I gave him months ago. I made sure of it when I found out the truth about him."

"He must have had a copy made before he gave your keys back."

She was silent for a moment. Gradually the confusion gave way to anger. "That rat!"

There were several other more colorful epithets Del would have used. "I'll stay here until your lock is changed, okay? I could install an alarm system, too."

She raised her eyebrows. "An alarm system? In this tiny place?"

"I could get a good deal on the electronics."

The corners of her mouth trembled in what could have been the hint of a smile. "Maybe I'll just tell the superintendent to call the exterminator back in. That should help keep the rats under control."

Del couldn't help it. Before he could think, he lifted his hand to wipe a tear from her cheek with the pad of his thumb. "You're taking this well, Maggie."

"No, I'm not." She sniffed again. "The front of your shirt is soaked."

"It'll dry."

"It's the hormones, you know. I just can't seem to control my emotions."

"It's understandable. You have every reason to be upset. Now I'm sorry I didn't break his arm, after all. He had it coming."

"Break his... Del, what did he mean about charging you with assault? What happened when he got here?"

"Nothing."

The smile that had been hovering around her lips finally broke through. "On your white charger riding to my rescue once more, huh?"

Oh, damn. He wanted to kiss her. If that made him an insensitive jerk, then that's what he was. The urge was as overpowering as the need to breathe. She felt so soft and feminine, the way she was nestled in his arms, with her hands on his chest and her chin tilted up, that his entire body was humming with awareness.

The urge was so much stronger than it had been earlier, in her bedroom. She was wide awake. Her eyes were sparkling as she looked at him. Her cheeks, still wet from her tears, dimpled with her smile. Del knew that if he didn't move away in the next second, there would be no stopping, no turning back.

Think about Delilah, he told himself. *Think about the baby, about Maggie's dream of having a family and forever, two things you could never promise her.*

But, damn, her mouth was so near and already moist and supple and inviting....

"Thanks for being my friend, Del," she said. She patted his cheek and stepped back. "Who says chivalry is dead?"

Chivalry? The hell with chivalry. He wanted to kiss her. Hard. Deep. Now.

Instead, he called the locksmith.

Chapter 6

Maggie stood outside the diner, looking through the window at the activity within. A middle-aged woman Maggie didn't recognize was clearing the dishes from an empty table. Behind the counter, Laszlo was fixing a fresh batch of coffee while Joanne chatted to a pair of customers who stood by the cash register. It was mid-morning, so the breakfast rush was tapering off and the noon-hour scramble hadn't yet begun.

The last time she had been here was almost four weeks ago, the day Delilah had been born. It was all so familiar, and yet so different. Maggie glanced at her reflection in the glass. Her hair was the same short, practical style, although a bit longer. Her cheeks seemed thinner, but that was nothing compared to the drastic reduction in size everywhere else. The last time she had walked through that door, she had been so pregnant she'd practically filled up the door frame and blocked the daylight.

Yet the biggest difference was that this time, she wouldn't be entering the place alone. Smiling, she looked at her daughter.

Delilah was lying on her back in the stroller, her gaze intent on the string of colorful beads that hung above her. A lace-trimmed pink bonnet shielded her face from the breeze, and a blanket embroidered with pink teddy bears kept her cozy. It was one of those perfect May mornings, the sky so clear and fresh that even Manhattan smelled as if spring was well and truly blossoming.

Yet Maggie's good mood today was due to more than the weather; it was because of Del. Ever since Alan's unexpected appearance at the apartment last week, Del had been exceptionally gallant, treating both her and Delilah with attentive consideration. Thanks to the naps Maggie had been able to take during Del's daily visits, she had been catching up on her sleep to the extent that she was feeling like a human being again, instead of a half-conscious zombie. In fact she was feeling so good, she was even looking forward to hearing Laszlo growl. ''Well, Delilah?'' she asked, steering the stroller toward the door. ''Want to see where we first met?''

The bell over the door tinkled as the customers who had been at the cash came out. Joanne looked up the moment Maggie wheeled Delilah inside.

''Maggie!'' she cried, hurrying out from behind the counter. She pulled Maggie into a quick embrace. ''I didn't know you were coming in today. What a treat! And you brought the baby!''

''Hi, Joanne,'' Maggie said. She paused to raise her voice. ''Hi, Laszlo.''

He turned. His mustache twitched in what could have been a smile. ''Maggie, you are well?''

''Yes, I'm fine, thanks.''

''Let me see kid,'' he said, wiping his hands on his apron as he walked toward her. He peered at Delilah. The baby peered back solemnly, her eyes crossing briefly in concentration. A thick, rumbling sound that was Laszlo's version of a chuckle arose from his chest. ''Ah, she is the clever girl.''

''A veritable genius,'' Maggie agreed.

''Good, good.'' He pulled aside his apron and withdrew a coin from his pocket. ''Here,'' he said, pressing the coin into Maggie's hand. ''For baby's piggy bank.''

"Laszlo, for heaven's sake," Joanne said. "A quarter? That's all?"

"Silver for baby is the tradition," he said, tilting his head as he wiggled his eyebrows at Delilah.

Maggie laughed and stretched up to plant a kiss on Laszlo's cheek. "Thanks, Laszlo. From both of us."

He grunted. A glint from his gold tooth appeared beneath his mustache before he resumed his work behind the counter.

The woman who had been clearing the table paused on her way by. "What a healthy-looking baby. Is she yours?"

"Yes, she's mine," Maggie said proudly, reaching down to lift Delilah out of the stroller.

"Oh, let me hold her," Joanne said. She took the baby carefully from Maggie's grasp and cradled her in her arms. "Hello, sunshine," Joanne said. "How's my cutesy wootsey wittle sweetie?"

"I hope you don't mind me saying this, but you really shouldn't use baby talk with the child," the other woman said. "Studies have shown that it could delay speech development."

Joanne rolled her eyes at Maggie. "That's Edith," she whispered as the woman moved away. "She's filling in for you. This week, anyway."

Maggie raised her eyebrows. "This week?"

"She's the fifth waitress we've hired since you left," Joanne explained. "I'd be surprised if she makes it through to the weekend."

"Why? What's wrong with her?"

"According to her, nothing. She's perfect, you see. Edith and only Edith knows the right way to do everything."

Cutlery splashed into the sink, sending water slopping onto the floor. At Laszlo's growl, Edith made a *tsk* noise. "You might want to consider installing a dishwasher," she pronounced, "or perhaps redoing the plumbing so there's more space for the sink."

Laszlo muttered something in Hungarian and glared. "Mop is in the back room."

"I hope you don't mind if I make a suggestion, but the back room needs to be better organized," Edith said. "It took me ten minutes to find the box of paper towels yesterday."

Laszlo's glare deepened. "I have the system."

"Oh, I'm sure, but I think I could improve it. We could store the supplies alphabetically, starting on the right and working around to the desk."

"If Edith had been here three weeks ago,"

Joanne muttered, ''she would have filed Delilah under B for Baby.''

There was another spurt of Hungarian from Laszlo. He swung his gaze to Joanne.

She laid the baby in the stroller and put her arm around Maggie's shoulders, turning her toward the door. ''C'mon, let's get out of here before he fires her, too.''

''Joanne!'' Laszlo bellowed.

''I'm taking my break,'' she said, yanking open the door.

Maggie pushed the stroller outside, holding in her laughter until they reached the sidewalk. Once there, both she and Joanne burst into giggles.

''Oh, Maggie,'' Joanne said finally, wiping her eyes. ''I've missed you. It's not the same here without you.''

''I miss you guys, too,'' Maggie said.

''I doubt that. Your little angel here probably keeps you too busy to think much about us at all. You're looking great, by the way.''

''Thanks.''

''And I'm completely envious. How did you manage to lose all that weight in only three weeks?''

''I haven't lost it all. My old pre-baby clothes still don't fit.''

"That's true. You kept it in all the right places. Still breast-feeding, huh?"

Maggie glanced at the buttons that strained over her bosom and laughed again. "What was your first clue?"

"Aside from the obvious? I'd say it was the glow you've got about you. You really are looking great, as if all your energy fields are perfectly balanced." Joanne took off the apron she wore over her brown uniform and stuffed it into the pouch behind the stroller as they moved along the sidewalk. "Motherhood definitely agrees with you, in spite of all the sleepless nights you must be having. I really don't know how you manage."

"It's all for Delilah, so I barely notice the work. Besides, Del's been a big help."

"Del?" Joanne repeated. "As in cowboy Del?"

Maggie shook her head. "He's more like a knight, Joanne. Sweet, kind and considerate. He's a very nice man."

"Nice? Maiden aunts are nice, Maggie. Guys who look like Del are a lot more. And they usually want a lot more."

"Not Del. He's been a really good friend. He dotes on Delilah. He gave her the bonnet she's wearing today and that blanket with the teddy bears, along with about a million rattles and stuffed toys.''

''No. Really?''

''And he's been fixing dinner for me at least three times a week.''

''So that's why he hasn't been around the coffee shop as often lately.''

''He's really wonderful. He changes Delilah, and sometimes he even does my laundry. He made sure to get the locks changed after Alan showed up and—''

''Wait a minute,'' Joanne said, placing her hand over Maggie's where she gripped the stroller handle. ''Alan was nosing around here last week but I wouldn't talk to him. The fourth girl who was filling in for you did, though. She got fired because she ate more food than she served. Anyhow, I can't believe he had the nerve to show up at your apartment. What happened?''

''Nothing. I told him to get lost, and Del made sure he left.''

''Del was there at the time?''

''He comes over every day.''

''And he's just a friend?''

''Yes.''

''Are you sure?''

''Positive.''

''And is that what you want?''

She hesitated for a telling instant. "Yes, of course."

Joanne pursed her lips and made a sound of disbelief.

Maggie exhaled impatiently. "This is ridiculous. I'm not interested in getting involved with any man. Look at me. Despite the boobs to die for, I'm a stew of uneven hormones raging through lumpy cookie dough. My priority is my baby. Getting mixed up with a romance is the last thing I need."

Joanne regarded her in silence. People streamed past them as the light on the corner changed.

"Really, it would be stupid," Maggie went on. "I can't trust my judgment when it comes to men, anyway. Alan was a mistake. He should have cured me of any illusions about finding Prince Charming."

Joanne started to smile.

"Stop smirking," Maggie said. "I know that as far as starting a serious relationship, the timing is all wrong. Even if I dredged up the energy to think about Del that way, I wouldn't be able to do anything about it without rupturing something. And Del is such a sweet man."

"He's sweet?"

"Yes. Terribly sweet. You should see how he blushes whenever I talk about nursing Delilah."

"Cowboy Del blushes?" Joanne's smile grew to a grin. "I wouldn't have guessed that."

"Well, it's not really a blush. It's more of a flush."

"That's…interesting."

"It's kind of endearing. The veins at the base of his throat start to pulse a little faster and harder. His voice gets a bit deeper, too. He has a wonderful voice. It's soothing and stimulating all at once. It's like his touch."

"Ah. He touches you."

"Only as a friend."

"You're sure of that?"

"Positive. He'd be shocked out of his Dockers if he knew how I sometimes look at his hands and think…well…"

"What do you think, Maggie?"

"About how strong and gentle his hands are and how good they would feel…somewhere else. Somewhere with fewer clothes."

"Oh, honey," Joanne said, giving her arm a gentle shake. "Listen to what you're saying. You're half in love with him already."

Maggie groaned. "No, I'm not. I couldn't be. That would be a disaster."

"It sounds as if you're trying to convince

yourself more than you're trying to convince me. Why is that?''

Joanne was right, Maggie realized. She *was* trying to convince herself. Could she really be falling in love with Del?

Oh, yes. All too easily. Given a wonderful, sweet, nice man like Del, any woman would be hard-pressed *not* to fall in love, and it couldn't be blamed merely on postpartum hormones. ''But I told you,'' Maggie said. ''I'm not in any shape to think about a relationship. I'm not looking for a man to come and rescue me. Delilah and I will be fine on our own.''

''But you'll get back in shape soon, and if the right man has already happened to come along, maybe you should hang on to him.''

''But he's *not* the right man,'' Maggie said desperately. ''He's only in New York temporarily. He's going to leave. And he doesn't want to be anything more than my friend.''

''You're sure of that?''

''Yes.''

''Hmm.''

''What's that supposed to mean?'' Maggie demanded.

''He's not married, is he?''

''He claims he isn't.''

Joanne lost her smile. ''You're not certain?''

"He doesn't talk about himself much, and I don't ask. Much. It isn't my business. Actually, I still don't know exactly where he works or where he lives when he's not traveling for his job."

"Why not? If he's coming into your home on a daily basis and getting close to you and your baby, don't you have the right to know more about him?"

"After all the nice things he has done for me, I'd feel disloyal if I pried."

"Go ahead and pry, hon. What are you worried about? That he's another Alan?"

"Alan was a liar. Del doesn't lie. He's just...reserved."

"Do you think he's hiding something?"

Maggie paused. "He couldn't be. He's such a nice man."

"But?" Joanne prompted. "I hear a but."

"Nothing. He's a nice man, a good friend," she said firmly.

"You keep saying that, but I hear something else. If you have doubts about him, you owe it to yourself to find out." Joanne took her apron out of the stroller pouch and put it on. "If he's really such a great guy, then you'll know it for sure. If he isn't, then wouldn't it be better to find out sooner rather than later? Like before you fall all the way in love with him?''

''What do you think I should do? Sit Del down in a straight-backed chair and shine a light in his face while I interrogate him? Work him over with a rubber hose?''

''No, but for starters, you could find out where he goes when he isn't with you.''

''And how would I do that?''

''Easy.'' Joanne motioned with her chin toward the other side of the street. ''You could follow him and see for yourself.''

''What?'' She spun around. ''Oh!''

As if their conversation had conjured him up, there was Del, big as life, striding along the sidewalk with his cell phone pressed to his ear.

Maggie chewed her lip as she watched him go past. She should have realized she might run into Del in this neighborhood. After all, he worked around here somewhere. That's why he had frequented the coffee shop in the first place.

But why had he never told her the address of his office, or even the name of his company? Why did he still tend to change the subject when the conversation turned to his profession? And why hadn't he given her the number of his cell phone yet? He'd taken calls on it several times while he'd been at her apartment, and every time he had dropped what he was doing and left immediately.

What kind of emergency did a consultant for an electronics company get called out to? If he was meeting a shipment of parts, wouldn't the flight schedule or the shipping manifest be known already?

Unless those calls weren't from his office at all. What if he really did have a wife, the way Alan did? Or what if he was doing something illegal? Maybe he had been lying about everything. Maybe she was wrong to trust him.

But he was so *nice*. The only reason she had the energy to undertake this outing today was Del's help with Delilah. How could she doubt him like this? How could she repay his friendship with suspicions?

But after the lesson she'd learned from Alan, how could she trust anyone blindly again? Maggie had to admit that Joanne's advice made sense. If only she didn't feel so guilty about it....

"Go on," Joanne said, giving her a nudge. "He's heading for the subway. This is your chance."

Del deposited the token in the slot and pushed through the turnstile. After scanning the crowd on the subway platform, he took up a position with his back against a pillar to wait for the next train. The rendezvous was set for eleven-fifteen. That gave him a good half hour to work his way to the site.

He didn't usually handle information drops—that was left up to the intelligence-gathering specialists—but when the opportunity had arisen, he'd quickly volunteered. He was getting sick of staring at an empty apartment. He might be serving by standing and waiting, but his patience was wearing thin.

A hunter had patience, Del reminded himself. A hunter had self-control.

Sure, but it had been more than four weeks since Simon had gone underground after the warehouse blast, and nothing was happening. There hadn't been any significant activity at the other surveillance sites, either—agents had been tailing Simon's tattooed associate who had swept for bugs in the apartment, but the man had continued to divide his time between strip bars and peep shows. Repulsive, yes. Illegal, no.

Something had to break soon. It had to. Each night when Del returned to his hotel room, the tension that tightened his muscles couldn't be completely relieved, no matter how much he exercised. Trouble was, Del knew most of the tension wasn't due to the frustrating wait for Simon.

No, his main problem was Maggie. She was on his mind constantly. She and Delilah were rapidly becoming a major part of his life. He treasured the time he spent with them both, even though it was starting to drive him mad.

It was getting more and more difficult to control his urges every time he saw Maggie. He still wanted to kiss her. Hell, more than that. He just plain wanted her. But he had painted himself into the proverbial corner. She thought he was chivalrous. She depended on his help. He couldn't take advantage of her. He had a conscience. He had scruples.

He had patience, he had self-control.

Del swore under his breath and clenched his jaw. Shoving his hands roughly into his pockets, he did another scan of the platform. Nothing suspicious, nothing threatening, just the usual mix of people. Business suits and briefcases, baggy jeans and bandannas. A petite blond woman with a stroller, two old men with canes...

Del snapped his gaze to where he'd spotted the woman. For a moment, he thought he'd seen Maggie. His view was obscured by a group of passing teenagers momentarily. When they moved on, he saw that the woman pushing the stroller was a brunette accompanied by an older child.

Damn. His preoccupation with Maggie was intruding into his work—he was imagining her even here. The floor vibrated with the arrival of the uptown train. Del exhaled hard and forced himself to relax as he boarded. He had to put Maggie out of his mind. She was part of his off-duty life. Until he finished his shift, he'd better keep his mind on his job.

One car down from Del, Maggie maneuvered past several teenagers to claim a seat as the train started to move. She drew the stroller close and set the brake. Through the grimy windows in the doors that separated the cars, she caught a glimpse of Del's back.

He was wearing a cream-colored shirt and khakis today. He looked as appealing and clean-cut as always, with his nondescript clothes and his close-cropped hair. Yet he seemed different from the man who visited her every day at her apartment. He seemed…harder, more alert. The way he moved, the way he held himself, he looked like the cowboy she had first thought he resembled, a ruthless gunslinger scanning the horizon for his prey.

Maggie leaned back against the seat and blew her bangs out of her eyes. Was she nuts? What on earth was she doing, spying on Del? What could she say to him if he saw her?

On the other hand, Joanne had a good point. Maggie had to do this, for Delilah's sake as well as her own. If she was starting to fall in love with this man, she had better know who he was. She hadn't bothered to discover the truth about Alan, and look what had happened.

Besides, it was too late to turn back now. Del was already getting off the train.

Maggie quickly released the stroller brake and blended into the crowd, assuming Del would leave the station. Instead, he worked his way to the opposite platform and caught the next train.

Over the next half hour, they changed trains three more times, seemingly at random. Her lack of stature made it a challenge to keep Del in sight, but if she had been taller, he probably would have spotted her half a dozen times. And if she hadn't been a native New Yorker and so adept at navigating the subways, she never would have been able to keep up with him. When they returned to midtown and he finally exited the subway only one stop away from where he had entered, she began to suspect that he might be lost.

She emerged into the sunlight and hurried along the sidewalk after him, pausing to stand on her toes. He disappeared briefly when he crossed the street and a bus blocked her view, but then she spotted him heading for the mid Manhattan branch of the New York Public Library.

Instead of going inside, Del paused at the base of the steps and took a map from his back pocket. Unfolding the map, he bent his head to read. An elderly couple, tourists by the look of them, stopped in front of him. Del gestured vaguely with one hand, then shrugged apologetically before they went on their way. He lingered for a few minutes, then folded up his map and started off once more.

Maggie sighed and pushed the stroller forward. Even though Del obviously had been confused by the transit system, he still was, well, nice enough to attempt to give directions to complete strangers.

She followed him from the library to a restaurant near the theater district. It appeared that he wasn't there to meet another woman. He went directly to a table that was already occupied by a balding, middle-aged man who reminded Maggie of her old high school English teacher.

The buoyant mood with which she had started out today slowly subsided under a weight of guilt. So far, Del had done nothing to warrant her distrust.

Yet he had done nothing to dispel her distrust, either. She could follow him around for days and still not know for sure whether he was hiding anything.

The problem here was *her,* not him. It all came down to a matter of faith—in Del as well as in her own judgment.

So if she wanted to trust Del, she had to trust herself.

At the table in the far corner of the restaurant, Del withdrew the encrypted message the tourists had slipped into his map. He concealed it in his palm as he passed it to Bill. "Are you going to decode it yourself?"

"I might as well. You know what they say about idle hands."

"Yes, I do, but I figure you're going to remind me anyhow."

Bill dipped his head. "'Idle hands are the devil's playground,'" he intoned, smoothly slipping the message into his pants pocket.

"Somehow, that doesn't sound like Shakespeare."

"No, it was my grandmother," he said. "How did the drop go?"

"Like clockwork." Del's lips twitched as he thought about his convoluted approach route. "I used the subway to get to the rendezvous."

"The subway? You could have walked there faster."

"It's standard operating procedure, the best way to ditch a possible tail."

"It's also more interesting than staring at the blank walls of that apartment."

"You said it. Those video cameras we set up are already doing what we're doing."

"Ah, but a camera couldn't pull a trigger."

Del nodded. "That reminds me. I've arranged to do my long-range target practice tomorrow morning."

"I'll talk to the other team and rearrange your shift."

"Thanks."

"No problem. I doubt if you'll miss anything exciting."

"This waiting is wearing on my nerves. I'll be glad when it's over."

"Seems to me you've been keeping yourself busy enough during this assignment. How are Maggie and the baby?"

"They're both fine," Del said. He rubbed his eyes briefly. The strain was really starting to get to him. For a second there, he thought he had seen Maggie's reflection in the small mirrored tiles that covered the wall. "Delilah's thriving. I have some new pictures. I'll bring them in tonight—"

"No, no, that's okay," Bill said quickly. "Don't trouble yourself."

Del smiled inwardly. He was beginning to enjoy boring his partner with baby pictures. A small revenge for the endless quotes he'd endured over the years. "It wouldn't be any trouble. I have an extra set of prints."

"That's not necessary." Bill looked past Del's shoulder. "Not when I can look at the real thing."

"What do you mean?"

Bill nodded toward the restaurant entrance. "Isn't that Maggie over there behind that plant?"

Del twisted around. This time it wasn't an illusion. Maggie was actually here. She was standing just inside the door, evidently studying the menu that was scrawled in chalk on the blackboard there.

"Did you ask her to meet you?" Bill asked.

"No, of course not," Del said.

"And how many times did you change trains?"

Del frowned. "It has to be a coincidence. She couldn't have followed me. Why would she?"

Bill chuckled. "No wonder we haven't been

able to corner Simon if a pint-size waitress from Queens can outwit a top-level operative.''

Del didn't join in Bill's laughter. He didn't find the situation amusing in the least.

Maggie looked up at that moment. Through the drooping leaves of a potted fern, she met his gaze.

Del really had no choice. He lifted his hand and waved a greeting.

This wasn't supposed to happen. Until now, Del had managed to keep Maggie's world completely separate from the world of SPEAR.

But now those worlds were on a collision course.

Chapter 7

"Maggie," Del said, rising from his chair as she approached. "What a pleasant surprise."

"Hi, Del." Her smile looked strained. "I don't mean to intrude."

"You're not intruding. We were just about to order coffee." He gestured toward Bill. "This is...a colleague of mine. Bill Grimes."

"Hello, Maggie," Bill said, putting on his most benign expression. "You might not remember me, but I used to come into the coffee shop when you worked there."

"That must be why you look familiar," Maggie said. "It's nice to see you again."

"Same here. And congratulations are in order. That's a fine daughter you have there."

"Thank you."

Bill pushed out an extra chair. ''Why don't you join us?''

''Oh, I can't stay. I have to get Delilah home soon. I was just downtown to visit some friends and thought I'd take a little walk when I saw Del come in here and decided to say hello.''

Her words were rushed, her voice pitched higher than usual. Del realized she was concealing something. Had Bill been right? Had she followed him in here? How much had she seen, and had she actually understood what she'd seen? He moved the stroller to one side and took her arm, guiding her to sit. ''I'll take you home in a taxi when you need to leave,'' he said.

''That's really, um, nice of you, Del.''

''I wish I'd run into you sooner,'' he said, watching her face carefully. ''Somehow I got turned around and could have used a guide.''

She pressed her lips together briefly, then glanced at him with an expression that looked almost guilty.

Damn, he thought. She must have seen the route he'd taken. She *had* been following him.

But for how long? And why?

Her penetration of their security was completely innocent, of that he was certain. He would stake his life on it. Maggie knew nothing of SPEAR. She couldn't. Only a handful of top govcrnment people were aware of the organization's existence.

Bill caught his gaze then, his eyes twinkling with barely suppressed humor. Evidently he still found the situation amusing. ''Yes, Del is still just a farm boy at heart. The big city confuses him.''

Maggie's smile wasn't quite as tight as before. ''It must be difficult having a job that involves so much traveling. It wouldn't give a person the chance to get to know any one place very well.''

''Ah. I assume Del has told you about our work, then?'' Bill asked.

''A little. Are you a consultant, too?''

''We share the same office,'' Bill said smoothly.

''You must be really busy. There's so much demand for that kind of thing these days.''

''Yes, that's true. Business is booming.''

Del glanced at his partner in irritation. He knew Bill was alluding to the warehouse explosion—sometimes his sense of humor was definitely warped. ''Electronics is an expanding field,'' Del said.

''Cutting edge, all right,'' Bill added. ''Why, just the other day—''

Whatever Bill was going to say was interrupted by a sudden wail. Both men looked down at the stroller.

Delilah was lying on her back, her eyes squeezed shut as she inhaled in preparation for another cry.

Maggie leaned over to scoop her up. The baby calmed somewhat as soon as she was held, but she bumped her head restlessly against her mother's shoulder. "I'm sorry," Maggie said, getting to her feet. "I'd better get her home."

Five minutes later, Del settled beside Maggie for the taxi ride to Queens. He wasn't disappointed to have the conversation with Bill cut short. He hadn't had a chance to brief his partner on the cover story he'd given Maggie. Considering the mood Bill seemed to be in, the lies would only end up getting more and more complicated.

This was why agents in SPEAR didn't usually develop relationships with outsiders. Apart from the problem of cover stories, there was always the risk of discovery. Until now, Del had been fortunate that his and Maggie's paths hadn't crossed, since she had been more or less limited by the baby to outings close to home.

Fortunately, from the looks of things, no harm seemed to have been done this time. The information drop had gone off as planned, and in his easygoing way, Bill had provided Maggie with an explanation for Del's erratic route to the rendezvous.

But what if it *hadn't* been simply a routine drop? What if Maggie had innocently followed Del into something more serious? Because of him, she could have put herself and Delilah in danger.

Delilah's fussiness increased as the taxi maneuvered its way through the midtown traffic. Del's concern over Maggie's unexpected appearance became replaced by alarm. He turned to face Maggie. ''She sounds upset,'' he said.

''She is,'' Maggie agreed, jiggling the child up and down. ''And it's all my fault. I never should have stayed out so long.''

''Can I help?''

''Thanks, Del, but there's not much you can do, not unless...'' Her words trailed off as she looked from him to the cabdriver. ''As a matter of fact, there is something you can do.''

''Sure. Do you want me to take her for a while?''

''No, I'd like you to sit in front of me.''

''What?''

''Right here,'' she said, patting the edge of the seat as she squeezed herself into the corner.

''Why?''

"I need you for a screen."

"A scream?"

"No," she said, raising her voice over the noise that Delilah was generating. "A screen."

"I don't understand."

"She's hungry. That's why she's crying. I stayed out past her feeding time."

It took a moment for her meaning to register. When it did, Del felt a slow flush work up his neck. "You want to feed her?"

Maggie nodded quickly. She reached for the buttons at the front of her blouse. "It's an emergency. I don't think either of us can wait until we get home. I would have brought a bottle, but I hadn't planned on being gone so long."

Del shot a glance at the driver, then twisted sideways and moved over to Maggie's side. Bracing one hand against the front seat with his back toward her, he positioned himself on the spot she had indicated.

She shifted her legs to one side of his hip. "Can you lean a little more to the right?"

He complied, placing his other hand against the door.

"That's it," she said.

Del felt her elbow bump into his back. Delilah's cries became frantic.

"Uh, you're going to have to lean forward a bit," Maggie said.

Del did. There was a rustle of movement, and Maggie's forearm pressed just above his waist. Two seconds later, Delilah's cries abruptly stopped. The silence was startling. The only sound, apart from the traffic outside and the drone of the taxi's engine, was a soft, rhythmic sucking.

She was nursing the baby, Del thought. Right here, right now. Close enough for him to hear. Close enough for him to feel her arm where she held Delilah to her breast.

Her breast. She had opened her blouse and bared her nipple. Inches away from his back.

Maggie sighed. "Thanks, Del. I thought I was going to burst."

No, don't think about it, he told himself. He kept his hands where they were. He couldn't move, he didn't dare. "Don't mention it," he said through his teeth.

"I really should have gone home sooner," she said. "Poor Delilah. She's drinking as if she's half-starved."

Del squeezed his eyes shut. No, he would not imagine what was happening. He wouldn't think about nipples or breasts. She was simply feeding a hungry baby, participating in a function that was wholesome and natural for a woman's body....

It wasn't working. He could think of other functions for a woman's body, for Maggie's body. The cab was one of the vintage yellow behemoths that cruised New York, so it had more room in the back seat than newer cars, yet Del could feel Maggie's thigh rub against his hip as she angled her legs next to the door. The extra pounds from her pregnancy had been melting away in the last week, but she still had retained enough to form curves that made his mouth water.

How would it feel if she wrapped both legs around him? His imagination all too readily supplied the answer. He could smell her bare skin beneath her opened clothing, and he felt sweat break out on his forehead. What she was doing, the way she was sitting so near...he had never been so achingly conscious of her femininity.

Oh, yeah, she would be a passionate lover. Earthy and sensuous, with no false modesty or shame about her physical needs. She was so generous and giving, any man would be honored to share her bed.

Any man? No, not just anyone. Not that jerk who deserted her. She needed a man who would respect her for the woman she was, who admired her, who cared about her, who could match her passion....

Del dug his fingers into the back of the front seat, surprised he hadn't punctured the vinyl by now. This was torture, plain and simple. Did she think he was made of stone? Didn't she know what she was doing to him?

No, of course she didn't know, Del thought immediately. It was that damn corner he'd painted himself into. She trusted him. She wouldn't be doing this in his presence in the first place if she thought of him as anything but a friend.

The taxi swerved as it turned a corner, and Del's eyes snapped open. He met the interested gaze of the taxi driver in the rearview mirror.

"Don't worry, pal," the man said. "Seventeen years driving this cab, I've seen it all."

Del knew that the width of his shoulders blocked Maggie from anyone's view, but his reaction was instinctive. He bared his teeth.

The driver was astute enough to realize it wasn't a smile. He returned his gaze to the road.

Del didn't know how he endured the rest of the trip. By the time he walked Maggie to her apartment, Delilah was sleeping contentedly against her mother's shoulder and Del felt as if every muscle in his body had tensed into steel.

He waited in the living room as Maggie went to change Delilah and put the baby in her crib. This couldn't go on, he thought, pacing to the window. The way Maggie had breached his security this morning was bad enough, but he couldn't continue this charade of friendship much longer. The best thing he could do, for both their sakes, would be to say goodbye now.

The tinkling sound of a lullaby drifted out of the bedroom from a music box Del had bought. The melody was bittersweet, a fleeting echo of childhood, a reminder of all that Maggie and Delilah had given him. Warmth, peace, contentment...all the things he lacked in his life with SPEAR. He pinched the bridge of his nose. He knew he was only delaying the inevitable—once the assignment ended, he would leave for good— but damn it all, he didn't *want* to say goodbye now.

Maggie returned and came to stand directly in front of him. Her eyes were brimming with tears. ''Oh, Del.''

He caught her by the shoulders. ''What's wrong?''

''I feel so awful. I owe you an apology.''

''You?'' He let his hands slide down her arms. ''You couldn't possibly have done anything to apologize about.''

"Oh, yes, I did. It's about what happened this morning."

"Maggie, you couldn't help it. Delilah was hungry."

"What? You mean the way I nursed her? No, that's not what I meant. You weren't offended, were you?"

Offended? Hardly. Try fascinated. Stimulated. Frustrated as hell. "Of course not," he answered.

"It's about what I did before." She looked away. "I lied to you."

She lied to *him?* "Maggie, whatever it was—"

"Please, just let me get this out, okay? I hate lies, I really do," she said fiercely.

Del's body flooded with guilt.

"Alan lied all the time," she went on. "Our entire relationship was a lie. I never want to go through that again. That's why I want to be honest with you."

"Maggie—"

"I value your friendship, Del. I don't know what I would have done these past weeks without you. You're the kindest, most considerate man I've ever known, and you don't deserve to be lied to."

Why didn't she just pull out a gun and shoot him? he thought miserably. "All right," he said. "Tell me what happened."

"This morning I...I didn't just happen to see you going into that restaurant. I followed you."

"Is that all?"

"All?" She jerked her gaze to his. "Del, don't you understand? I followed you all the way from the coffee shop."

That far? So it hadn't been his imagination, after all. He really had seen her on that subway platform. He was torn between berating himself for being so sloppy...and admiring Maggie for being so resourceful. Not only could she teach some of his fellow agents about courage and enduring pain, she could give them pointers on tailing a subject.

"I'm sorry, Del," she continued. "It was so underhanded and sneaky. I'm ashamed—"

"No, Maggie." Del moved his hand to her cheek. He wiped a tear away with the tip of his thumb. "Please, don't upset yourself over this."

She pressed her cheek against his palm and gave him a wavering smile. "After the way you were so sweet about helping me with Delilah in the cab, I felt so rotten, I knew I couldn't live with myself if I didn't confess. I owed you the truth."

Sweet? She thought he was *sweet?* If she could have read his mind... "I'm glad I could help."

"It served me right for trailing you like some

kind of, well, secret agent. I just wish that I hadn't made Delilah suffer.''

''Delilah seems to be fine.'' He realized his thumb was straying dangerously close to her lips, but he couldn't bring himself to pull away. He settled for stroking her hair behind her ear. ''But why did you follow me, Maggie?''

''Because I wanted to know where you went.''

''Where I went? What do you mean?''

She blinked hard, as if debating whether to answer, but then she inhaled sharply and spoke in a rush. ''I was curious. I wanted to know where your office was, where you go when you get those phone calls, whether you have a girl-friend or a wife or—''

''A wife? Maggie, there's no one. I swear that to you.''

''But don't you see? It wouldn't be my business if you had an entire harem, Del. You're my friend. Whatever you do in your private life—''

''Maggie, *you* are what I do in my private life. You and Delilah. Other than the two of you, all I have is my work and an impersonal hotel room,'' Del said, realizing he was telling the absolute truth. ''I know I don't talk about my work very much, but that's because I like to forget it when I'm here. I—'' He hesitated. ''I try my best to keep those two worlds separate.''

She stepped back and turned away, clasping her hands in front of her. "I'm sorry, Del. Ever since Alan, I've had a problem with trust."

"That's understandable."

"But I hate being this way. That's how my mother was, and I've tried all my life not to do the same."

"Your mother?"

"Don't get me wrong," she said quickly. "I loved my mother. She was a wonderful person. She passed away three years ago, and a day hasn't gone by that I haven't missed her. It's just that she had this…tendency to look on the bad side of things."

"How so?"

"My father died when I was five, and he didn't have any insurance or any family, so it wasn't easy for my mother to manage. She did the best she could, supporting us on her own, but I think the pain she felt when my father died turned her into a pessimist. She always assumed the worst. That way, she wouldn't be disappointed."

"That must have been tough on you. You're such a positive person."

"It was harder on her than on me. I realize it was how she coped with her difficult situation, but she missed out on so much because of her attitude. She wouldn't only look a gift horse in the mouth, she would demand to see its dental X rays. She was so bent on looking for problems that she refused to believe in happiness, even when the chance was right there in front of her. It got to the point that she didn't even want to try anymore. After my accident, she just gave up.''

''What accident?''

Maggie moved to where she had left the stroller, dipping her head as she focused on the handle. ''I was twelve,'' she said. ''I was on my way to school one morning when a car swerved onto the sidewalk and hit me.''

''God, Maggie,'' Del said. ''How bad was it?''

She lifted a shoulder. ''I don't recall much about the accident itself, but I do remember it was right off the old pinprick-to-root-canal scale. My injuries were so bad the doctors said I'd probably never walk again.''

He tried to imagine this vibrant, energetic woman spending her life in a wheelchair, but he couldn't.

''My mother didn't want me to go to rehab because she was so sure it was pointless,'' she went on. ''I can't blame her—I know she was only trying to save me from being disappointed.

Luckily, I was only twelve, so I didn't believe the doctors. I kept trying and eventually got better.''

She said it so easily, trying to downplay the trauma she had endured, but Del knew the courage she must have needed to fight her way to a full recovery. He'd seen the results of impact injuries, and he'd known agents who had spent years in slow, painful rehabilitation. He moved behind her, slipping his arms over hers and pulling her back against his chest. ''You're a very special woman, Maggie Rice.''

Her hair brushed his chin as she shook her head. ''Oh, no. I'm as ordinary as they come. I just took one day at a time—that's all I could do. I can't count the number of times I fell flat on my face, but I figured it was better to try than to simply give up.''

''Making lemonade out of life's lemons,'' he murmured, remembering what she had said about the way Robbie had aced being an orphan. She had more in common with her neighbor's foster child than he had realized.

''I guess. On the day I managed to walk on my own, I promised myself I would never do what my mother did. Life is precious, and I wasn't going to waste it by being afraid to take chances. That's why...''

"That's why you took a chance with Alan," he finished for her.

"Yes." She leaned back with a sigh. "I did have my suspicions about him, but I let myself be fooled. I *wanted* to trust him. I wanted to love him. I wanted to grab my chance at happiness."

He pressed his cheek to the side of her head. There was so much strength beneath her good-natured approach to life. Her spirit, her zest for living, her determination to be a good mother to Delilah, all of it made so much sense, now that he knew what she had been through.

Maggie didn't accept his embrace for long before she sighed and turned in his arms to face him. She placed her palms lightly on the front of his shirt. "That's why I'm doubly sorry for not trusting you, Del."

"Please, Maggie. Don't apologize."

"I have to. Friends are honest."

She was tearing him apart. The fact that she had succeeded in following him today only illustrated how risky their association could be. There were so many good reasons it would be best for both of them if he ended this relationship.

But how could he say goodbye after she had opened up to him this way? When his feelings for her were only deepening? For a crazy instant, he wanted to confess everything to her, tell her that she was right to doubt him, that when it came to liars, he was way out of hers or even Alan's league.

But he wasn't at liberty to tell her about his life. He couldn't compromise his mission and SPEAR that way.

Still, maybe it was time to come clean about what he could. She deserved that much, didn't she?

He eased his fingers into her hair, tipping her face toward his. "Maggie, I treasure the time I've spent with you and Delilah, and I feel privileged that you consider me your friend."

"Oh, Del, you're the best friend I have."

"No, I'm not."

"But—"

"Since we're into confessions, maybe you should hear mine."

Her gaze searched his, her blue eyes growing darker. "All right."

"I don't feel particularly friendly right now."

"You don't?"

He slid his other hand behind her, splaying his fingers over her back. "No."

"Then how do you feel, Del?"

He smiled and gave her an honest answer. "I feel like kissing you."

Her lips parted. Her gaze lowered to his mouth. "You shouldn't."

"You're right, I shouldn't. But I do."

"I've just had a baby."

"I know. I was there. Only a kiss, Maggie, that's all."

"And I like being friends. I don't want to start any other kind of relationship."

"Me, neither." He drew her closer. "But I still want to kiss you."

Tentatively, she slid her hands up his chest. "This really would be crazy," she whispered.

"Then you can blame me."

"No."

"No?"

"I can't blame you, Del. Not when I've been crazy enough to think about the same thing for weeks." Locking her fingers behind his neck, she tugged his head down.

It was a day for acting on impulse, Maggie thought. Her first impulse, the one that had sent her trailing after Del, had been a mistake. No doubt this second one might be a mistake, too. But as soon as his mouth touched hers, she decided to put aside her misgivings and simply enjoy the moment.

She should have known his kiss would be like

this. Sweet, warm and gentle. He didn't push or
prod or hurry. Instead, he...savored. Yes, that
was it. His lips whispered over hers. He took his
time, as if he had been anticipating this in his
mind as long as she had.

It seemed to be a day for honesty, too. Yes,
she had been thinking about this. Even before
Delilah was born, she had been looking at Del
this way, but she hadn't wanted to admit it. She
didn't want to trust her feelings. She didn't want
to trust Del, because she didn't want to be hurt
again.

But right now he wasn't hurting her. He was
making her feel...cherished.

Del lifted his hands to frame her face, cradling
her cheeks as he slowly increased the pressure of
his mouth. She sighed and arched her back, fitting her body to his, and warmth unfurled deep
inside her. For the moment she didn't think about
being a mother, she thought about being a
woman.

It had been so long since she'd allowed herself
any pleasure. Could this be wrong?

His tongue traced the seam of her lips with a
gentleness that had her opening her mouth before
she could even think about it. The pleasure expanded, spreading through her veins like hot
syrup. No, this couldn't be wrong. It felt right.

Perfect. As if she had been waiting all along just for the sensation of his lips molding to hers. He slid his tongue deeper, the moist abrasion sending ripples of delight all the way down to her toes.

She squeezed herself closer. Her breasts, so sensitive and so recently emptied, flattened against his chest. The nipples tingled. It was similar to the tingles she felt just before Delilah latched on, but so much more. There was nothing maternal about the sensation, nothing at all.

It had only been three weeks since she had given birth, but Maggie felt her body slowly awaken as parts that had lain dormant for more than nine months stretched and stirred. She knew it was too soon to consider sharing anything more than a kiss, and yet she couldn't stop the sound of need that rose in her throat.

Del slid his hands to her back, his palms burning through her blouse. She could feel his body tightening. A tremor shook his frame. And yet he didn't deepen the kiss. He eased back gradually until all she could feel was his breath on her lips. "Maggie," he whispered.

She opened her eyes. When had she closed them? "Mmm?"

"I'm sorry."

"No, Del, please don't apologize. That was… nice."

"I'm not apologizing for the kiss, Maggie," he said, rubbing his thumb across the moisture that clung to her lower lip. "I'm sorry because I have to get that."

Only then did she hear the ringing. It was his cell phone.

He reached up to grasp her wrists and eased her hands apart, unlocking the grip she had on the back of his neck. He held her gaze, his eyes filled with regret, as he brushed a kiss over each palm.

The tender gesture made her feel like melting. But then he released her hands, pulled his phone out of his pocket and turned away. He listened, said a few words in response, then walked to the door.

"Del?" she asked.

He paused, his hand on the knob. "I'm sorry, Maggie. I'll call you as soon as I get a chance, okay?"

It was just like the other times, Maggie thought numbly as the door closed behind him. And as it had happened so often before, the warmth she was feeling gave way to uneasiness.

How could he have walked away like that, with barely a word? Where was he going? Whom

was he meeting? Why was he so darn...
secretive?

"Oh, hell," she muttered, collapsing onto the
couch. She couldn't very well follow him again,
could she? Maybe she should try *trusting* him.

After all, hadn't that apology she had made to
him minutes ago meant anything to her?

But how could he simply leave after kissing
her so sweetly? Had she been the only one whose
world had just shifted? Hadn't he felt anything?

Sure, he had. Unless her judgment when it
came to something even that basic couldn't be
trusted, either.

"Oh, hell," she repeated on a sigh. It was just
as well they had been interrupted. The kiss
couldn't have gone any further, anyway.

Besides, she needed some time to think about
this. She wasn't going to look for problems, but
there was no point rushing into anything. She had
done that with Alan, and it had led to disaster.

Of course, Del wasn't at all like Alan.

*If the right man has already happened to come
along...*

Joanne's words teased at Maggie's mind. So
did all the reasons Maggie had given her that Del
wasn't the right man.

But, oh, it would be easy to fall the rest of the
way in love with a man like Del Rogers.

Much, much too easy.

Chapter 8

The scent of early morning rose from the ground, the tang of grass still heavy with dew, the dark aroma of soil just starting to warm in the sun. Del stretched out on his stomach on the top of the rise. Dampness seeped through his clothes as a flock of crows squawked from the trees behind him. The sounds and smells were so familiar, he could have been back home, watching the sunrise from the hill behind the barn. Except back home, he didn't generally greet the sunrise with a high-powered rifle.

An indoor firing range couldn't accommodate the distances Del required to practice, so SPEAR had found a deserted quarry an hour out of the city. Del slipped on his hearing protection, fitted the rifle butt to his shoulder and focused on the target.

Without the telescopic sight Del peered through, the white square with the concentric black circles would be no more than a speck on the distant hillside. At a thousand yards it was at the limit of the range for the .308 caliber weapon he held, but for him it was no problem. His index finger squeezed the trigger.

Even though the rifle's stock was steadied by the two-legged support stand, the recoil had the kick of a mule. Del rolled with the blow and brought the muzzle down to keep the target in his sights. There was a new shadow in the center, a sharp-edged circle the bullet had punched.

He felt no elation that he'd made what some would consider an impossible shot. He regarded his accuracy as a given. This was what he did, who he was. He loaded another round into the chamber and aimed an inch above the first hole.

Squeeze the trigger, check the target, reload. The rhythm was a familiar one. To insure his skills stayed honed, for every one shot he fired on an assignment, he took at least a hundred in practice. He kept going until a new ring of evenly spaced holes surrounded the bull's-eye, then pulled off his hearing protection, secured the rifle, retrieved the spent shell casings and targets and recorded each shot in his logbook.

Wind conditions, temperature, time of day, distance from the target. All the information was relevant, enabling him to keep track of not only his performance but that of his weapon. He had a record of every bullet that had been fired through this barrel so he would know when it would be necessary to replace it.

Yes, this was what he was good at. This was his job, his life. For eight years, this had been his world.

But as Del loaded his rifle into the car he had requisitioned for the day, he wasn't thinking about his job. He was thinking about Maggie.

She would have enjoyed coming out here today. She could have spread a blanket over the grass and watched the clouds roll by, or tickled Delilah's toes with some clover, or laughed at the antics of the crows.

They would have had a picnic, and then they would have put Delilah in her infant chair for a nap. And then Del would have stretched out beside Maggie on the blanket and kissed her in the sunshine and slowly peeled the clothes away from her ripe, ripe body....

And Maggie's soft whimpers of pleasure

would turn to horror when she saw the targets and the bullets and the gun.

The fantasy dissolved like a puff of smoke from the muzzle of a hot barrel. Del leaned his elbows on the steering wheel and raked his hands through his hair. After a minute, he started the engine and drove back to the city.

Bill was waiting for him in the alley that flanked the surveillance site. He motioned him over with a jerk of his head. "Are you alone?" he asked.

Del did a quick check of the perimeter. "Yes."

"You're sure you weren't followed? Maybe by a little old lady with a guide dog this time?"

"Bill..."

"Or perhaps a fellow wearing a fluorescent orange jumpsuit and a clown nose? I know that would be rather difficult to spot in a crowd."

Del swore under his breath and turned to go.

Bill snagged his arm to stop him. "Heads up," he said, his voice turning serious. "Two o'clock."

Del melted into the shadows of the alley and moved his gaze across the courtyard to his right. "Who?"

"Not who. What. At ten o'clock now."

Bill's statement had nothing to do with the

time. It was noon. Del scanned the area in front of him and to the left but couldn't see anything unusual. The traffic in the area, both vehicular and pedestrian, was doing its usual crawl. He squinted into the gleam of sunlight that reflected from a car windshield. A red spot winked from the hood of a taxi. "Laser?"

"Right."

"Ours?"

"Nope. It belongs to our friend with the tattoo who visited before."

Del searched again but couldn't spot the source of the laser beam. "Where is he?"

"In the subject apartment."

That explained why Bill had been waiting for him here, Del thought. This alley was out of the direct line of sight of that apartment.

"He's been there for the past twenty minutes," Bill continued. "He checked for bugs again, then went to the window with what appeared to be a scope. By the way, intelligence figured out who he is. Herbert Hull. Ex Marine."

Unfortunately, that in itself wasn't so unusual, Del thought. Many former servicemen who were disaffected with the military for some reason or another ended up hiring out their skills to the highest bidder. "Anything else?" he asked.

"He got a dishonorable discharge after the

Gulf War. It seems he liberated more cash than he did Kuwaitis.''

''That sounds like the kind of scum Simon would hire.''

''There's more, and you're going to love this part. He was a Marine scout. A sniper.''

A red dot appeared fifty yards away, on the plaza across First Avenue. It steadied for a second on a tourist who was taking a picture of the approach to the UN headquarters, then tracked along the ground and disappeared into the distance. Although it was no longer visible to the naked eye, Del had no doubt that it was still there.

Del felt a hunter's tingle of anticipation. Most people wouldn't notice those laser spots, and even if they did, they wouldn't realize their significance. Only someone trained in the one shot, one kill method of sniping would know what those flashes of light indicated.

In order to make every shot count, a marksman needed to know the range with pinpoint accuracy. Ideally, the distance to each strategic point—each possible target location in an area—would be determined ahead of time. ''He's using a laser range finder to index the shots,'' Del said.

''That would be my guess.''

"We suspected it, but now we know for sure why Simon wants that apartment."

"Exactly."

"An overt assassination," Del said, his gaze going to the row of flagpoles. The colors of every country represented at the United Nations fluttered bravely in the sun. "That's not Simon's style."

"He's getting desperate. We've backed him into a corner," Bill said. "Too bad we still don't know the intended target."

"Who would Simon want dead that badly?" Del asked.

"Good question. Perhaps a diplomat? Do you think he's attempting to extort money that way?"

"Possibly. Again, though, that's not his style. So far, everything he's done seems to have been targeting SPEAR."

"Intelligence is working on it."

"Whatever it is, we've got to stop Simon this time, Bill."

"We will. You're the best there is." Bill stated it as a fact, not a compliment. "You never miss."

Del thought about the perfect circles in the targets he'd retrieved that morning, the logbook of perfect scores, and he nodded. Yes, this is what he did, who he was, what he was good at.

And when he met his prey, he would be ready.

* * *

Maggie picked up the next diaper from the laundry basket and had just begun to fold it when she was interrupted by a brisk knock at the apartment door. Automatically, she checked to make sure Delilah was safely strapped into her infant chair before she went to answer.

A young woman in a bright green jumpsuit with the name of a local florist printed on the breast pocket stood in the corridor. In one hand she managed to hold a clipboard while in her other hand she balanced a huge arrangement of flowers.

"Oh, my gosh," Maggie said, opening the door.

"Maggie Rice?" the delivery woman asked.

Maggie nodded, her eyes widening. The heady scent of hothouse blooms was already wafting through the doorway.

"I'm sorry," the woman continued. "I tried buzzing you but I guess you didn't hear me. Your super said you were here so she let me in."

"I must have been on my way back from the laundry room. Those couldn't be for me, could they?"

The delivery woman checked her clipboard,

then smiled. "They sure are," she said, handing them over. "Enjoy yourself."

"Oh, my." Maggie struggled to get a good grip on the arrangement as she bumped the door closed with her hip. She carried the flowers to the table, pushing aside a pile of folded diapers to make space for the vase.

Robbie came running from the bathroom and skidded to a stop beside the table. His red hair was slicked down with water, and the ends of a towel were tucked into the neck of his T-shirt. As he had informed her when Armilda had brought him here after school, today he was a superhero. Evidently he had completed his costume.

"Did somebody die?" Robbie asked, eyeing the flowers.

Startled, Maggie squatted in front of him and caught his hands in hers. "Of course not, darling. Why would you ask that?"

"When Mom and Dad died, everyone sent tons of flowers."

"Oh, Robbie," she said, giving him a hug. "There are all kinds of reasons people send flowers."

"I know that."

"Flowers are meant to make you feel better because they're so beautiful." She reached out to pluck a chrysanthemum blossom from the arrangement. "Here. Take a look. Isn't it pretty?"

He looked carefully at the bloom she handed to him. "Yeah, I guess so. You're sure nobody died?"

"Positive."

"So why do you got flowers?"

"Why? Well, let's just see." She straightened up and looked through the arrangement for a card. The flowers were stuffed into the short vase so thickly that she didn't find anything immediately. Then she spotted a pink envelope deep inside the greenery. "Aha!" she said, ripping the envelope open and withdrawing the card.

My dearest Maggie, the note read. *Once more I apologize for the way we parted, and I'm counting the hours until I can see you again.*

The note was signed with a scrawled initial that she assumed was a D. Maggie didn't need to see a name to know who these flowers were from. Only one man would do something this sweet.

Del must still feel bad about leaving her so quickly after their kiss yesterday. But he obviously didn't regret what they had done. The wording of this note implied he wanted to change their relationship. He didn't sound like a friend, he sounded like a lover.

Or at least a potential lover.

"The flowers are from Del," she said finally.

"Yeah?"

"Uh-huh."

"Uncle Del's cool," Robbie said, twirling the blossom she had given him between his fingers. "He made me a fort out of the pillows on the couch."

Maggie remembered. Del had been here the last time she had baby-sat Robbie, and they had gotten along so well that as soon as Robbie had learned that Del was Delilah's honorary uncle, he had decided to make him his, too.

Poor Robbie. He was so eager to have a family that he wanted everyone to be his relative. Maggie understood that all too well. "Del's good at using his imagination, isn't he?" she said.

"Yeah."

"I'll bet he'd find a way that a superhero could use that flower."

Robbie thought for a moment, then thrust out his arm, holding the flower aloft. "Zap!"

"What's that?"

"It's my secret weapon. It shoots power rays." He brandished the flower and ran off, his towel cape flapping behind him. "Wait till I show Uncle Del!"

Maggie smiled at the recovery of Robbie's

good humor and at his eagerness to see Del. Even though Del said he hadn't had much experience with babies or children, he was proving to be a natural with both. He would make a great father. And lover. And maybe even a husband…

Deliberately, she slammed the door on that direction of her thoughts. She was jumping the gun just a tad here, wasn't she? For heaven's sake, all they had done so far was kiss. And these flowers weren't a proposal. She should take things slow, figure out where this was leading before she risked her heart.

Nevertheless, when Del arrived that evening, a bag from a Chinese restaurant in each hand, she couldn't prevent the rush of excitement that tripped her pulse. Yet on the heels of the excitement came a sudden self-consciousness. Had she remembered to comb her hair? Had the spit-up stain come out of this blouse? Were the dark circles under her eyes as repulsive as they had looked the last time she had peeked at a mirror?

It was so much easier when they had been simply friends.

Still, even without the note, the bouquet Del had sent her carried a message loud and clear….

Oh, the heck with analyzing this to death, she thought. They had done fine with honesty before.

She might as well try the same thing today. "Del, I think we should talk."

He shifted the bags to one arm and locked the door behind him. "What about?"

"About...what we did yesterday."

He looked her square in the eyes. "You mean when I kissed you."

Merely hearing him say it made her knees go weak. She clasped her hands in front of her. "Yes. I don't want you to get the wrong idea."

He smiled slowly. "You'd be surprised at the ideas I get."

"Del, you're the best friend I have, and I don't want to lose that, but I don't want to rush into anything more serious."

His smile faded. "Neither do I, Maggie."

His ready agreement should have pleased her. Why didn't it? "Uh, great. So it might be best to just go on like we were before and forget about that kiss."

"I'll always be your friend, Maggie, but that doesn't mean I'm going to forget what it felt like to kiss you." He ran his fingertips lightly along her cheek, then dropped his hand to his side. "I'm not going to press you for more, though. I'm aware of your physical condition."

His directness made her blush. "Oh. I thought your expectations were different, but—"

"My expectations? Why would you think that?"

"Because of those flowers you sent."

"Maggie, I didn't send you any flowers."

"But…" She turned her head to look over her shoulder. The arrangement sat in the center of the table.

"I didn't send them," he repeated.

"But your note…" She paused. "It wasn't signed. I just assumed it was from you."

Del took the bags of food to the table and picked up the card. His expression hardened. "I didn't write this."

She should have known better. The message in that bouquet wasn't from Del. Of course, the flowers wouldn't have been from him. He was too nice, too honorable, to try to push her into a more serious relationship under these circumstances.

So if Del hadn't sent the flowers, who could have?

"Oh, no," she breathed. She hurried across the room and took the card from his hand, squinting over the initial that had been used in place of a signature. She had thought it was a D. But now that she looked more closely, she could see it was slanted backward, and the ends of the letter extended a little too far. "It's an A," she murmured. "Not a D."

"Could they be from Alan?" Del asked.

Alan. The warmth she had been feeling at seeing Del dissipated. Oh, God. It had to be Alan. Who else? She thought of the wording on the card. *Once more I apologize for the way we parted.* He was referring to his last visit here. The flowers were a peace offering. A bribe. A down payment. Whatever distasteful term she wanted to use, the purpose was the same. He hadn't taken no for an answer.

Until I can see you again.

She crumpled the note in her fist and threw it across the room. "How dare he," she said, her voice shaking. "How can he pretend he cares about me after all his lies. Oh, damn! Damn! I should have known he wouldn't give up."

Del caught her shoulders. "Maggie, I won't let him bother you."

"But what if he comes over again?" She gasped as another thought occurred to her. "Oh, Del, what if he decides he wants Delilah?"

"He won't. Think, Maggie. Alan wouldn't do that. He wouldn't want his secrets exposed to his wife and family."

The panic that had stirred instantly at the thought of losing Delilah quickly retreated.

"You're right. Of course, he wouldn't want Delilah. He never did. I was such a fool," she said for what had to be the hundredth time.

"You're an open, generous-hearted woman, Maggie. You saw a shot at happiness and you took it. Don't blame yourself for that."

He really did understand why she had made the mistake with Alan, she realized. And he didn't condemn her for it. Gratitude surged through her, along with something deeper, something she didn't want to think about just yet. "It's such a jumble," she said. "I regret Alan, but I can't regret Delilah."

"Delilah's a wonderful child."

"Yes, she is. I just hope...."

"What?"

"That she doesn't take after her father."

"She won't. You can already see that she's going to grow up to be a terrific person, just like her mom." He leaned down to smile at her. "Don't be so hard on yourself. We all make mistakes."

He'd said that before, she realized. "Have you?"

"What?"

"Have you ever loved the wrong person?"

He looked at her in silence as a flicker of what appeared to be pain crossed his face.

"Oh, Del," she said. "I'm sorry. I didn't mean to upset you."

"It's all right, Maggie." He released her shoulders and turned to open the bags he had brought. "Yes, I was mistaken about someone I loved."

It was on the tip of her tongue to take back her question. She didn't want to make him relive any painful memories. But hadn't she wanted to know more about his life? She waited for him to continue.

"I was engaged once."

It shouldn't have been a surprise. Considering what a great guy Del was, it would have surprised her if some woman *hadn't* recognized that by now. "Who was she?"

"Her name was Elizabeth. I had known her since we were kids. We got engaged after high school. It didn't work out."

"What happened?"

He set out cardboard containers of food in an orderly row. The aroma of sweet-and-sour sauce drifted through the air. "It wasn't her fault. I couldn't give her what she wanted. She found someone else and I moved away. The last I heard, her youngest kid had already started kindergarten at the school where we met."

How could anyone have rejected a man as

wonderful as Del? Maggie wondered. He was such a kind, generous person. What possible fault could this Elizabeth have found in him? "I'm sorry," she murmured.

"It was a long time ago."

"That's why you don't visit your sister and her children often, isn't it?" she said. "You don't want to go home because of the bad memories."

He rubbed the back of his neck and turned to face her once more. "When I told you that all the traveling I do keeps me too busy to get back to Missouri, that was only part of the truth. You're right. Even without the demands of my job, I would prefer to stay away."

"I can understand that, but you're so great with kids, Del. It seems like a shame that you don't see your nieces and nephews—"

"My sister and her family live in my house, Maggie."

"You mean with your parents?"

He shook his head. "When Elizabeth and I were engaged, I started building a house on a section of my parents' farm. It wasn't fancy, but it had plenty of bedrooms for the kids we had hoped to have someday. It wouldn't have been practical to let it go to waste, so when my sister got married, she and her husband moved in."

Despite his stoic demeanor, she could see the pain on his face. "What an awful situation."

One corner of his mouth lifted in a sad smile. "I told you about that old Missouri homesteader tradition, didn't I? Raising your own farmhands? Since I wouldn't be filling all those bedrooms with Elizabeth's children—"

"Oh, Del," she said. Friends or not, she was unable to keep her distance any longer. Without hesitation, she put her arms around him and pressed her cheek to his chest.

No wonder he was so fond of Delilah, she thought. He had so much love inside him, but he hadn't had the chance to share it. That Elizabeth must be a fool to have had his love and thrown it away.

And no wonder Del was so reserved when it came to talking about himself. After his broken engagement and the poignancy of having to abandon the house he had built, he had as much reason as Maggie to be cautious about whom to trust. He wasn't secretive, he was just...private.

And now she could understand why he put so much importance in his job. He had probably turned to his work as a way to mend his broken heart.

"When Robbie saw the flowers today, he thought they were for a funeral," she said.

"Because of his parents?" Del asked.

"Yes. He associated flowers with something painful, and that's understandable, considering what he's been through. But I tried to explain that flowers can mean other things, too."

"Robbie's a good kid."

"He needs to make some positive memories to replace the negative ones."

"That makes sense."

She felt the weight of Del's chin settle on top of her head. "I hope I got through to him," she said.

"I'm sure you did. He adores you."

"He likes you, too. And I hope that someday you'll have some good memories of your home to replace the bad ones."

He leaned back and tipped her chin so she would meet his gaze. "Trying to talk me into adopting your positive attitude?"

"Works for me."

"Yes, it does," he said. "Maggie, you're quite a woman, you know that?"

"Well, thank you. You're quite a guy."

He smiled. It wasn't merely a sad lift of one side of his mouth but spread all the way to the crinkles at the corners of his eyes. "So does this mean you're going to keep Alan's flowers?"

"What?"

"Positive attitude, good memories over bad and all that."

"Hell, no."

He laughed. "I'll carry them to the trash for you."

"I'll hold the door."

"And Maggie?"

"Mmm?"

"Don't worry about Alan. He's not going to bother you or Delilah again. That much I can promise."

"But how…"

"For starters, I'm going to stay here tonight."

Chapter 9

Del pressed his forearm over his eyes and drew up one leg. If he didn't breathe too deeply and angled his hips just right, the broken spring on the back of the couch didn't dig into his ribs. Much. And if he concentrated real hard on the multiplication tables, he could almost ignore the sounds of the creaking mattress in the next room. But there didn't seem to be anything he could do to block out the images that teased his brain, images of Maggie on her bed, her body relaxed in sleep, her lips softly parted....

It had been a week since he had kissed her, seven days of exercising more self-control than he'd ever needed to call on in his eight years with SPEAR. She wanted to stay friends. He knew it was for the best. But that didn't make the nights any easier.

Gritting his teeth, he sat up and rubbed his face. Well, it had seemed like a good idea at the time. Moving in with Maggie was the simplest way to discourage Alan from making contact again and to insure she didn't have to face him alone if the bastard made another one of his surprise visits. Besides, apart from going back to the hotel room for a shower and a change of clothes when he finished his shift at the surveillance site, Del had been practically living here for weeks already. By moving in, he would be able to help Maggie with Delilah even more.

Sounded reasonable, didn't it? he asked himself. And it had worked out well for Maggie, hadn't it? Delilah was thriving, and Maggie was continuing to grow stronger. Alan had tried calling twice, and both times Del had answered. Nevertheless, the calls had upset Maggie. She wouldn't feel completely at ease until she knew that Alan was out of her life for good.

According to the background material that SPEAR intelligence had gathered, Alan Blackthorn was more of a nuisance than a real threat. He had no criminal record, and there had been no hint of dangerous or obsessive behavior in the past. He was a successful, upwardly mobile insurance company executive with a twenty-year marriage who was going through a mid-life crisis. Since Maggie had thrown Alan out, he had had a hair weave and had begun sneaking off to strip clubs on his lunch hour.

Compared to the kind of people Del usually had to deal with in his profession, Alan was a harmless, almost pathetic cliché. All the indications were that Alan hadn't been in love with Maggie. Instead, he had been infatuated with the clandestine adventure of his affair with her.

Both Maggie and Delilah deserved far better than that, Del thought. She was too warm and loving a woman to remain alone for long. Once Del moved on to the next assignment, Maggie would probably meet someone new and—

As always, Del's mind shied away from carrying that thought to its logical conclusion. He didn't want to imagine what kind of man Maggie would end up with, who would give her the stable home and the family she wanted. Because if he let himself think about it, he would feel like breaking someone's arm again.

He tossed aside the light blanket, giving up on sleep. Clad in only his boxer shorts, he didn't bother turning on a light. After one week straight of the same routine, he no longer tripped over the furniture. He pushed the coffee table aside and dropped to the floor.

Try to be positive, he reminded himself. He might not be getting much sleep, and all this extra exercise wasn't doing much to lower his stress level, but thanks to Maggie he was able to bounce a dime off his abs. He counted off two sets of push-ups, then rolled to his back. Hooking his ankles on the arm of the couch, he laced his fingers behind his neck and curled his shoulders upward.

Del was just getting started on his third set of curls when there was a sudden crash from Maggie's bedroom. Adrenaline surged through his system. He shot to his feet, closing the distance to the doorway in less than a second. He burst through the door and flattened himself against the wall to scan the room, prepared for anything.

In the glow of the night-light, he immediately saw that Delilah was still safe in her crib. She whimpered crankily a few times, drawing her knees to her chest, but she seemed unharmed. Her cries were sleepy and halfhearted, subsiding quickly.

Del's gaze moved to the bed. It was empty.

His heart rate, already elevated by his workout and by the adrenaline, kicked into double time as he took a step farther into the room. And that's when he saw Maggie. She was kneeling on the floor between her bed and the window. Pieces of the lamp she kept on her bedside table lay scattered around her.

Clearly, there was no intruder. Nothing sinister or dangerous had occurred. Maggie had accidentally knocked over a lamp, that was all.

Del really should apologize for barging in on her and go back to the living room.

Yet he couldn't move. The way she was kneeling twisted her long flannel nightgown snugly over her hips and thighs, outlining her lush body. The soft illumination of the night-light etched fascinating shadows on her face. The hush of the late hour and the intimacy of the darkened bedroom only served to increase his awareness.

Oh, hell. He could exercise until he was exhausted. He could pretend to be noble. But he was still a man. It would be easier to glue that shattered lamp back together than to continue to keep himself from touching her.

Maggie knew she should stop staring. She should apologize for waking Del with her clumsiness and clean up the shards of the lamp. She wasn't some blushing virgin. She had seen a half-naked man before.

Sure, but she had never seen Del half-naked.

She had known he was in good shape—just seeing the way he moved had told her that. She had already noticed and admired his large hands and muscular forearms. Yet the loose polo shirts and pleated khakis he usually wore had served to camouflage the rest of his build.

He was magnificent. There was no other way she could describe him. His shoulders were broad, in perfect proportion to his narrow hips. His upper arms were carved from muscle, not the puffy lumps of a bodybuilder but the firm, sinewy curves of a man who used his body often and used it hard. Dark hair dusted his chest and narrowed to a tantalizing line that bisected a set of six-pack abs.

He was wearing black boxer shorts. Until now, she had never considered boxers an appealing garment, but on Del they looked incredibly sexy. Riding low on his hips, skimming the tops of his thighs, they only hinted at what might lie beneath. From what she could see of the rest of him, he was probably as spectacular *there* as everywhere else.

"Maggie? Are you all right?"

His whispered question made her start. She snapped her gaze to his face, grateful for the shadows that concealed what had to be the mother of all blushes. She nodded.

He squeezed past the crib and squatted beside her. "You're sure?"

In the tight space between her bed and the window, she could feel the heat from his body. The air stirred up from his movement carried a whiff of soap and male skin...and Maggie felt warmth kindle deep inside. This wasn't the first time she had felt a sexual twinge because of Del, but it had never before been so strong.

Was it the setting? The atmosphere? A natural consequence of her healing body? Or was it due to an entire week of not so much as a kiss? "I'm fine," she finally managed to say.

"What happened?"

"I was reaching for the light and missed. Sorry to wake you up."

"I wasn't asleep."

"Oh."

He watched her in silence. Crouched on the floor with him like this, she was close enough to see the gleam in his eyes. She could also see the exact moment his gaze dropped to her lips.

Oh, God, Maggie thought. She had wanted to take things slow. She had told him she wanted to remain friends. She wasn't ready, either physically or emotionally, for anything more.

But would another kiss do that much harm? They were adult enough to ignore the fact that they were both undressed and only inches away from a warm bed, right?

Wrong. Even if she were a hundred years old, she wouldn't be adult enough to ignore Del when he was practically naked and close enough to smell.

His fingertips brushed her cheek. He stroked her hair behind her ear, then caught her earlobe and squeezed gently, rolling the lobe between his thumb and forefinger.

It was only her earlobe, she told herself. It had never been an erogenous zone for her before. Nevertheless, a shiver of anticipation trembled through her.

She reached up to grasp his hand.

And something hot dripped down her wrist.

She pulled back and turned her hand over, tilting it toward the light. There was a dark gash just below her thumb.

Del must have seen it the same time she did. "You cut yourself," he stated.

"It must have been from one of the pieces of the lamp. It doesn't look bad."

He placed his hand under her elbow and helped her to her feet. Without pausing, he slipped one arm around her back and the other behind her knees, then effortlessly scooped her up and moved toward the door.

"Del!" she exclaimed.

"Shh." He dipped his chin toward the baby. "You'll wake up Delilah."

"Put me down," she whispered. "You don't have to carry me. It's only a scratch."

"I don't want you to cut your feet. Those lamp shards are all over the floor." He tightened his hold on her as he maneuvered past the crib.

Maggie didn't really want to argue. It would be dishonest to pretend she wasn't enjoying this. His muscles were even more impressive up close and flexing.

He carried her through the living room to the corner that served as her kitchen and sat her down on the edge of the table. He went back to close the bedroom door, then flipped on the light and returned with the first aid kit she kept in her bathroom.

"It really isn't that bad," she said. She could see how minor the cut on her thumb was.

"Then it won't take long to heal," he said. Despite her objections, he proceeded to clean and disinfect the wound.

"You do that as if you've had experience in first aid," she said, noticing the careful efficiency of his movements.

"I've had some in the course of my work," he said.

"I wouldn't have thought there would be much need for that in the electronics business."

His hands stilled for a moment. "No, there wouldn't be. I meant I learned this when I worked my parents' farm."

"Oh, right. I should have guessed that."

He smoothed a bandage over the cut and released her hand, yet he didn't move away. Under the harsh brightness of the overhead bulb, the intimate mood that had begun in the bedroom should have dissolved. Instead, Maggie found the added illumination only made Del's body more appealing. She tried to think of something else to say. She felt the need for conversation to keep herself from...ogling him. Yes, that's what she was doing. She had progressed past staring all the way to ogling.

He could have posed for some ancient Greek statue, or he could have served as the mold for those armored breastplates the Romans used. He was classic male perfection sculpted in taut flesh. Without thinking, she reached out to touch him with one finger.

His skin was hot and damp, silk over steel. A shiver of anticipation made her hand tremble. She wanted to place her lips where her finger was. She wanted to know how he tasted.

"Maggie," he said, his voice rough.

She pulled back her hand and put her finger in her mouth. She tasted salt and a trace of something else that had to be pure Del. It was a unique, erotic flavor, like a whisper in the dark.

Del leaned closer and caught her wrist. Holding her gaze, he turned her hand around and bit gently on the finger she had just licked.

Pleasure skittered down her arm. ''I bet you didn't learn that on the farm,'' she murmured.

His lips curved as he sucked her finger into his mouth.

The pleasure spread. She swung her foot forward so that she could rub her toes on his shin.

He released her finger with a pop and placed one palm on her hip.

Maggie smiled. ''I guess we shouldn't really be doing this, Del.''

''Probably not,'' he agreed. He splayed his fingers. ''But if I don't touch you, I'll definitely go mad. Damn, it's been a long week.''

''It's been long for me, too,'' she said.

''I'll stop anytime you say.''

Her breath hitched at the tingles that chased over her hip where his hand rested so possessively. ''I know, Del. I trust you.''

Was it her imagination, or did a shadow flit across his face? She didn't have time to check.

He dipped his head and brushed a butterfly kiss over the hollow of her throat.

Maggie lifted her hands to his hair, sliding her fingers through the short, resilient strands. To her surprise, she caught the scent of the baby shampoo she and Delilah used. On another man, the scent might have been a turn-off, but on someone as unmistakably masculine as Del, it was curiously appealing.

Face it, Maggie told herself. *Everything about him is appealing.* She lifted her chin, enjoying the moist heat of his mouth at the opening of her nightgown. Oh, this was wonderful. Why had they deprived themselves of this pleasure for so long?

Del rubbed his nose up the side of her neck and nibbled at her ear.

Maggie sighed.

He pulled back to look at her, one eyebrow lifting in a wordless question.

"I can't believe my ear can feel like that," she said.

"Like what?"

"Lean over again and I'll show you," she replied, tugging his head down. She flicked the tip of her tongue over his earlobe, then nibbled and tasted until they both were out of breath. This time it was she who pulled back, not because she wanted to stop, but because she wanted more.

Del must have read the desire in her face. He braced his hands on the table on either side of her and brought his mouth down on hers.

Oh, yes, Maggie thought, parting her lips. This was what she wanted. Her memory hadn't deceived her—it was as good as she remembered. Better. He was as controlled and gentle as the last time, his mouth coaxing hers in a sensual dance, an exploration as basic as time.

She moved her hands to his chest, her palms tracing the outline of his muscles. She could feel his heart racing with the same crazy rhythm as hers. What had she been so afraid of? she wondered dimly. She hadn't wanted to rush into anything with Del, but she wasn't rushing now, was she? She had restrained herself for a whole week.

Gradually, the pressure of his lips changed. It was no longer tentative or gentle. It wasn't the kiss of a friend.

It was the kiss of a half-naked man in the middle of the night.

He stepped closer and splayed his fingers over the tops of her thighs. The firm warmth of his palms burned through her nightgown as if it weren't there, and Maggie felt quick heat pool between her legs. It was exhilarating. With a throaty moan, she swayed into him, tilting her head to find the best fit for their mouths.

Del tightened his grip on her thighs and stepped between her knees. He eased her backward until she was reclining on the table. Fabric bunched as he pulled her nightgown upward and touched her bare skin.

Need, swift and sharp, sizzled through Maggie's heart. Oh, it was glorious, this blossoming inside her. Being a mother was fulfilling, but her sexuality was a part of her, too. She wanted to see where this would lead, she wanted to let it continue to its conclusion....

But while her heart might be willing, her body wasn't ready. The swelling heat between her legs turned to a stinging ache. Her breath hitched. She broke off the kiss and gulped in air. "Del..."

His face was hard as he leaned over her. His eyes were more golden than amber. There was no humor or friendship in his gaze, only acute desire.

She had never seen him like this before. He didn't look chivalrous, he looked...dangerous. Ruthless. Like a gunslinger.

Oh, God. Did she really know him? Not what he did or where he went, but who he was, deep down inside? For the first time since she had met him, Maggie felt a tickle of unease.

His thumbs stroked boldly across the sensitive skin on the inside of her thighs.

She put her hands over his to keep him from going higher. "Del, no."

He was fighting for control. She could see it in the muscle that twitched in his cheek and the tendons that corded along his neck. Beneath her fingers, she felt a tremor go through his hands.

"I'm sorry," she said softly. "I can't...I mean, I think it's still too soon."

Slowly, oh, so slowly, the passion that sharpened his features dimmed. He moved his hands aside, bracing them on the table to push himself upward. His chest heaved as he took several deep breaths before he straightened and took a step backward. Finally, he held out his hand to help Maggie sit up.

Maggie exhaled hard, feeling her uneasiness fade. She must have imagined the hard stranger. This was Del, her friend, the nicest guy in New York. She did know him.

"Hell, Maggie," he said finally. "I didn't mean to go that far."

"It's okay, Del. Things happened kind of fast."

"I apologize. I shouldn't have touched you."

She glanced at his arms. His muscles were tensed, standing out in ropy ridges from his shoulders to his wrists. She swallowed. "But I wanted you to, Del."

"Ah, Maggie. You're not making this easier."

"Neither are you."

"What do you mean?"

"Now I know what you've been hiding."

He pulled back swiftly, his expression suddenly wary. "What makes you think I'm hiding something?"

"You could have warned me you had a body like a Greek statue."

"Like a…"

"Only yours is a lot warmer than marble, that's for sure." She looked at his chest. "I've just had a baby, Del, but I'm not dead. You should have known this would happen if you paraded around in front of me half-naked."

"I wasn't parading around. This is how I sleep."

"But you said you weren't asleep."

"I was working out."

Maggie had a sudden image of Del's body flexing, his skin gleaming with a sheen of sweat. She sighed and echoed the words he had said to her. "Ah, Del. You're not making this easier."

He gave a startled laugh, then lifted her hand to his lips. The long, strong fingers that had gripped her thighs so boldly were incredibly tender as he turned her hand over and placed a gentle kiss on her bandaged thumb.

Maggie relaxed. Yes, it must have been her imagination. How could she possibly have considered Del dangerous?

Wind gusted through the glass and brick canyons of Manhattan in a teasing foretaste of summer, carrying the smell of warm asphalt and the cacophony of car horns. Maggie slapped a hand on top of her head to hold down her hat as she stopped at the corner.

She had told Del she didn't need a hat, but he had insisted that with the hot weather approaching and her fair complexion, she needed to protect herself from the sun. That was the reasoning he gave, anyway, but she knew there was more to it than that. He just didn't want to admit he had given in to a spate of pure whimsy.

The hat was made of the softest brushed cotton in a white as pure as the top of a cloud. The brim was wide enough to keep the sun off her nose, yet curled up at the edge to make a flattering frame for her face. A wide satin ribbon embroidered with violet and pink flowers circled the crown and trailed merrily down the back of her neck.

Yet what made it most appealing of all was

the fact that a miniature version graced Delilah's head.

Del had brought her and Delilah downtown to do some shopping today, ostensibly to replace the lamp she had broken yesterday, but somehow they had gotten sidetracked into F.A.O. Schwartz. Among the giant stuffed animals and the crowds of dolls, he had spotted the mother-daughter hats before she did.

He might have the body of a Greek statue or a Roman warrior, she thought, but at heart he was a genuine marshmallow. He enjoyed spoiling his honorary niece as much as he spoiled his niece's mother. Smiling, Maggie peeked around the ruffled awning of the stroller to check on Delilah.

"How is she doing?" Del asked.

"Adorable, as always."

"And that's an objective opinion."

"Of course."

Del looked carefully up and down the street, then pushed the stroller forward as the light changed to green. "She must be getting hungry by now."

"I'm sure she'll make her wishes known any minute. Laszlo won't mind if I use the back room of the diner. It'll give me a chance to visit with Joanne."

"I could take you home, if you like."

He had shown up with a car today. He had explained it belonged to the company he worked for and that they wouldn't object if he borrowed it now and then. No wonder he was so dedicated to his job—his company certainly didn't skimp on the fringe benefits they gave their employees. "Thanks, but it would be silly not to drop in since we're in the neighborhood."

"Okay, if that's what you want."

Was it only her imagination, or had he grown tenser the closer they had gotten to the diner? Or was the tension because they were getting closer to his office? Still hanging onto her hat, she tipped her head to look at the tall buildings that surrounded them. "Which one of these do you work in, Del?" she asked impulsively.

"You can't see it from here. It's on the next block. Watch out for the curb," he said, grabbing her elbow.

"What? Oh!" Her toe hit the edge of the curb, and she stumbled onto the sidewalk. "Oops."

Still hanging onto the stroller with one hand, he clamped his other arm around her waist to steady her. She flattened her palm on his chest and looked up, prepared to thank him.

But his sudden proximity drove all thought out of her head. Now that she knew the spectacular build his nondescript polo shirt concealed, all she could think about was getting her hands on him again. Before she remembered what she had asked him, they arrived at the diner.

As soon as they got through the door, they were greeted by a blast of Gershwin. The source of the noise was a boom box that had been wedged between the cash register and the pie keeper. A young man with baggy pants and a build like Fred Astaire, his upturned hand balancing a trio of plates heaped with French fries, tap-danced his way across the floor. Maggie watched, spellbound, as he deposited the plates with a flourish and took a bow.

Laughing, she joined in the burst of applause from the customers. "He's great," she said to Del.

"Yeah." He looked around the interior of the diner, then half-turned to leave. "The noise is going to upset Delilah. We shouldn't stay."

"She's okay. She loves music. Besides, they've just turned it down," she said, nodding toward the counter.

Joanne adjusted the volume and waved happily at Maggie as she hurried forward to greet them. "Hey, Mags, I love the hat. And the little sweetums has one, too."

"Thanks. Del got them."

Joanne grinned at Del. "Oh, that's too cute.

The flowers in the band even match Maggie's outfit.''

She was right, Maggie thought. The colors in the hat matched the dusty rose tunic and dark violet leggings she had put on that morning. Yet another example of how...sweet Del was.

He shrugged. ''The hats are practical. They'll keep the sun off.''

''What do you think of our new waiter?'' Joanne asked.

''He's wonderful,'' Maggie said. ''But what happened to Edith?''

''Edith the Perfect got fired when Laszlo caught her substituting tofu for the beef in his hamburgers. Luckily, José over there witnessed the whole thing and applied for the job on the spot.'' Joanne lowered her voice. ''José's not really a waiter, you know. He's a Broadway dancer. This is his day job until he gets his big break.''

''How long has he been here?''

''It's a new record. Eight days and counting, and Laszlo only came close to firing him once.''

''Why?''

''José used to be in the chorus of *Cats*,'' Joanne explained. ''He got into his role a bit too deeply and pounced on the counter on all fours.''

Maggie bit back a snort.

"He was great," Joanne continued, "but he spilled coffee all over a couple of cops. Laszlo had to promise them free doughnuts for a month to keep them from giving him a ticket."

"No one ever arrested me when I spilled things."

"Not for spilling coffee, for providing entertainment without a license."

"Oh, my," Maggie said, laughing.

"Laszlo puts up with it because he knows José's dancing is bringing in more customers than ever."

"I can see that," Del said. "We'd better come back another time, Maggie. The place looks full."

"No, there's a spot in the far corner," Joanne said.

Maggie thanked her and started forward when she spotted a familiar face. Bill Grimes was sitting at a table by the window, his balding head gleaming in the sunlight. "Isn't that your friend over there?" she asked.

Del swallowed a resigned sigh and nodded a greeting to Bill. Judging by the smirk on his partner's face, Bill was fully aware that Del had already spotted him and had attempted to steer Maggie out of the diner.

Before he could move forward, though, Delilah let out an insistent wail. Del had enough experience with her to realize it was a cry of hunger. He made another offer to drive Maggie home, but she declined. Linking her arm with Joanne's, she maneuvered the stroller between the tables toward the privacy of the diner's back room.

As soon as Maggie and Delilah disappeared through the swinging door, Del went over to join his colleague.

"Don't tell me, let me guess," Bill said, gesturing with a forkful of apple pie. "She followed you in here, right?"

"The joke's getting old, Bill," Del muttered. He stacked the shopping bags he was carrying on a chair beside him. "What are you doing here?"

"Eating pie and watching the waiter's free show," Bill answered. "That music also serves as great interference to casual eavesdropping. What are you doing here?"

"We were shopping."

"You're getting quite domesticated, aren't you?"

"I'm just helping Maggie out," Del said.

"May is rapidly going past. If you want a June wedding, you'd better get busy."

Somehow, Del wasn't in the mood for more of his partner's ribbing. "That joke's getting old, too, Bill. You know anything permanent between me and Maggie isn't going to happen.''

Bill set down his fork. ''You have feelings for her,'' he stated.

''She's a remarkable woman,'' Del said. ''But she knows nothing about me. There are too many good reasons to limit our relationship to friendship.''

''Ah, do you know what Lord Byron said about friendship?''

''Bill...''

'''Friendship is Love without his wings!'''

Del frowned. Love? No, it hadn't gone that far. He couldn't let it. He knew where that road led. ''Give it up, Bill. SPEAR agents aren't suited to love and marriage.''

''Don't tell that to Tish Buckner,'' Bill said.

''What?''

''Didn't you hear the news? Tish is pregnant.''

Del was startled. Tish? Pregnant? How could that be? Tish Buckner was the agent who had been caught in the warehouse explosion last month. Del had burned his hands pulling her to safety. The last time he had seen her, she had just come out of a coma. Her husband, Jeff Kirby, had immediately rushed to her side.

As a matter of fact, the last time Del had seen Tish had been on the day Delilah was born. He had just come from visiting her in the hospital when he had decided to stop into the diner…and had ended up delivering Maggie's baby.

Del cleared his throat. Even after all this time, he still felt a lump there when he thought about the wonder of Delilah's birth. "Tish was in bad shape after the explosion. I'm glad to hear she recovered so quickly."

"Actually, she was already pregnant when you pulled her out of that fire," Bill said. "That's what Jeff told me. They had been keeping the news to themselves until they were sure she was out of danger."

"How about that," Del murmured. For a man who normally did his best to avoid dealing with babies, it appeared he had ended up rescuing not one but two pregnant women in the past month.

Jeff Kirby and Tish Buckner were a good match, Del thought. They were both SPEAR agents, so there weren't any secrets between them. Still, having a child was bound to curtail their activities. They would have to tone down their careers. They wouldn't be able to take the dangerous assignments and risk leaving an orphan. With a baby to care for, they would have to give up the excitement of the chase, and what would they have in return?

They would have the simple pleasures of holding their baby in their arms, of watching it grow up, of sharing a home and planning a family and forever together....

No. That train of thought was pointless. Other people could plan a future like that, not him. With an effort, he turned his attention to what Bill was saying.

"...but I don't believe in coincidences."

"Sorry," Del said. "What did you say?"

Bill pushed his empty pie plate aside and crossed his arms on the table, leaning closer to Del. "Word has it that there's going to be a special session of the UN security council here in New York next week."

"Concerning what?"

"World terrorism."

"Apart from contributing to the problem, what connection would Simon have to that?" Del frowned and answered his own question. "Unless his intended target is attending."

"That's exactly what I figured. As I said, I don't believe in coincidences. Whatever Simon is planning is going to happen during that session."

"We'll need a list of the speakers and attendees."

"The meeting has just been scheduled. We'll know more in a few days."

"Good."

"If my hunch is right, it would appear that by next week at this time, our waiting will be over."

Could Bill be right? One week to go, and what had been almost a year of near misses by SPEAR would be finished. The hunt for Simon would end.

And so would Del's time with Maggie.

Suddenly, the idea of being through with the endless hours of surveillance wasn't as appealing as it had once been. When once he had wanted to hurry the time along, now he wanted to slow it down.

He looked toward the door that led to the diner's back room. He had planned to take Maggie and Delilah straight home when she finished her visit with Joanne. After the way he had come so close to losing control the night before, he had even been considering the idea of moving back into his hotel room. But now he changed his mind. With his assignment in New York rapidly drawing to a close, he didn't want to squander one second of the time he and Maggie had left.

Twenty minutes later, when Maggie finally joined them, instead of taking her and Delilah home, Del took them to Central Park. Although Delilah was too young to care about the animals in the children's zoo, Maggie enjoyed showing them to her anyway. Del did, too. He felt like a kid again as Maggie talked him into riding the park's famous carousel. He pushed thoughts of his work to the back of his mind and let himself be swept along by her enthusiasm.

By the time they arrived at Maggie's apartment, dusk had fallen. Delilah, exhausted after the long outing, settled down to sleep with a minimum of fuss.

Del sipped a beer and eyed the couch. His back was already twinging at the prospect of the night ahead, but putting up with that broken spring in the couch would be better than the sterile four walls of his hotel room.

"Whew!" Maggie said, collapsing into the rocking chair. "I hadn't realized how out of shape I am."

"I'm sorry," Del said immediately. "I should have realized you were getting tired."

"No, no," she said, waving away his apology. "I had a great time and I wouldn't have cut it short for the world. Do you know how long it has been since I took a day off for fun?"

"No, but if it's been as long for you as it has for me, I'd say we were both overdue for it."

She smiled. "Yes, I think we were. Thanks again for those hats."

Del sat on the coffee table in front of her and

leaned forward, dangling his beer can between his knees. He returned her smile as he thought about how she and Delilah had looked on the carousel, with their violet ribbons fluttering behind them. He wished he had thought to take a camera from the equipment pool when he had requisitioned the car today. "The pleasure was all mine, Maggie."

"I should have remembered to get some new sneakers while we were out," she said, toeing off her shoes. "I think all that extra weight I was carrying around a month ago made my feet spread. Or maybe I should go back to wearing sandals."

"Are your feet sore?"

"Oh, it's nothing a soak in the tub won't fix. I used to do that after a long day at the diner. I'm just too lazy right now to move off this chair."

"Allow me," Del said, setting his beer aside in order to pick up her right foot. Angling himself to the side, he propped her heel on his thigh.

She grabbed the arms of the chair. "Del, what are you doing?"

"Relax, Maggie. You need a massage." He reached down to pick up her left foot and set it beside the right one. He tugged off her socks, then folded his hands over her toes and squeezed gently. "How's that?"

She heaved a noisy sigh and let her chair rock backward. "Heaven."

He felt her skin warm beneath his touch as he slowly eased away the stiffness. "Better?"

"Mmm. Much."

He wiggled her toes, his lips twitching as he saw the purple nail polish. Despite Delilah's demands on her time, Maggie still managed to keep her toenails painted.

That was part of her nature, he thought. She set out to enjoy each day, to live life to its fullest. "I need to go into the office tomorrow morning, but if you can wait a few days, I'll take you shoe shopping on the weekend."

"Thanks, that would be nice." She fell silent as he kneaded his way from her toes to her heels. When he rubbed his thumbs into the balls of her feet, she gave a low moan of pleasure.

At least, he assumed it was pleasure. His hands stilled as he thought about how he could have hurt her the night before when all he had wanted was to give her pleasure. He lifted his head and looked at her.

Maggie smiled. "Don't stop, Del. It feels so good."

He grasped her ankles and turned to face her. "Let me know if I hurt you, Maggie."

"My feet are feeling better by the minute."

"I would never want to hurt you. If I do, just tell me to stop, all right?"

The amusement faded from her face. "Okay."

"I can't keep from touching you, Maggie."

Her grip on the chair arms tightened as she regarded him in silence. Obviously, she realized that he was talking about more than a foot rub. Her reply, when it came, was as straightforward and uninhibited as the way she had handled their kiss the night before. "I won't lie to you, Del," she said. "I like it when you touch me. I always have. I'm just not ready to...well..."

"Let me worry about that," he said, giving her toes another squeeze as he set her heels on the coffee table. He left her briefly, then returned with a towel and a bottle of Delilah's baby oil.

Her eyes widened. "Del? What are you doing?"

"Only as much as we're able to," he replied. He spread the towel over his legs and lifted her feet onto his lap, then uncapped the bottle and drizzled oil into his palm.

Maggie stared, motionless. And fascinated. Somewhere in a corner of her mind, an annoying little voice was telling her that she should get up and run.

But she didn't really want to. Besides, she couldn't, could she? Trying to run now would be hazardous. Del had already spread baby oil on the soles of her feet.

She sighed and dropped her head against the back of the rocking chair. His hands should be registered as lethal weapons, she thought. Her skin tingled with little spurts of pleasure as his clever, nimble fingers worked the oil between her toes.

She had never given much thought to reflexology, but people who practiced it were definitely on to something. The feet really were packed with bundles of nerve endings. What else could explain the echoes of sensation that were coursing to other parts of her body with every shift of his hands?

First her earlobe, now her feet. If they kept this up, how many more erogenous zones would he help her discover?

He lifted his gaze to hers, and her breath caught. Naked passion coiled in the depths of his eyes. For a moment she thought she glimpsed the hard stranger who had pinned her to the table last night, but then the tiny laugh lines at the corners of his eyes crinkled, and he tickled the arch of her foot.

Another sensation echoed along her nerves, but this one targeted the most erogenous zone of all. It went straight to her heart.

Chapter 10

"What a darling baby. How old is she?"

Del glanced at the heavily pregnant woman who had paused in front of him. "She's six weeks old today."

"Oh, that's the best age. They're so easy."

Del thought of the night feedings, the diapers and the endless laundry baskets full of baby clothes. "Uh, really?"

"They stay wherever you put them and they don't talk back." She turned, grasped the arms of the chair beside him and carefully levered herself down to sit. "Ah," she murmured.

There was a shriek from the other side of the waiting room. A girl with black pigtails and two missing front teeth raced around the miniature parking garage that sat in the center of the floor.

Behind her trailed an overalled boy of about three. He grabbed in vain for the plastic dump truck she held.

The woman sighed. ''Emma, stop teasing Bruce and give him back his truck.''

The girl grudgingly complied. As soon as he got the toy, the boy plopped down on the floor and started to make what were probably supposed to be engine noises.

Delilah lifted her head from Del's shoulder to follow the boy's progress. She emitted a gurgle that could have been a burp but sounded more like a reply.

Del turned her around, holding her under her arms so that she could see the action more easily. She braced her feet on his lap and flexed her knees in a miniature jumping jack, then gave his hand a splayed-finger pat, as if in approval.

The woman laughed. ''I wish my husband was as good with our kids as you are. Is this your first?''

Del ignored the sudden shaft of pain her words caused. Her mistake was understandable. Anyone seeing a man sitting with a baby in an obstetrician's office first thing in the morning would naturally assume he was her father. ''She isn't mine. I'm just watching her while her mother's in with the doctor.''

"Oh." She paused. "Well, you could give my Stanley some tips, anyway. Bruce, not in your mouth," she called suddenly.

The toddler on the floor grinned, the corner of a magazine clamped in his teeth.

"Bru-cee! I got your truck," the pigtailed girl called, grabbing his toy and skipping out of reach.

The boy spat out the magazine and started to cry.

"Oh, God," the woman moaned, levering herself out of the chair. "And I wanted a third? I must be nuts."

In spite of her perilously swollen abdomen, the woman squatted beside her son and gave him a hug. Her daughter joined them, and after some patient negotiations, some more hugs and a small plastic bag of animal crackers the woman took from her purse, the children calmed down and snuggled against their mother as she read a cardboard book.

As Del watched the family interaction, he thought about Maggie. He had a vivid image of Maggie years from now, her belly swollen with her third child, acting as referee between a pigtailed Delilah and a sturdy little toddler.

She wanted more children, and she would undoubtedly adore them all as much as she did Delilah. Her home would be filled with noisy, loving chaos, just like his sister's. Just like Elizabeth's.

Another shaft of pain, deeper than the last, stabbed through his heart. Why was he torturing himself this way?

Del focused on Delilah's wispy blond curls, then closed his eyes and inhaled deeply, drawing in the clean, soft baby scent of her scalp.

Maggie tucked her blouse into her skirt and took a seat in front of the desk, craning her neck as she tried to read the notes the doctor was making in her file. "I'm getting plenty of rest, Dr. Hendricks. Really."

"I'm glad to hear that. Exhaustion is one of the most common problems with new mothers." Dr. Hendricks scribbled something undecipherable. "Do you have any help at home?"

"Oh, yes," Maggie said. "I have a wonderful friend who has been giving me a hand since Delilah was born. And now that Delilah's practically sleeping through the night, things are almost too easy."

"Too easy?" The doctor set down her pen and folded her hands on her desk. "That's one complaint I haven't heard before."

"Oh, I'm not complaining. Not really. I just...oh, I don't know, sometimes I worry."

"That's because you love your child and you want to be the best mother possible for her, right?"

Maggie sighed. "I wonder whether I'm trying hard enough, Dr. Hendricks. I've heard babies are supposed to be so difficult to take care of and so much work, but so far Delilah has given me nothing but joy."

The doctor smiled. "Babies *are* joy, Maggie. Why do you think most of my business comes from repeat customers?"

"I'd love to have more."

"And there's no reason you shouldn't, once you give your body a year or two to recover."

"Do I have to wait that long?"

"The choice is yours, of course, but pregnancies spaced too closely together can drain a woman's reserves of strength and put too much strain on a system that is already weakened." The doctor drew a brochure out of a stack on a shelf behind her and passed it to Maggie. "This details the birth control options that are available. Have you given any thought to which one you would like to use?"

Maggie held the brochure in her lap but didn't

open it. "I wanted to ask you about that. When will it be safe for me to, um…"

"Resume sexual relations?"

She nodded. It sounded so clinical when put like that, Maggie thought. It was a far cry from the warm, tingling awareness that she felt whenever Del was around.

Over the past weeks, that awareness had been growing at a breathtaking rate. Neither one of them could pretend that the kisses and caresses they shared were merely friendly. Although Del had restrained himself from pressing her for more, he didn't try to hide the desire he felt. Nor did she. They both were adult enough to realize where their intimacy was inevitably leading.

It was such a major step to take in any relationship, somehow it didn't seem right to be thinking about it here.

"The timing varies with each woman, Maggie," the doctor said. "In your case, I would say there's no physical reason to delay any longer, if that's what you want to do."

"You mean I could start right away? Tonight?"

"Whenever you want," the doctor said. "But please, while I do like repeat customers, I strongly advise you to consider some kind of contraception. It's not impossible to conceive while you're still breast-feeding.''

Maggie knew the doctor was right, but she couldn't help imagining what it would be like someday to have a little sister or brother for Delilah, another baby to love, perhaps a child with dark hair and warm amber eyes....

She knew what she was doing. She was picturing Del's baby.

Well, why shouldn't she? If ever there was a man who was meant to be a father, it was Del.

And babies were the natural consequence of sexual relations, weren't they?

Although a doctor's office really wasn't the place to be thinking about lovemaking, Maggie found herself doing just that as she went to join Del in the waiting room. He was sitting in a chair near the door, Delilah on his lap with her head nestled in the crook of his arm. He had tipped his head back against the wall behind him and closed his eyes, but she could tell he wasn't asleep by the way his fingers moved in Delilah's hair.

What would it be like to make love with Del?

Anticipation shot through her as she realized that there was no longer a physical reason to keep her from finding out. Yet although she might be physically capable, was she emotionally ready to take a step like that? To some people, sex was merely an enjoyable activity, but to Maggie, it was so much more. To make love, she had to *be* in love.

Had she fallen the rest of the way in love with Del?

Whenever Del was near, he drew her gaze like a lighted window on a dark night, as if he were surrounded by one of those auras Joanne was always talking about. The sound of his voice never failed to set her heart vibrating. His touch was something she was coming to crave, even if it was no more than the casual brush of his hand against her cheek as he smoothed a curl behind her ear.

Maggie didn't need to see him to be aware of his presence. These past few weeks while he had shared her apartment with her, whenever he was near she felt a warm glow in the pit of her stomach and the core of her bones.

Six weeks ago she hadn't known his last name. Wasn't it too soon to think about love?

On the other hand, six weeks ago she had known Delilah for less than a day. Her heart didn't have a timetable. Love simply happened.

So, was she in love with Del?

Nothing had really changed. He still was planning to leave when his work in New York was over. He still was maddeningly private about so many things. He had never talked about commitment. The odds were stacked against a future together. It would be risky to take a chance on loving him. She would probably end up falling flat on her face.

Yes, well, she had never paid much attention to the odds before, had she? Life was meant to be lived. If she hadn't believed in taking chances, she wouldn't be able to stand here today on two healthy legs. She wouldn't have known Delilah.

The brightly lit waiting room was filled with strangers and the sporadic fussing of tired babies, yet it all faded from her consciousness as Maggie stood very, very still and watched Del's strong hands tenderly cradle her child. The wave of certainty that surged over her was so strong, it made her shudder.

Oh, yes. She loved him.

Del opened his eyes, his gaze finding hers as if he could sense her presence as easily as she sensed his. He picked up Delilah's diaper bag from the floor beside him and rose to his feet. "Are you ready?"

Oh, yes. She was not only ready, she was willing and able. And tonight, when Delilah was asleep and the two of them were alone, she would show him how much. Maggie smiled and took his arm.

"'Something wicked this way comes,'" Bill murmured, lifting the binoculars to his eyes.

Del grunted. Shakespeare again. But he couldn't argue with Bill's choice of quotation. Through the light drizzle that streaked the car windows, he could see Herbert Hull step onto the sidewalk. The dented steel door swung shut behind him as he paused to ogle the glossy teaser photos of the performers displayed under the marquee.

The former Marine sniper was keeping to his usual schedule this afternoon. He had shot a few games of pool and had his typical lunch of beer, nuts and pickled eggs before coming to this peep show. True to habit, he had required far less time to finish his business at the peep show than he had to finish his beer.

Since the day Hull had used the laser range finder to index his shots, he had been steering clear of the apartment near the UN, but something was definitely going to happen soon— SPEAR intelligence had observed a number of Simon's known associates arriving in the city. In his last briefing tape, Jonah had ordered the agents to double-team all the suspects. At this point, SPEAR didn't want to lose track of anyone who could turn out to be a key player in Simon's plans.

"Is Horton in place?" Bill asked as Hull started down the sidewalk.

Del looked at the doorway of the adjacent building. A small man in a ragged sweater, a brown paper bag containing a bottle clutched in his hand, a grimy baseball cap pulled down over his eyes, sat huddled against the rain. As Hull passed by, the derelict staggered to his feet and wove away in the same direction. "Yeah, he's got him."

"I don't see Lamere."

A white van drove past and turned at the next corner. "She just went by."

"All right. They'll take over from here." Bill put down the binoculars and pulled his pipe out of his jacket pocket.

Del drummed his fingers on the steering wheel. "Something's going to break soon," he muttered. "I can feel it."

"Patience, my man. 'They also serve who only stand and—'"

"Shut up, Bill," Del said mildly.

Bill chuckled and filled the pipe bowl with tobacco.

Del started the car, then cracked open a window to let the pipe smoke drift out. A passing delivery truck splashed past, throwing up a sheet of spray. Bill chuckled again as Del wiped his face and switched on the wipers.

He was about to pull away from the curb when Del saw a man in a tan trench coat hurry past on the sidewalk, a black umbrella over his head. Del frowned and followed his progress toward the topless bar across the street from the peep show Hull had just exited. The man seemed to be too well-dressed for this seedy neighborhood—he was probably some executive type who wanted to walk on the wild side. The trench-coated man closed his umbrella and looked over his shoulder nervously. Del had no more than a split second glimpse of the man's face, but it was enough.

"I don't believe it," Del muttered.

"What?" Bill asked, looking up.

"That was Alan Blackthorn."

"Blackthorn? The name doesn't ring a bell."

"He's Maggie's old boyfriend."

"That married guy who ran out on her?"

"Yeah. I had SPEAR intelligence run a check on him. They said he's been going to strip clubs on his lunch hour. What are the chances of him showing up here?"

"Where does he work?"

"An insurance company on Forty-second Street."

"Then the chances are pretty good. That's only a few blocks from here. Why did you do the check?" Bill lowered his pipe, his expression losing amiability. "Is the bastard bothering Maggie?"

"You guessed it. He wants to pick up where they left off."

"She strikes me as too intelligent a woman to get taken in by him again."

"She is. But each time he calls it upsets her." Del pondered his options. So far, he had shielded Maggie from Alan's persistence, but he wouldn't be able to run interference for her indefinitely.

The idea of roughing Alan up was tempting, but that would be more for Del's satisfaction than Maggie's. Throwing around his weight as a SPEAR operative was tempting, too, but besides compromising the agency, using that approach would be overkill. Alan was a nuisance, not a threat.

Still, this was too good an opportunity to pass up. Del turned off the engine and reached for the door handle. "Wait here."

"No problem. What are you going to do?"

"Alan doesn't seem to take it seriously when

he hears no over the phone. Maybe I can find a way to make him pay attention in person.''

"Let me know if I can be of assistance," Bill said.

"Thanks. I might do that.''

Del turned up the collar of his windbreaker, hunching his shoulders against the drizzle as he strode toward the bar. Even though the day was dull with a low overcast, the interior of the bar was many times darker. Rock music throbbed through the dimness as Del paused inside the entrance to give his eyes a chance to adjust.

Alan sat at a table in the far corner. He hadn't taken off his coat. A bored-looking waitress moved toward him, her full breasts gleaming red in the light over the bar. Her face was carefully made up and her hair teased to alarming heights, but Alan didn't lift his gaze above her neck.

The sight of all that naked flesh didn't affect Del in the slightest. He kept his gaze on Alan as he crossed the room, pulled a hundred from his pocket and held it out to the waitress. "Take a break, miss," he said.

"Now, just a minute," Alan began.

The woman placed the beer on the table, then plucked the bill from Del's fingers and tucked it into the waistband of her skirt. "Sure thing, hon,'' she said, walking away. ''Whatever gets you off.''

Del pushed the table to one side and slid into the seat beside Alan, boxing him in against the wall. ''Hello, Mr. Blackthorn. Remember me?''

For a moment all that showed on Alan's features was irritation, then suddenly recognition dawned. ''You! What are you doing here?''

''I could ask you the same thing,'' Del said. ''But I don't really want to know. You turn my stomach enough as it is.''

''What I do is none of your business.''

''When it concerns Maggie it is. She asked you to leave her alone. I'd like you to do it.''

Alan shifted as if he were about to stand up. ''I don't have to listen to this. She liked my company well enough before. Maybe you're just jealous because you want her for yourself.''

Despite his resolve to simply talk to Alan, Del felt a sudden spurt of anger. He clamped his hand over Alan's wrist and twisted just enough to make the bones squeak. ''The last time I saw you, I wanted to break your arm. I didn't because it would have upset Maggie. She isn't here now, and I don't think your new D-cup friend over there would care if I took you apart and mailed the pieces to a blood bank.'' He released his grip and wiped his hand on his pants leg. "Do I have your attention?"

Alan paled and rubbed his wrist.

"Good," Del said. "You've been married, what? Twenty years? And you have a son and a daughter, right?"

"What? How do you know that?"

"You haven't been as clever as you think you are. Secrets have a way of coming out."

In the dim light, the sweat that broke out on Alan's forehead looked oily. He stared at Del. "What's this going to cost me?"

"Cost you?"

He reached for his beer mug and took a quick gulp. "How much do you want to keep your mouth shut?"

Del scowled impatiently. "I'm not interested in your money, Alan. I'm trying to make a point. You have a wife and two healthy children who need a stable home. Instead of spending your time and energy chasing after young women to give your ego a boost out of your mid-life crisis, why don't you work on your marriage?"

Alan's jaw slackened with confusion. "I don't understand."

"Listen, Alan," Del said, leaning closer. "As far as I'm concerned, you're a piece of scum because of the way you took advantage of a kindhearted woman like Maggie, but she must have seen some goodness in you at one time. I'm hoping that she wasn't all wrong, that underneath your silk suit and bad hair weave you've still got a few ounces of decency.''

Alan blinked and touched his fingertips to his hair, as if to check it was still there.

''You must still care about your wife and family,'' Del continued, ''or you wouldn't have been so concerned about hiding your affair from them. Do you really want to hurt your wife? Do you want to see your children turn against you?''

A crack appeared in Alan's bravado. He glanced furtively around the bar.

''You get your kicks by sneaking around and cheating on your wife,'' Del continued. ''You figure it's all right as long as no one finds out. Well, you're a fool, Alan.''

''Now just a minute—''

''You think your secrets are safe, and no one's going to find out about your double life, but secrets and lies are no way to build a relationship,'' Del said, realizing again how much he had in common with this man. Damn, he didn't like thinking about that. ''The longer the lies go on, the worse it's going to get.''

''Are you blackmailing me or not?''

Del sat back in disgust. ''For the last time, I

don't care about your money. I only care about Maggie.''

''Then why were you talking about my wife?''

''For some reason, I thought that if you work things out with your wife, you'll quit trying to reestablish your affair with Maggie.''

''And that's what this was all about?'' Alan asked. ''You accost me and practically break my wrist in order to give me *marital* advice?''

''Yes.''

Alan hesitated. For a moment it looked as if he actually might be mulling over what Del had said. ''Why the hell would you do that? Why do you care?''

Del wouldn't care if Alan ended up ruining his marriage and making his children hate him. He didn't care if Alan threw away the very thing that Del yearned for but could never have. All Del wanted was to insure the man stayed out of Maggie's life. ''I care about Maggie,'' he said.

''So do I.''

''Then leave her alone.''

Alan took another swallow of beer, his throat working jerkily.

''Think about it, Alan.'' Del got to his feet, his anger spent. In its place was a creeping emptiness. ''You already have what some people can only dream of. As long as you continue living a lie, you risk losing it all."

Del returned to the car, the words he had spoken repeating in his head like the steady drizzling of the rain. Living a lie. Living a lie. That's what he was doing, too, wasn't it?

No, it was different. He wasn't like Alan. He never intended to hurt Maggie....

But in the end, he feared the result would be the same.

Chapter 11

Maggie moved the curtain aside to look out the window for what had to be the seventh time in the past hour. The drizzle that had begun that afternoon had turned into a steady rain. Headlights shone in jagged streaks as a car shushed past three stories below. There was no lightning or thunder. Maggie knew that the electric tingling she felt zipping along her nerves wasn't due to the weather.

Ever since she had left the doctor's office this morning, she had felt on edge, jumpy, as if all her senses were heightened. It was the same kind of breathless tension she felt on the up slope of a roller coaster, when the cars were being winched to the top of the first rise. The decision had been made to take the ride, but the ride hadn't yet truly begun.

Six weeks ago, she had thought the hormones associated with her pregnancy had been responsible for the ups and downs of her emotions. What she felt now was different. She wasn't afraid of trusting her emotions now. Besides, she had always loved the swooping exhilaration of a roller coaster. It was a lot like making love.

"When is Uncle Del going to come home?" Robbie asked, bumping into her hip as he skidded to a stop by her side. He pressed his nose against the glass and looked out into the night beside her.

Home. Despite the bleak weather, Maggie felt a warm glow ignite inside her. She liked the sound of "Del" and "home" together.

Now that she had finally admitted to herself that she was in love, everything seemed so much clearer. It was as if a weight had been lifted from her heart, allowing her the freedom to dream once more.

A home. A family. Forever. That's what she had sought when she'd allowed herself to believe Alan's lies. This time, it would be different. She had chosen the right man, a man she could trust. What she had felt for Alan was nothing compared to her love for Del.

"Auntie Maggie?"

She reached out to ruffle Robbie's red hair. "He had to work late," she answered. "He won't be here until after your bedtime."

"Is he gonna bring ice cream?"

"I don't know. If he does, I'll save you some, okay?"

"Cool." A knock sounded on the apartment door. Robbie pushed away from the window and ran to answer it. "Gramma's here."

"Hold on, Robbie," Maggie called. "Check to make sure first."

He made a face, but jumped up and peered through the peephole anyway. "Told ya," he said, yanking open the door.

Armilda gave Robbie a hug and propped her dripping umbrella in the hallway before she stepped inside. "What an awful night. I'm sorry I'm late, Maggie. The bridge game went on longer than I expected."

"It's okay, Armilda."

"Well? Where's the little angel?" She looked around the room, then headed for the infant chair Maggie had set beside the couch. She tipped her glasses down her nose and smiled. "Hello, Delilah."

Delilah gurgled in pleasure at the familiar face and made a grab for Armilda's glasses.

Maggie went over to lift Delilah from her chair. "Are you sure you're not too tired for this, Armilda?"

"We'll be fine, Maggie. Besides, Robbie promised he would help."

"Yeah," Robbie said, puffing out his chest proudly. "I'm gonna baby-sit."

"Because if you run into any problems, remember I'm only thirty seconds away."

"Maggie, you deserve a break," Armilda said, reaching out to take Delilah from her arms. "Considering the way you've been taking Robbie all these weeks, you should have asked me sooner."

"It's only for a few hours," Maggie said, running her hand down Delilah's arm.

"Take as long as you want."

"She's just finished nursing, so she probably won't be hungry again until after midnight. I've mixed up a bottle of formula just in case, but I don't know whether she will take it. Make sure to call me if she needs me."

"I'm sure we'll get along fine," Armilda said. As Robbie ran off to gather his toys, she leaned closer to Maggie and lowered her voice. "And unless it's an emergency, I'm not going to be interrupting you. In my opinion, it's high time you and Del had some time alone to concentrate on each other.''

Maggie felt her cheeks heat. Were her reasons for asking her neighbor to baby-sit Delilah really so transparent? ''Thanks, Armilda.''

''Del's a good man. From what I've seen of him over the past six weeks, I'd say that he's one fellow you'd be smart to hang on to.''

''I intend to,'' she said, smiling despite her blush.

''You'd better.'' Armilda winked. ''If I were thirty years younger, I might go after him myself.''

Maggie cocked her head and put her fists on her hips. ''You'd have to get past me first.''

''That's the spirit.'' Armilda hooked the diaper bag with her free hand and ushered Robbie out the door. ''Good luck!''

As soon as she was alone, Maggie glanced at the clock. The roller coaster cars winched upward another notch closer to the summit. Butterflies milled around her stomach.

There was so much to do if she wanted everything to be ready. The stacks of folded baby clothes on the table and the bags of diapers in the corner weren't exactly romantic. Neither was the spit-up stain on the shoulder of her T-shirt. Candles and soft music would help to set the mood, and if she hurried, she would be able to squeeze in a bath and do her nails, but what on earth should she wear?

Maybe there was no need to go to all this trouble. Given the way she felt, making love with Del was inevitable. They had been struggling to restrain themselves for weeks. Perhaps she should simply relax and let nature take its course.

Still, as Joanne would say, there wouldn't be any harm in giving the karmic wheel a little grease, would there?

Del sat on the edge of the bed and lifted the glass. The aroma of aged whiskey slithered through his senses, promising a temporary respite from his thoughts.

This wasn't what he wanted.

But there was a hell of a difference between what he wanted and what he could have. He'd learned that lesson eight years ago. The visit to the doctor this morning—and his run-in with Alan later—had served as a refresher course.

He lifted the glass just as the telephone on the night table began to ring. He looked at it without moving for a moment. Although he was off duty, he was always officially on call, yet if this was SPEAR business, the call would come through on his cell phone.

It was Bill. "Del, I've got some news."

Del frowned. "Not over an unsecured line, Bill."

"This is off the record."

"Okay, what?"

There was a pause. "Are you all right?"

"Yes, I'm fine." The glass clinked against the whiskey bottle as he set it down. "What's up?"

"Our friends at the airport reported an interesting development ten minutes ago."

He was talking about the SPEAR intelligence people who were watching for Simon's men, Del realized. But why wasn't Bill using the cell phone with its scrambling system?

The answer was clear with Bill's next words.

"The reservation computer shows a certain insurance company executive just booked four tickets to Orlando for next Wednesday."

"Insurance...do you mean Blackthorn?"

"Uh-huh. After you two had your little chat, I had intelligence put a flag on his name, just to keep tabs. Seems the tickets are part of a package deal, a family vacation at Disney World."

Del exhaled in a slow whistle. Evidently, their chat had been more effective than he had thought. From the sound of it, Alan was about to pay some long overdue attention to his wife and children. "It's not a permanent solution, but it's a step in the right direction."

"Sure is. I'm curious, Del."

"Yes?"

"What the hell did you say to him, anyway?"

He looked at his glass. "Just reminded him about something he already knew."

Del hung up the phone thoughtfully. Wouldn't that be something if Alan managed to mend his marriage, despite the fact that he was a self-centered jerk? Maggie would like that. She was so kindhearted, she wouldn't want to see anyone miserable, even Alan. It was too bad Del couldn't tell her about Alan's planned vacation, but that would mean having to come up with yet more lies to explain how he knew.

"'O what a tangled web we weave, when first we practice to deceive!'" he muttered. He laughed without humor. He'd been holed up with Bill Grimes too long. Now he was starting to issue quotations himself—and Sir Walter Scott, no less.

Before Del could retrieve his glass, the phone rang again. This time it was Maggie.

As always, the sound of her voice warmed Del faster than any whiskey ever could. "Hello, Maggie."

"Del." She hesitated. In the background, he

could hear music. Not the tinkling sound of one of Delilah's toys, but soft jazz. "I was worried about you."

"I called earlier."

"I must have been in the bath." There was a long pause. "Were you planning on coming over here tonight?"

He hadn't. He had planned to stay here and remind himself of all the reasons he *shouldn't* go over there tonight. He looked at the bottle beside him, then slowly screwed the cap on.

It was bad enough lying to Maggie, but there was no point lying to himself. He didn't care about the pain that was bound to come. He didn't care if he was repeating the mistake he'd made eight years ago. He was neither smart enough nor noble enough to keep away.

When Maggie met him at the door of her apartment, Del didn't know what to say. He knew he was staring like a fool, but he couldn't seem to help it.

She had done something to her hair. Her short curls were fluffier, softer looking. They framed her face like a blond halo. Her face was different, too. Her eyes seemed larger, her cheekbones higher, her lips fuller.

She was wearing makeup, he realized. By this

time of the evening, she was usually already pre-
paring for bed, her face fresh-scrubbed and rosy.

"Are you going somewhere?" he asked.

"No," she said, reaching for his jacket.

As he shrugged out of his wet windbreaker,
his gaze dropped. Rather than one of the wash-
and-wear tunics or shirts she typically wore, she
was wearing a silk blouse. It was the color of
fresh cream, making her skin glow like satin.
And there was a lot of skin to see—she had left
the top three buttons unfastened. As she lifted her
arms to hang up his jacket, the blouse gaped
open.

Del felt his mouth go dry. Damn, he was re-
acting like an adolescent getting his first peek at
a centerfold. Those ripe, generous curves, that
deep cleavage, the glimpse of black lace...

Since when were nursing bras trimmed with
black lace?

Maggie took his hand and tugged him into the
living room. "Would you like some wine?"

He cleared his throat. He hadn't done more
than inhale whiskey fumes earlier, but he felt as
if his brain were already shutting down. His
body, though, was wide awake. "Wine?"

She left him by the couch while she crossed
the room to the refrigerator in the corner and
leaned over to take a bottle from the lowest shelf.

Her skirt draped softly over her hips in a tempting display of feminine roundness. ''I hope you like it.''

''Oh, yeah,'' he murmured.

''It's white,'' she said, straightening up with a bottle in one hand. ''Red wine gives me migraines.''

''Anything's fine.''

''Great.'' She held the bottle under one arm as she opened a drawer. ''Where's that corkscrew. I know I have one.''

Del tore his gaze away from Maggie. The lamps were dark. The only illumination came from a dozen squat candles in glass holders that had been distributed around the room. Two mismatched wineglasses rested in the center of the coffee table. From the small portable stereo near the window came the strains of a plaintive ballad.

Her apartment had always seemed cozy and welcoming to him. He had become accustomed to the clutter of baby paraphernalia. Tonight, though, the place looked as different as Maggie did. If he didn't know better, he might think she was trying to set the scene for a...seduction.

But Maggie wouldn't do that, would she? She knew how hard it was for him to keep the chemistry between them under control. She wouldn't deliberately set out to tease him with implied promises she couldn't keep, would she? Unless...

Unless she wasn't trying to tease him.

There was a frenzied rattling from the kitchen. "Ah, here we go," Maggie said, withdrawing a corkscrew from a tangle of cooking implements. She opened the wine and went over to pour it into the two glasses on the coffee table. She held one out to Del and smiled.

He approached her slowly, taking the glass she offered. "What's going on, Maggie?"

"What do you mean?"

"Are you celebrating something?"

"I guess you could say that."

"Want to let me in on it?"

She took a sip of her wine. "That's the general idea, yes."

"Well?"

"I..." She took another sip, then drew her lower lip between her teeth and looked away. "I don't know how to say this. I mean, we're always so honest with each other, but this isn't something...."

He put his index finger under her chin and gently turned her face toward him. "Maggie?"

She sighed. "Oh, Del. I guess I'm not doing a very good job of this."

"What are you trying to do?"

Her sigh turned into a wry laugh. "If you have to ask, then I *know* I'm not doing it right."

He glanced at the candles and the wine, then once again focused on Maggie. "I can see that you've gone to a lot of trouble to make the place inviting," he said.

"Thank you."

"And you look beautiful."

"Thank you."

"But you look beautiful first thing in the morning, too."

"Del..."

"It's the truth. You do." He moved his hand into her hair, splaying his fingers to let the curls slide through. "I like seeing your hair tousled and the pink creases from your pillow on your cheek."

"You do?"

"Yes, I do." He dropped his hand to her shoulder and ran his palm down the silk that covered her arm. "I like the way you look right after you've given Delilah her bath, too, when the steam in the bathroom dampens the curls around your face and drops of water make your shirt cling to your body."

She took a hurried gulp of wine. "Oh."

"This blouse you're wearing tonight is very

flattering, Maggie. I don't think I've seen you wear it before.''

''It wouldn't have been very practical.''

''Not for bathing or burping a baby, no.'' Holding her gaze, he brushed his knuckles along the side of her breast. ''But if you're trying to make me crazy, it's very effective.''

A pulse beat hard at the side of her neck. She moistened her lips with the tip of her tongue. ''Good.''

''Maggie…''

''The doctor said it was okay,'' she murmured, moving her shoulders so that her breast rubbed more firmly against his hand. ''I have every intention of driving you crazy.''

Del's hand stilled. He leaned down to look into her face to be certain he hadn't misunderstood.

Even in the candlelight he could see her cheeks were flushed. Her eyes sparkled. ''Tonight I don't have to be just a mother, Del. I can be a woman.''

No, he hadn't misunderstood. The invitation in her eyes was as clear as a banner. Anticipation coiled through his muscles so swiftly his breath caught. ''Do you mean we can—''

''Uh-huh.'' Maggie clinked her glass against his and smiled. ''Want to help me celebrate?''

Oh, hell, he thought. They had agreed they

wouldn't deepen their relationship. He hadn't meant to lead her on. There was no future for them. This could never work....

The familiar refrain sped through his mind on one final burst of conscience, but it was quickly overwhelmed by a pounding, primitive desire. He took her glass and set it with his on the table, then cupped her bottom and lifted her off her feet to fit her against him. "I don't want to hurt you, Maggie," he said hoarsely. "I never wanted to hurt you. Whatever happens, I hope you remember that."

Maggie hooked her legs around Del's waist to hold him closer, his words barely registering over the sensations that clamored for her attention. She could feel him swelling, his erection pressing into the front of her skirt in a blatant promise. His fingers tightened, and he lifted her higher, rubbing his length along the junction of her legs. A sudden stab of pleasure at the intimate contact made her cry out in surprise.

He leaned back to look at her. "Maggie?"

"Don't stop, Del," she said breathlessly. "Please."

He didn't. He backed up and sat on the arm of the couch so he could support her weight on his thigh. Then he cradled her face in his hands and kissed her.

It had started at last, Maggie thought. And just like a roller coaster, she didn't want it to stop. Sure, there were risks in loving Del, but there were risks in anything worthwhile. She parted her lips eagerly, loving the way he made her feel so...alive.

He slipped his fingers beneath the collar of her blouse, lowering his hands until his thumbs traced the valley between her breasts. He opened her remaining buttons, easing the silk over her shoulders until it caught at her elbows. His hair brushed her chin as he pressed his lips to the slope of her breast.

''Ah, Maggie,'' he murmured against her skin. ''Do you have any idea how long I've wanted to do this?''

She couldn't have answered. It was all she could do to remember to breathe. Those long, agile, clever fingers of his had unhooked her bra and were cupping her swollen flesh.

His breath tickled across her chest. ''You are exquisite,'' he whispered.

There was a time when she might have argued with that. She knew that childbirth and breast-feeding had changed her body. To her, all the extra inches hadn't made her feel beautiful. She had felt...functional. With Del, she felt different.

All along, he had reminded her that there was more to her life than being a mother.

The wonder of it was, she felt no guilt. She loved her daughter—she had lived most of the past year just for the baby she carried and bore—but she had denied this aspect of being a woman for too long. With Del, she wanted to embrace it. She wanted to revel in it. She thrust her hands into his shirt, laughing when she heard a pair of buttons pop and bounce across the floor.

He closed his lips around her nipple, and her laughter changed to moans. She arched into him, wordlessly offering him more. He took more. With the tip of his tongue he traced the hard nub in lazy circles, pressing, laving, making her shiver and burn.

"Oh, Del," she whispered, moving her hands to his head. She tunneled her fingers through his hair to hold him steady. "Oh, Del, that feels…" She gasped with pleasure.

"Good?" he asked.

"Yes. Oh, my, yes."

Smiling, he lifted her breast to his lips. His cheeks moved as he drew on her. His eyes half closed in pleasure, and a low growl rumbled from his throat. Maggie was amazed at the intensity of the sensation. Her flesh, so swollen and sensitive, sent wave after wave of enjoyment through her body. It didn't seem to matter where he touched her, where he tasted, the delight continued to grow.

Maggie shuddered and slid her hands to his chest. She had only touched his bare chest once before this, but her fingers followed the molded, muscular contours as if the memory was burned in her brain. It probably was. Closing her eyes, she took her time exploring the broad expanse of taut skin, then rested her fingers over his heart.

It pounded firm and steady. Could he hear her heart pounding in return? Did he know how much she yearned for him, how much she loved him?

Holding her by the waist, Del slid off the couch arm to lie back on the cushions, bringing her down on top of him so that her knees straddled his hips. She took full advantage of the change in their positions, sitting on her heels so she could lower her hands to his waist. She pushed his shirttails aside and skimmed her fingertips along his belt.

They had been living together for weeks. They were more comfortable together than Maggie had thought two people could be…and yet there was nothing comfortable about the excitement that sparked between them now. The strength of it was taking her breath away. Her hands trembling, she unfastened his belt buckle.

"Maggie." His voice was low, stroking over her sensitized nerves like wet velvet.

She wriggled backward toward his knees and lowered his zipper.

"Maggie, I hope to hell you're sure of this, because I don't think I'll be able to stop if you touch me—"

"Who said anything about stopping?" she murmured, running her fingers over the long, hard length that pushed against the black cotton of his boxers.

The next sound Del made was too guttural, too urgent for language, but Maggie understood it perfectly. She slid her hand beneath the elastic waistband of his underwear, her knuckles brushing across the tip of his arousal for a long, tantalizing moment before she sighed with pleasure and wrapped her fingers around him.

How could it be possible to love him more? This is what lovemaking was all about, wasn't it? A physical expression of what was held in the heart. She was communicating her love for him without words, yet it seemed to shout a chorus that echoed in the air around them.

The power of his excitement increased her own. He swelled and jerked within her grip. She felt a series of quick contractions low in her belly and a pulsing need at the junction of her legs. Her hold on him tightened as she curled forward to press her mouth to his chest.

Del caught her by the shoulders and urged her upward until he captured her lips once more. The kiss was openmouthed and hot, a surrender and a victory at the same time. When Maggie felt Del's hands push beneath her skirt, her pulse skipped with eagerness. No, there would be no stopping this time, she thought. She wanted this. She wanted Del. It was as simple—and as necessary—as drawing her next breath.

Her skirt pooled over his wrists as he stroked his way up the insides of her thighs. Gently, he pushed her panties aside with his fingers until he found the sensitive bud that was hidden within.

Desire ripped through her, mindless and intense. She knew Del felt it. He had to. His tongue swept into her mouth at the same time his fingers probed further.

"Del," she cried, her voice shaking.

He didn't misinterpret her plea. He lifted her just long enough to help her get rid of her underwear, then guided her down on top of him. They didn't take off the rest of their clothes. They didn't need to. With a tilt of their hips, their bodies joined.

For a suspended instant, Maggie looked into Del's eyes. If she'd had any lingering doubts, what she saw there would have banished them. His amber gaze glowed with pure, honest passion...and a need as undeniable as hers. As if they had been lovers for years, they moved together, finding a rhythm that built with every slick, throbbing slide of their bodies. Tension spiraled and stretched until every nerve was screaming for release.

The climax that shuddered through both their bodies brought a cry of satisfaction to her lips and tears of emotion to her eyes. Maggie gave a long, low purr of delight and collapsed on Del's chest. Beneath her ear, she could hear his heart drumming hard and steady. His skin was hot and damp against her cheek. She inhaled the scent of soap, sex and Del, and a delayed tremor shook her body.

She felt full, complete. If she could meld herself to the large, strong body on which she lay, she would. She had never felt this way before. She didn't think it was due to her long abstinence, or to residual hormones or anything physical.

It was because she was in love.

Del moved his hand to her hair and tenderly

stroked her curls away from her face. "Are you okay?"

She nodded. "Very."

"I'm sorry if I was too rough."

"You weren't," she said, turning her face to plant a kiss in the center of his chest. She rubbed her nose against his springy hair, smiling at the way it tickled. "I'm glad you cooperated."

"Cooperated?"

"In my seduction of you. I wasn't quite sure how to go about it. I'm glad *I* didn't have to get rough."

Quiet laughter rumbled through his chest. "Maggie, you're something else."

"Thanks. I think." She stacked her hands under her chin and lifted her head to look at him.

Oh, he was a glorious sight. In the flickering candlelight, his broad, muscled chest was sculpted bronze. His shirt, minus a few buttons, was twisted crookedly, half on, half off his shoulders. Shadows softened his chiseled features and darkened the smile lines around his lips. His eyes were half-closed, not with fatigue but with a lazy gleam of satisfaction.

Another aftershock of pleasure trembled through her thighs. She had to be honest with herself. While her love for Del might have intensified the sex, there was no denying that his magnificent body had contributed greatly to the experience. Goodness, wasn't it lucky for her that the man she loved happened to be handsome as sin?

"What are you smiling about?" he asked, tracing her lips with his fingertip.

"Just thinking about your luscious body."

"Luscious?" He stretched to grasp the hem of her blouse, tugging it over her head and down her arms. Her bra followed. Grinning, he tossed the garments to the floor and slid his hands between their bodies so that his palms cradled her breasts. "Now, these are luscious," he said, squeezing gently.

She wiggled her shoulders. "Mmm."

He shifted his hips. "Maggie?"

"Mmm?"

"Let's use the bed this time."

This time? Her pulse did an odd flip as she felt him harden again.

"Or would you be worried that we might disturb Delilah?"

"Delilah's with my neighbor," she said. "Armilda's baby-sitting her."

"She's…" He sat up, moving her to his lap. "Do you mean we're alone?"

Looping her arms around his neck, she nodded. Again, she thought that she probably should be feeling guilty for thinking of her own pleasure, but she didn't. ''Her next feeding isn't until after midnight.''

Del quickly shrugged out of his shirt, then scooped her up and rose to his feet. His belt clunked to the floor as his pants, still unfastened, fell to his ankles. His eyes met hers, his expression a potent mixture of humor and passion as he kicked his pants aside. Naked, he carried her to the bedroom.

The candle that Maggie had placed on the night table sputtered in a pool of hot wax. The fresh sheets she had put on the mattress that afternoon were a damp, tangled heap at the foot of the bed. The picture that had hung over the headboard was on the floor—the rocking of the bed had knocked it off its hook an hour ago.

Lacing her fingers over her head, Maggie rolled to her back and stretched luxuriously. ''Mmm.''

Del curled over to place a wet kiss on her navel. ''Do you know how many times you've said that tonight?''

''No. I think I lost count.''

''Well, I suspect we might have set some kind of record.''

She giggled. ''Okay, I confess. I did count.''

Del kissed his way upward, then lay down on his side, flung one leg over hers and propped his head against his hand. "This could be habit-forming."

"Only if we practice." She put her hand on his cheek. The shadow of his beard rasped against her palm.

He caught her finger between his teeth and bit lightly, then sucked on it.

"A lot," she said, her stomach contracting with heat. "We have to practice a whole lot."

"Good idea." He released her finger and leaned over to give her a long, thorough kiss.

Record or not, by the time he lifted his head, Maggie would have wanted him again if she wasn't getting warning twinges from areas that were already tender. With a sigh, she snuggled against his chest. "I never knew it could be like this."

"Neither did I, Maggie," he murmured. He moved his hand to her hip, splaying his fingers possessively.

"Sometimes, when I think about you, I can't understand how I got so lucky." She brushed a kiss over his heart. "You're my best friend, Del. I've never had a man be my best friend before, but you've been there for me from the day Delilah was born."

His fingers tightened on her waist. "I'm glad you still consider me your friend, Maggie."

"Oh, you are. I don't know how I would have survived these past six weeks without you."

"I didn't do that much. You would have managed on your own," he said.

"Maybe. But I don't want to be on my own." She arched backward to look into his face. "Stay with me, Del."

There was a brief silence. "I have been staying with you."

"That's not what I mean. I know that you said you'd be leaving when your work in New York was done, but—"

"Maggie," he said, his tone hollow. "Don't. Please."

She heard the warning in his voice, and it sent fear tiptoeing down her spine. They had just made love. They had been as close as two people could get. And yet even though he wasn't moving, she felt him draw away.

She came up on her knees. Whether he wanted to hear it or not, she wasn't going to let this opportunity pass by. She might lose him, but the bigger the stakes, the bigger the risk. And for a future with Del, she was willing to risk it all. She leaned over, caught his face in her hands and smiled. "I love you, Del."

For an instant, pure joy shone from his eyes. The hard line of his jaw softened and he covered her hands with his. He parted his lips.

In the breathless silence as she waited for his reply, she slowly became aware of the distant, muffled ringing of a cell phone.

Del muttered a curse and pulled her hands away. "I'm sorry, Maggie."

"Del—"

"I'm sorry." He jackknifed upward and left the bed. Moments later there was the clunk of his belt buckle on the floor, a rustle of fabric, and then the sound of Del's voice.

Maggie knelt in the center of the mattress, stunned by how swiftly everything had changed. Part of her wanted to curl up in a ball and pull the sheets over her head and pretend this was all a bad dream.

How could he have done this? How could the tender lover of minutes ago transform into a cold, distant stranger? What kind of phone call could possibly be more important than her declaration of love?

Or maybe it wasn't the phone call at all. Maybe it was what she had said that had sent him running. Of course! she thought desperately. That had to be it. Plenty of men got scared off by the L-word. Because of his broken engagement, Del was even more cautious than most. She should have realized that.

Grabbing her robe, she sprinted barefoot to the living room.

He was already dressed. If it weren't for the missing buttons on his shirt and the wrinkles in his pants, she might have wondered whether she had imagined the whole evening.

"Del, wait," she said.

He rubbed his hand roughly over his face. "Maggie, I have to go."

"I'm not going to betray you."

"What?"

"You can trust me, Del. We've always been honest with each other, and we always will be. I'm not like that other woman."

"What are you talking about?"

"I'm not like Elizabeth, that woman who broke your heart."

"Maggie—"

"I know you've been hurt, and that's why you've been so cautious about what's going on between us, but don't let what happened in the past keep you from taking a chance on our future. I didn't." She moved closer and lifted her hands to his shoulders. "I love you, Del. Please, don't run from that. Stay and give us a chance."

"You don't understand," he said, his tone fast

and harsh. "This isn't about us, it's about business."

"What?"

"I have to get to the office."

"Why?"

"Something urgent just came up. It's my job—"

"Your job?" She gave him a shake. "A job is just a way to make money, it's not your life."

"It is my life, Maggie."

"You're wrong. It can't take the place of a home and children and someone who really loves you."

His eyes snapped with a look of raw pain. "It does for me."

"But, Del—"

He grasped her wrists and pulled her hands away. "I'm not the man you think I am."

"Then tell me who you are. Tell me what you're hiding."

His nostrils flared as he drew in his breath. "I can't, Maggie."

She looked at him in dawning horror. Over the past six weeks, she had convinced herself that she was imagining his secrecy, that her misgivings sprang from her problem with trust. She had done her best to rationalize her doubts away.

But now he hadn't even tried to deny that he was hiding something.

"Why not?" she demanded, feeling her temper rise. She curled her hands into fists, angry at herself as much as at him. "Why the hell not? Doesn't what we just did mean *anything* to you, Del? If you're hiding something, don't you think you owe me the truth?"

For an instant, he wavered. But then he dropped her wrists and turned toward the door. "I'm sorry, Maggie. I can't," he repeated.

All the suspicions, all the gut-clenching fears that she had dammed up in the back of her mind came flooding out. Was he really married? Did he have a double life? Was he doing something illegal?

Oh, God. She had been a fool for the second time. She had been willfully deluding herself. It was Alan all over again. She had managed to recover the last time, but the way she felt about Del, the pain was already ripping her heart in two.

He opened the dead bolt and slid the chain off its slot. Regret hardened the angles of his face. "I never meant to hurt you."

He had said that before, she realized suddenly. Just before they had made love the first time. She hadn't thought anything about it then, but had he been trying to warn her? She had made love, but had it only been sex to him?

She clutched the lapels of her robe together. Despite the modest garment, she felt naked. "Yeah, right," she said, hating the way her voice shook.

"Maggie..."

Reaching past him, she turned the knob and flung the door open. "If you're leaving, then leave. Just go away. That's what you want to do, isn't it?"

He clenched his jaw and stepped into the hall. "I don't want us to part this way, Maggie. I'll come back when—"

"No, Del. Don't come back."

"Maggie—"

"You were right," she said, blinking back her tears as she stood in the doorway. "You're not the man I thought you were." She closed the door.

Chapter 12

Del could see from the number of wet footprints leading up the stairs that at least six agents had recently arrived at the surveillance site. Evidently, SPEAR intelligence had notified all available personnel.

The phone call Del had received had been brief but to the point.

Their quarry had been spotted.

Simon was on his way to the Manhattan apartment.

After months of tedious waiting, Del should have been elated to hear the news. This was what he wanted, wasn't it? He had chafed at his enforced inactivity. He had been eager to end the hunt. There had been nothing more important in his life than the satisfaction of his position in SPEAR. It was what he did, who he was—

It's not your life.

The helpless frustration he'd felt since he'd left Maggie's—no, since she had thrown him out—escalated to rage. Del hit the side of his fist against the stairwell wall.

Damn it, could the timing have been any worse? He had just experienced the most incredible lovemaking of his life, and he'd had to end things with all the finesse of a kid late for curfew.

Maggie deserved better than that. She deserved better than *him.* And judging by the pain on her face when he'd left her, she'd finally come to that conclusion herself.

Del reached the sixth floor and hit the wall again, barely noticing the pain that hummed up his arm.

Someone grabbed his elbow as he stepped into the corridor. "Hey, take it easy."

Del spun around, pressing his forearm across his assailant's windpipe as he slammed him into the wall. A split second later, he recognized the face. Muttering an oath, he dropped his arm.

"Geez, Del." Bill rubbed his throat and regarded him warily. "Save it for the other side."

"Sorry," Del said. "Are you hurt?"

"No. But you could have snapped my neck," Bill said. "What's wrong with you?"

"Nothing," Del said, turning away.

"Like hell." Bill caught his elbow again. "What's going on?"

"Just trying to do my job," Del snapped. "That's what this is all about, after all, right? The job?"

"Then get a hold of yourself. You're no use to us like this."

Del knew his partner was right. He had hoped he could burn off some of his frustration on the way over here. He had to focus on the task at hand. His life and everyone else's could depend on it. He tipped back his head and inhaled through his teeth, searching for the control he was famous for.

Bill lowered his voice. "Is it Maggie?"

What was the point of lying? He was sick of lies. "Yes."

"Did the call come at a bad time?"

"The worst," Del muttered, heading for the apartment.

For once Bill didn't pursue the subject as he fell into step beside him. Obviously, he realized Del was too close to the edge as it was.

As soon as Del stepped through the door to the apartment, he saw that his estimate of the number of agents who had arrived before him was low. He counted three people gathered by the surveillance equipment at the window. Four more clustered in front of the flickering screen of the video monitor, and two were assembling weapons in the kitchen.

Tension crackled through the room. There was no lighthearted banter as there had been this afternoon in the van. This was no lark, no dry run, and the knowledge was reflected in the expression and posture of every agent present. Not only were they wearing their game faces, they were wearing full assault gear.

Del went directly to the equipment shelf and stripped down to his underwear. His fingers faltered briefly as he felt the empty buttonholes on his shirt—the buttons would still be on Maggie's floor. Her laughter when she had ripped off those buttons had been the most erotic sound he had ever heard....

No, he couldn't think about that now. This was the moment he had been waiting for. It demanded no less than one hundred percent of his attention.

Setting his jaw, Del pulled on his black jumpsuit and rubber-soled boots. The black bulletproof body armor came next, then the earphone and throat microphone that would keep him in contact with the rest of the team.

More agents arrived. Del pulled on a black ski mask, picked up his sniper's rifle and moved aside to give them enough space to suit up. Despite the gathering crowd, though, the place was eerily quiet. Only the hiss of clothing sliding on, the click-chunk of weapons being readied and tersely muttered directions broke the silence. Del made his way to the window, lifted his gun's scope to his eye and sighted on the lighted apartment across the courtyard.

He spotted Herbert Hull immediately. The tattooed ex Marine was stationed beside the apartment door, an M16 slung on his shoulder. Hull appeared to be acting as sentry tonight rather than sniper—the 5.56 mm rifle he held was better for stopping power than for long-range accuracy. As Del watched, a pair of men were admitted to the apartment by Hull, bringing the number of subjects there to eleven. And like Hull, they all appeared to be armed.

Del traded his rifle for binoculars. He recognized several faces from the briefings he'd received from intelligence. These were Simon's associates who had recently arrived in town. From the looks of things, they were gathering for a meeting.

The agent who had been monitoring the parabolic microphone pulled off her headphones and channeled the feed from the recording equipment into a speaker. Instantly, the air was filled with the chatter of conversation.

"...how much longer he expects us to wait."

"He'll be here," Hull said.

"I don't like it," another voice said. Del moved the binoculars to see who was talking. A short man lounged against the wall, a cigarette dangling from the corner of his mouth. "I can't see the profit in this plan."

"Then take it up with Simon."

The short man puffed nervously on his cigarette and glanced around him. "Hey, I got no problem with Simon. I just want to know what's in it for me...."

The conversation continued to ramble on. Nothing specific was said. Hull and his friends appeared to be waiting for Simon.

Then again, wasn't everyone? Del thought.

Over the next half hour, Hull continued to admit people to the apartment. The rain gradually tapered off, giving the agents an unobstructed view of the assembled men. The air of expectancy on both sides of the courtyard grew.

Finally, with no warning or fanfare, Simon was there.

The man SPEAR had pursued for almost a year strode confidently into the midst of his associates. He was a tall man in his fifties, still rock-solid judging by the coiled energy in his movements. A full beard, dark brown shot through with gray like his hair, covered the lower half of his face but couldn't hide the scars on his cheeks. From his jawline to his temples, Simon's skin was rippled with the shiny white-and-red mottling of a decades-old burn. His gaze was cold, flat and only half-human—one of his eyes was glass.

There was a low murmur from the agents around Del. Camera shutters clicked and film whirred forward as the surveillance teams made full use of this rare opportunity to record Simon's image.

This was it, Del thought. He felt a tremor of excitement, the controlled, adrenaline rush of the hunter. With hands that were rock steady, he retrieved his rifle and followed the progress of his prey.

It would be a simple matter for Del to kill him. One squeeze of the trigger and he could rid SPEAR of the enemy who had tried to engineer their downfall and had unleashed a year of terrorism. But Del wasn't an assassin. He wouldn't take a life. And he still needed to wait before he could fire the bullet that would put Simon out of commission. For all its power, SPEAR was bound by the laws it upheld.

Still, now that they knew the location of their quarry, SPEAR wasn't prepared to let him slip out of their grasp. One by one, agents left to take up positions around the building and draw the net tighter. It was well after midnight. In this area, few people were on the streets at this hour, but even those who were would have had difficulty spotting the black-clad agents as they melted into the shadows of doorways and alleys.

Apparently oblivious to the activity outside, Simon slowly revealed his plans.

For the most part, he only confirmed what Del and SPEAR had already guessed. Simon had arranged to rent that particular apartment because of its view of the UN headquarters. And the event that interested him was the security council session on world terrorism. Simon was indeed planning an assassination.

But the target, when he revealed it, was a complete surprise.

Simon's disembodied voice floated from the speaker. "He will be making a presentation to the council in two days," he said. "We'll hit him on his approach to the building. He's the head of a top-secret government agency called SPEAR and he's never seen in public. For the past ten years, he's gone by the name of Jonah.''

Bill came over to stand beside Del at the window. His unlit pipe was clamped between his teeth, an M21 semiautomatic cradled in his arm. Instead of one of his classy quotes, he muttered a short, crude oath.

Del echoed it. He'd known Simon was growing bolder with each of his schemes, but this? To go after the head of SPEAR itself? It was brazen and unprecedented. And in an open, public space like the approach to the UN, it just might work. ''Is headquarters patched into this audio?'' Del asked.

The agent monitoring the video camera responded. ''They're getting all the data that we are.''

Simon continued, his voice gaining in volume as he expanded on his plan. ''Hull, you'll be the primary shooter, but the rest of you will be in position around the approach route.''

The short man lit another cigarette from the butt of his last one. ''How much are we going to ask for?''

''Not a cent,'' Simon replied.

There was a brief silence, then a chorus of protests from the men gathered around Simon. He shouted for quiet, then fixed each one of them in turn with a stony glare. "We have shared many profitable ventures in the past," he said. "This time, it isn't business, it's personal."

Another round of protests, less vehement this time. Simon waited until they tapered off before he elaborated. "I want the man called Jonah dead. And I intend to be close enough to watch him take his last breath. That is my goal, and I am willing to give two hundred thousand dollars to whoever fires the fatal shot."

At the promise of a payoff, the discord disappeared. Simon smiled, the scars on his cheeks writhing grotesquely. Then he unrolled a map and began to lay out his plan in more detail.

The woman overseeing the SPEAR listening equipment checked the red light on the backup recorder and smiled grimly. "That's it, Simon. Talk to me," she said. "Lay it all out so we can make the charges stick."

And Simon did lay it all out. Either he was so emboldened by his past successes that he didn't believe he could be under surveillance, or he was too arrogant to care. Over the next seventeen minutes, Simon incriminated himself so thoroughly that even a tag team of Hollywood lawyers wouldn't have been able to mount a defense for him.

Del's earphone crackled with static for an instant before a deep voice came through. "Stand by, Rogers."

Del stiffened. He knew that voice. He'd only heard it on briefing tapes or on rare occasions over the scrambled line, but the steady, authoritative tone was unmistakable. It was Jonah himself.

As a rule, Jonah worked behind the scenes, trusting his agents to do the jobs they were trained for. Still, it was only fitting that he chose to get directly involved now—Simon had baldly stated that his desire to see Jonah dead was personal.

"Yes, sir?" Del said, pressing his throat mike.

"Can you take him alive?"

Moving smoothly despite the sudden increase in his pulse, Del cranked the window open and knelt in front of it. He rested the struts of the rifle's bipod support stand on the windowsill and focused his sights on a point above Simon's left ear. Fired from this range, a bullet would slow down marginally as it passed through the glass of the other apartment's window, but it would still have more than enough velocity to cause a concussion as it creased Simon's scalp. "Yes, sir. I have a shot."

"Assault teams, report," Jonah ordered.

More voices joined the frequency as the agents

who had deployed earlier confirmed they were in position.

"All teams prepare to move in," Jonah said. "Agent Rogers, take your shot."

The endless hours of training took over. Del closed out everything around him. The ongoing drone of Simon's voice over the speaker, the hardness of the floor beneath Del's knees, the cool dampness of the breeze that blew through the open window all faded away as his concentration narrowed to a point no larger than a dime. He knew that Bill was standing beside him, prepared to provide cover, he knew that eleven months of fruitless pursuit hinged on his marksmanship ability, yet that, too, was pushed to the back of his mind.

All that mattered was the job. This was what he did, who he was.

Del squeezed the trigger.

A neat round hole appeared in the glass of the lighted window. A narrow red line furrowed across Simon's temple, and a heartbeat later, he crumpled to the floor.

Pandemonium broke out as Simon's cronies scrambled for cover or raced for the door, but Hull had the presence of mind to douse the lights. When the SPEAR agents burst into the suddenly dark apartment, weapons aimed and ready, it was they who were the easy targets. Hull swung his M16 into position and fired at the first man in. The agent went down with an agonized cry, the body armor he had donned ripped open by what had to be an armor-piercing shell.

From his vantage point across the courtyard, Del watched in horror as what should have been a quick, clean strike turned into a firefight. The darkness of the apartment was broken only by intermittent muzzle flashes, not enough to give him a target. Abandoning his long-range rifle, he rammed an ammunition clip into a Heckler and Koch pistol. With Bill on his heels, he headed for the street.

Maggie licked at a tear that trickled to the corner of her mouth as she put the sheets in the laundry basket. She carried it to the door and set it down beside the garbage bag where she had tossed what was left of the candles.

If she could have afforded it, she would have burned those sheets. If those wineglasses hadn't been the only ones she owned, she would have thrown them against the nearest wall and happily watched them shatter. And if her fancy silk blouse hadn't cost her a week's worth of tips, she would have torn it into a thousand ragged little pieces to match her heart.

She picked up the hem of her T-shirt and wiped her eyes impatiently. Well, what had she expected? A fairy-tale ending? Midnight had come and gone. The ball was over. Time to return to the pumpkin reality of diapers and spit-up stains.

"You've been through worse," she told herself. "You'll get over this, too."

Of course, she would. She still had her health, she still had Delilah. So what if she no longer had her best friend? So what if she wouldn't have a lover who could make her knees melt? Sex was overrated. Chocolate was better. It was always there when you needed it, you enjoyed it at your own pace, you didn't have to worry about awkward mornings after or stilted conversations when the hunger abated. Yes, she would just indulge in a chocolate bar once a day until the craving for Del went away.

First thing in the morning, she would see about ordering a case or two. Or maybe fifty.

Another wave of tears flowed down her cheeks. Maggie sniffed hard and sank down to sit in the rocking chair. It was a good thing she hadn't thrown out her maternity clothes. Once she started on those chocolate bars, her waistline was bound to start expanding again.

On the other hand, considering the record she

and Del had set tonight, she might just need those maternity clothes anyway.

The chances of conceiving while she was still breast-feeding were slim, but the doctor had said it wasn't impossible. Maggie had meant to use birth control. She really had. That's why she had gone to the pharmacy on the corner and bought a box of condoms from the blushing, acne-plagued young clerk. Yet somehow, she hadn't used them.

It hadn't been a premeditated decision. It had just happened. What she and Del had done had seemed so natural, so *right* that she had been willing to take the chance of another pregnancy, because Del would have made such a wonderful father and husband....

"Oh, God," she muttered, putting her face in her hands. "I did it again."

Her dreams had gotten in the way of her brain again. She had wanted so much to believe that Del was the one she could build her future with, she had jumped right in with both feet...and her heart.

So much for her knight in shining armor. She had replayed their final confrontation over and over again in her head, but no matter how she looked at it, the facts remained the same.

Del admitted that he was hiding something.

And whatever it was, it was so serious that he had walked out.

Damn, she really knew how to pick them, didn't she?

Maybe her mother was right to always assume the worst. To hell with trust and taking risks. If she just stopped trying, she was sure not to be disappointed again. Safety wasn't such a bad thing, was it?

There was a cranky sob from the direction of the bedroom, and a heaping dose of guilt piled on top of Maggie's misery. Delilah had been fussy ever since Maggie had brought her home from Armilda's. Like most babies, she had the ability to sense her mother's agitation. So now, because of Maggie's blind infatuation with Del, she was making her child suffer.

As she picked up Delilah from her crib, Maggie's gaze was caught by a flutter of movement. The delicate unicorns that hung from the mobile at the side of the crib danced playfully on the air currents that she had stirred.

Del had bought that mobile three weeks ago. His face had softened with one of his wistful, adorable smiles as he'd fastened it in place and spun the unicorns for Delilah. He'd also bought the pink sleeper Delilah was wearing, and the menagerie of stuffed toys that hung from a ribbon in the corner, and the stroller, and the night-light, and that pair of frivolous, purple-ribbon-trimmed matching sun hats....

Maggie's heart clenched in pain. How could she have been so wrong? Del *wasn't* like Alan. He was sweet and gentle and considerate. Maybe she had been too hasty. If she gave him another chance...

Oh, face facts, she told herself harshly. He'd said all along he wouldn't stay. Whatever other things he had hidden, whatever other lies he had told, that much was the truth.

It was a scene from a nightmare. Men Del had known for years, solid reliable agents who had worked with him on countless occasions, lay wounded and bleeding in the stairwell and the corridor as Simon's criminal accomplices viciously fought their way out of the trap the apartment had become. Del worked his way along the corridor, choosing his targets with levelheaded deliberation despite the confusion around him. He felt a searing pain in his left arm just as Bill shouted a warning. Del pivoted in time to shoot the rifle out of Hull's hands before he could get off another shot. Bill was on the ex Marine in a flash, knocking him out with a karate chop to the side of his neck.

Finally, the tide turned. Black-suited SPEAR agents took control of the area, swarming among the fallen bodies. As the lights came on, Del stepped over the threshold into the apartment he had been watching for months. Simon's men, the ones still conscious, were quickly immobilized with plastic bindings around their wrists and ankles. Medics provided field first aid to the most seriously injured on both sides while the map that Simon had been using to illustrate his plan was carefully bagged for evidence.

"Is the area secure?" Jonah's question came through Del's earpiece.

He pressed his throat mike. "Yes, sir."

"What is the condition of Simon?"

Del tipped his gun toward the ceiling and scanned the crowd, looking for the large, bearded man his bullet had creased.

The place where Simon had fallen was empty.

"No," Del breathed, moving forward.

Tiny chips of glass from the hole in the window sparkled on the floor next to a smear of blood. But there was no body.

"That's impossible," Del muttered, looking around. "He was out cold."

"Rogers?" the voice in his ear barked. "Report."

He walked through the apartment again,

checking faces, turning over bodies, but he didn't find the one he was seeking.

His blood chilled. *No,* he thought. *Not again.* After all this time and effort and endless, soul-deadening waiting, it still wasn't over. He turned to face the window and stared straight into the video camera he knew was focused on the apartment. "He is not here, sir."

"Say again?"

"It appears that Simon has escaped."

There was a stunned silence. Shock, rage and bitter disappointment registered on the faces of the agents around Del. "How the *hell* did that happen?" someone asked, voicing the question that was on everyone's mind.

The answer came almost immediately. A young agent staggered to his feet, a swelling bruise over half his face, a dazed look in his eyes. His black vest and ski mask were missing.

No doubt an infrared analysis of the SPEAR videotape would provide the details of what had happened in the darkness. Right now, though, there was no time for questions or recriminations. Within minutes, a search was organized and the agents who were uninjured left to fan out through the neighborhood. They were betting that Simon couldn't have gotten far—with the headache from the concussion Del's bullet had given him, he would barely be able to walk.

Del tucked his gun into his belt and automatically turned to follow Bill when he was stopped by one of the medics.

"Give me your arm, Rogers."

Del looked down. The sleeve of his black jumpsuit was shiny with wet blood. The iron control he had been keeping over his body and his emotions finally slipped. Only then did he become aware of the throbbing ache in his flesh.

The medic guided him to a chair, slipped a scalpel into the hole in the fabric and calmly sliced off the sleeve. She grasped his arm to turn it over. "It's gone straight through. Doesn't look as if it hit bone." She shook her head and slathered disinfectant on the entrance and exit wounds. "Consider yourself lucky it didn't hit three inches to the right. That vest wouldn't have been any protection against the hot loads they were using."

Del's gaze went to the agent who had been first through the door. He was being lifted onto a stretcher. His face was white, his body limp, his bulletproof armor bearing a hole in the center of his chest.

"Is he going to make it?" Del asked, nodding toward the man on the stretcher.

The medic wrapped a bandage around Del's arm. "It doesn't look good," she said quietly.

It was like the aftermath of the warehouse explosion nearly two months ago. It was like all the operations over all the years. They could plan and prepare all they wanted, but nothing was ever one hundred percent certain. Then, like now, it had been only the luck of the draw that determined who lived and who died.

Was that agent on the stretcher married? Did he have a wife who would mourn for him, a child who would grow up fatherless?

This was why SPEAR agents shouldn't marry. The job was too dangerous. There was no guarantee of a future.

It was the same thing Del had reminded himself of countless times. The logic seemed sound, yet somehow, something was missing.

And suddenly, Del knew what it was. The future wasn't some distant worst-case scenario. It unfolded each and every day. It started *now*.

Del watched as the stretcher was maneuvered through the doorway, and he felt his view of the world shift.

Yes, it would be a tragedy if that man left a grieving family, but wouldn't it be a greater tragedy if he left no one at all? What if his life had been empty, if he'd never had the chance to share his life with the person he loved? What if he'd never known the joy of holding a newborn child in his hands, or hearing the passion-filled laughter of a loving woman?

Life was precious. It shouldn't be wasted.

But that's exactly what Del was doing.

Don't let what happened in the past keep you from taking a chance on our future.

Maggie's words came back to him, whispering through his head like the rain-scented breeze, cool, fresh and full of promise. He had told her she didn't understand, but he'd been wrong. She understood him better than he did himself.

There were no guarantees in life, no matter what a person did for a living. Take Maggie. She had been only a child when she had been gravely injured, but she hadn't given up. Instead, she had taken a chance and embraced life head-on and the hell with the odds. She was so passionate about everything she did. Was it any wonder he had fallen in love with her?

The realization was so easy, it must have been there all along, but he'd been too stubborn to see it. Looking death in the face tonight seemed to have cleared his vision.

He loved her.

But what about the children she wanted? When

she discovered he couldn't give them to her, what then? Would it be Elizabeth all over again?

I'm not going to betray you.... I'm not like that other woman.

Was that true? Would Maggie be willing to accept him as he was? Could he ask that of her?

Considering the mess he'd made of things when he'd left her, he might never get the chance to find out.

"Agent Rogers?"

Del started, returning his gaze to the medic.

"I'm taking you off active duty for forty-eight hours," she said.

"Now wait a minute. You can't—"

"I have the authority, and you know it. You lost a significant amount of blood. Your pressure's down. Once the adrenaline wears off, you're liable to collapse, and that's not going to do anyone any good. You should be in a hospital."

"It's just a flesh wound. It's not that serious."

"Somehow, I figured you would say that." She fashioned a sling out of a triangular bandage and fitted it around his neck. "At least keep this arm motionless. You shouldn't be on your feet, let alone on the street."

Del knew she was right. As he pushed himself out of the chair, he felt a cold tingling in the tips of his fingers. As much as he wanted to join the hunt for Simon, he would have to trust the rest of the team to finish the job.

Yet for the first time in eight years, Del didn't really *want* to finish the job. His job wasn't his life. He didn't want to be on duty or in a hospital or recuperating alone in his hotel room. What he really wanted was to go to Maggie.

The colored lights of patrol cars and emergency vehicles flashed in the courtyard, multiplied by reflecting puddles. As was always the case after a SPEAR operation, the local law enforcement people were running interference with the public and the media. Credit for the raid and the arrests would go to the police to insure the continued anonymity of SPEAR.

Del bypassed the waiting ambulances and returned to the surveillance site. He stopped there just long enough to change into his civilian clothes before he stepped back into the night. He hung onto a lamppost to steady himself against a brief wave of dizziness, then pushed off and headed for the subway.

The lights and sirens faded behind him. So did the past eight years. He wasn't concentrating on his surroundings; he wasn't thinking about his job. His mind wasn't on the hunt, it was already on Maggie and what he would say to her if she gave him the chance.

Would she see him? He wouldn't blame her if she refused, but he would try anyway. After daily dealing with one of the riskiest professions on earth, Del was finally going to risk what really mattered—his heart. He was going to tell Maggie the truth about everything. He only hoped he had half the courage she had.

Chapter 13

It was three o'clock when the key turned in the lock. Maggie dragged her foot along the floor to stop the motion of the rocking chair and twisted her head to look at the door.

She knew who it was. Del was the only person besides herself who had a key.

She seemed doomed to repeat her mistakes, didn't she? A spare key was how Alan had come in uninvited. Giving Del a key had seemed like a good idea at the time—once he had started spending the nights here, it was the only way he wouldn't interrupt her with his comings and go-ings when she was busy with Delilah. She had believed she could trust him with a key. After all, he'd been the one to install the lock in the first place.

Yes, well, she would remedy that as soon as the locksmith opened for business, she decided, watching as the door pushed open only to be stopped by the security chain.

"Maggie?"

The sound of Del's deep, rich voice murmuring her name sent tingles down her spine. She remembered how it had sounded in her candlelit bedroom, how it had felt with his lips against her skin. Had it only been four hours? She pushed the chair into motion, trying to tamp down the traitorous reaction of her body. Think about other things. Chocolate. She must have chocolate somewhere in this apartment. That would take her mind off him, wouldn't it?

"Maggie, please let me in."

Her eyes misted over. He sounded so sincere, so sweet, as if he really cared.

But she couldn't let herself trust him. She was through with trust. She was through with men. She would ignore him until he went away.

"I know you're awake, Maggie," he said, keeping his voice low enough not to disturb her neighbors. "I can hear the rocking chair creaking."

She pressed her feet flat on the floor and pulled her lower lip between her teeth. She didn't want to talk to him. More than that, she didn't want to listen.

But she wasn't the only female in this apartment who recognized the sound of Del's voice. Delilah, who had been dozing fitfully against Maggie's shoulder, lifted her head and let out a happy gurgle.

"Why is Delilah awake?" he asked quickly. "Is she all right? Does she need a doctor?"

Oh, damn. Damn! Just when she thought she might have the willpower to turn him away, he had to bring up Delilah. He might have deceived her about other things, but Maggie knew with a mother's instinct that Del's feelings for Delilah had to be genuine.

She hung onto Delilah as she rocked forward and let her momentum carry her out of the chair. She padded over to the door, her gaze going to the laundry basket that held the sheets she and Del had made love on all evening....

Gritting her teeth, she shoved the basket aside with her foot and stood behind the door. She wouldn't look at him. Hearing him was bad enough. "We're fine, Del. Thank you for your concern. Now go away."

"Not until you hear what I have to say."

"No."

"All I'm asking for is a chance."

"For what? To leave me again? I've been down that road before, Del, and I don't plan to return. I'm not going to wait around and pretend things will change."

"Maggie—"

"No. I may be a slow learner, but I'm not stupid," she said. "Please, just leave."

The chain tightened to its limit as the door panels rattled with a thump. Startled, Maggie took a step back. Del had the strength to force his way inside if he wanted, but she hadn't thought he would go that far.

"I'm not trying to excuse the way I acted," Del said, his voice barely above a whisper. "There's no excuse. I was an idiot."

"Then that makes two of us. Goodbye, Del."

"You said I owed you the truth. That's why I'm here."

"It's too late—"

"Don't say that, Maggie." He paused. In the silence, she could hear him draw in a labored breath. "Ten minutes. That's all I'm asking. Give me ten minutes to explain, and then if you still want me to leave, I'll go."

"Del—"

"Please."

It was only one syllable, yet the small word shook with sincerity. Maggie tipped back her head, struggling for the strength to resist him, but it was no use. With one hand on Delilah's back, she moved forward and looked through the narrow crack the chain allowed.

The moment she caught sight of Del, she gasped. Only four hours had passed since he had left her, but the change in him was frightening. His skin was waxen, his eyes too bright. He was leaning hard on his right shoulder, his body slumped against the door. He hadn't been trying to force the door open, he had fallen against it for support.

"Oh, my God," she breathed. "Del, what on earth happened to you?"

"I'll explain later." He paused. "And I mean it. I really will explain. No more lies, Maggie. I promise."

The left sleeve of his navy windbreaker was empty. She saw an edge of white fabric and realized his arm was supported by a sling. Was that blood on his hand?

Without pausing to think further, she shoved on the door with her shoulder, put enough slack on the chain to unhook it, then swung the door open.

Del swayed on his feet and grasped the door frame with his good hand. "Thank you." His nostrils flared as he straightened up and stepped inside.

"My God, Del. You're the one who needs a doctor," she said, backing up. "Go sit down and I'll call—"

Her breath caught on a startled cry. No sooner had Del crossed the threshold than a figure rushed toward them from the stairwell down the hall.

Disbelief kept Maggie frozen for a critical split second. Being a New Yorker, she had always taken precautions with security. She knew crime happened every day. But a mugger? Here in the corridor? Where she carried her trash to the garbage chute every day and Robbie played superhero? Oh, God, no! "Del!" she cried.

Del spun around, but her warning came too late. A tall, bearded man barreled into him, hitting him square on his injured arm. Maggie felt her stomach roll at the agony that creased Del's face, yet he recovered his balance quickly, placing himself between her and the stranger, whipping his right elbow in an arc toward the stranger's throat. "Maggie, run!" Del ordered. "Get out!"

Get out. It was what she had said to him only moments ago. But she didn't want to leave him.

With one arm in a sling, Del was hopelessly outmatched by this mugger.

But what could she do to help? She clutched Delilah to her chest. She had to protect her baby. She had to do what Del said, she had to leave. She could go to Armilda's. She could call the police from there.

Even as she made the decision, Maggie was bolting for the open door.

The stranger knocked Del to the floor with a vicious kick to the groin. Reaching out his arm, he snagged the back of Maggie's T-shirt as she tried to go past.

The sudden pain in her neck brought her up short. Choking, gasping for breath, she kicked out behind her, trying to break his hold. Her heel connected solidly with his kneecap.

There was a growl of pain, then Maggie felt herself pulled off her feet and flung backward through the air.

She screamed, curling her body to shelter Delilah as she felt herself falling. She hit the floor on her back, knocking the air from her lungs. Her head slammed hard into the corner of the coffee table. Delilah's panicked cries were the last thing she heard as darkness enveloped her.

*   *   *

It was worse than a nightmare. It was a living hell.

Del gritted his teeth against the agony in his arm and the pain in his crotch and rolled to his knees, his gaze riveted on the terrifying tableau in front of him. Maggie was crumpled on her side on the floor, her eyes closed, her breathing shallow. Yet even in her unconsciousness she was sheltering her baby in her arms.

"How touching. It's a regular little love nest you have here."

Using the wall for support, Del slowly pushed to his feet. He lifted his gaze from Maggie and stared into the flat brown eyes of the man he had been hunting for the better part of a year.

He had expected to confront his quarry on a dark street or a booby-trapped warehouse or any number of stakeout scenarios. Simon and his evil belonged in another world, the world of SPEAR.

But not here at Maggie's. Oh, *God,* not here. Seeing this man, this evil genius, in the same room with Maggie and her baby was wrong. It was obscene. It was hell. And he had no one to blame but himself. How could he have let down his guard and allowed this monster to follow him? But he'd be damned if he allowed Maggie and Delilah to pay for his mistake.

Delilah squirmed against her mother's breast,

her cries full of impatience and puzzlement, but not, thank God, bearing any trace of pain.

Del took a step toward them.

Simon pulled a gun from beneath his jacket and pointed it at Del. ''That's far enough, Rogers.''

''So you know who I am.''

''Naturally.'' He pressed the fingertips of his free hand to his temple and turned them outward to display the line of blood. ''You're the one who gave me this bitch of a headache. You're Del Rogers, the only man alive who could have made that shot.''

''I'm sorry I missed,'' Del said.

''You never miss. Jonah always did try to surround himself with the best.''

Del's arm felt as if it were on fire. He could feel fresh blood from the gunshot wound trickle hotly down his arm. He tried to shut it out and concentrate, to think rationally, to put his mind on the job. He needed control.

But damn it, how could he be cool? The bastard had invaded Maggie's apartment. He had hurt the woman Del loved. Del didn't want to line up a surgically perfect shot to knock him out, he wanted to leap across the room and rip Simon's throat out with his bare hands.

"Close the door," Simon said, motioning with the gun barrel.

Del didn't move. "What do you want?"

"I want you to close the door. We don't need any nosy neighbors complicating our business."

"First, let the woman and child go. They've got nothing to do with this."

"On the contrary. They are an important part of my plan."

"Give it up, Simon. We know all about your scheme to assassinate Jonah. We have all of your associates in custody. There's no point—"

"Oh, don't give me the you'll-never-get-away-with-it speech. We both know that I always do. Now go over there and shut the door." When Del still didn't move, Simon swung the gun barrel to point at the center of Maggie's forehead. "It makes no difference to me which one I use. If I shoot the mother, I've still got the baby."

Del trembled with suppressed rage. He was unarmed—he never brought weapons to Maggie's. Because of his wound, his reaction time was slower than normal and he only had the use of one hand. The chances of him reaching Simon and overpowering him before he could pull that trigger were slim to none. So, as much as every nerve in his body was screaming with the need for action, he could do nothing. He reached out and swung the door shut. "If you want a hostage, take me," he said.

"Oh, no. I have another use for you, Agent Rogers." Still keeping his gun trained on Maggie, Simon rounded the couch and sat down. He leaned over and gave Maggie's cheek a brisk slap with his free hand. "Wake up."

Del strained forward. "If you hurt her, I will kill you," he said.

"You never kill anyone," Simon began.

"I will kill you," Del repeated, slowly and distinctly, meaning every word.

Something in his tone must have convinced Simon it was no empty threat. He didn't slap Maggie again. Instead, he shook her shoulder.

Maggie's breathing quickened. Her expression changed from the slackness of unconsciousness into a wince. She blinked twice and gazed around blankly. As full awareness returned, her eyes widened and she clutched Delilah more securely to her chest. The baby's sobs tapered off.

Simon gave her shoulder another shake. "Sit up," he ordered.

Still cradling her daughter protectively in front of her, Maggie braced her back against the bottom of the couch and sat. Then she turned her head and sank her teeth into Simon's hand.

At Simon's shout of pain, Del sprang across

the room, ready to take full advantage of the momentary distraction.

But instead of trying to shake Maggie off, Simon merely moved his gun. The tip of the barrel nestled against Delilah's tiny ear. "Makes no difference to me," he snarled, his gaze on Del. "Tell her. If I shoot the baby, I've still got the mother."

Bile rose in Del's throat in a scalding rush. He stopped where he was. "No!"

Maggie whimpered and pulled her head back. She was breathing fast through her mouth, the color draining from her face. Her gaze darted wildly around the room until it steadied on Del.

Seeing her panic helped him find the strength he needed to tamp down his rising desperation. "Stay calm, Maggie," he said. "And do what he says. It'll be all right."

"Yes, listen to your boyfriend," Simon said.

Maggie gave a strangled sob. "Please, don't hurt my baby," she cried. "Take whatever you want. Just don't—" Her voice broke. "Don't hurt her."

Simon clamped his hand on Maggie's shoulder. The bite mark on his skin was welling with blood, but he didn't appear to notice it. "That's what I want to hear," he said. "You have a smart woman here, Rogers."

"What do you want, Simon?" Del asked.

"I want to finish the job you interrupted," Simon replied. "I want Jonah."

"I don't know where he is."

"No, but you can get him for me."

"I can't—"

"Of course, you can. All you need to do is use the special number on that cell phone you carry. You do still have it, don't you?"

As always, Simon's inside knowledge of SPEAR was as accurate as it was disturbing. The man had been one step ahead of them all along.

"I'm proposing a simple trade," Simon continued. "You give me Jonah, and I'll give you back the woman and child."

"You plan to kill him," Del stated.

Simon lifted one shoulder, keeping his gun trained on Delilah. "If I don't kill Jonah, then I'll kill these two. I have plenty of bullets. It's up to you."

"Del?" Maggie asked, her voice high-pitched with impending hysteria. "What's he talking about? Do you know him?"

"Oh, yes," Simon answered for him. "He knows me. And he also knows I never bluff. Well, Rogers? Make your choice. What will it be? Jonah's life or theirs?"

There was no choice, Del thought. Simon had

no reason to bluff. He also had no reason to keep his word. He would use Maggie and Delilah to get what he wanted, but then he would have no qualms about disposing of them at the earliest opportunity.

He was a conscienceless bastard. He was pure evil. And to keep Maggie alive, Del would have to bargain with him.

"All right," Del said. "Tell me what you want."

Simon's scarred cheeks deepened into a hideous smile. "Excellent. I want you to arrange a meeting. Just Jonah and me. Man to man. Think you can do that?"

"Yes," Del said, not letting any of his doubts show. He couldn't guarantee Jonah's appearance. No one could. "I can do that, but only if you let the woman and child go. I'll take their place as your hostage."

"Don't try my patience. We've already gone over this, and that's not how it works. You stay put. They come with me. I will call here in exactly one hour to tell you where and when the trade will take place. You follow my instructions to the letter, and no tricks, or I won't hesitate to kill these two." Simon moved his hand down to grasp Maggie's arm and stood up from the couch. "Come on, woman. On your feet."

Tears brimmed in Maggie's eyes. She pressed her lips together and shuffled in front of Simon as he guided her forward.

Del felt a damp heat building behind his eyes. Seeing Maggie's strength in the face of Simon's evil, seeing her fierce love for her child, made Del's admiration for her deepen with every panting breath he watched her take. He had never felt more in love...or more helpless.

He wanted to hold her, to love her, to tell her all his secrets and make all the promises he had been hiding inside for so long. He had already wasted so much time. What if it was too late?

But he couldn't afford to let his emotions loose now. If he did, they would all die.

Maggie was dry-eyed as she steered the taxi through the deserted streets. Sometime in the past hour, her tears had stopped. Not because they were used up. Oh, no. The urge to cry was still there, tangled with the urge to scream and the urge to twist in her seat and scratch out the eyes of the man who held her baby.

Yet somehow, she was keeping all that under control. She felt as if a hard, distant mask had come down over her features, the same way she had seen it happen with Del.

I'm not the man you think I am.

What kind of criminal activity was he mixed up in? Was this what he had been hiding? Did the business he'd never wanted to talk about involve dealing with men like this...this monster beside her?

This man was no mugger who had chosen her apartment building at random. This man knew Del. And Del had brought him into her life.

Why? How? Was Del a member of some rival criminal gang? Was he a cop? But if he was on the side of the police, wouldn't he have a badge and a gun? Wouldn't he have been able to *tell* her? And who was this Jonah character?

She wished she had never met Del Rogers. She wished she had never loved him. She had known he would be trouble, but she'd never dreamed in her worst nightmares that it could have led to this. Her safe, ordinary life had suddenly become filled with guns, violence and the threat of death. She should hate him for what was happening.

But she couldn't hate him. She loved him. He had tried to defend her. He had offered himself in her place. He had promised her she would be all right.

But he had been hurt. He had barely been able to stand. She had seen a dark red stain spreading over the sling that held his arm. If only she hadn't kept him standing out in the hall so long...

But if she hadn't let him in, none of this would be happening.

An involuntary sob escaped her throat. She couldn't think about Del now. She couldn't indulge in self-recriminations or questions with no answers. All she could do was survive.

"Pull in over there," the man instructed, pointing toward a darkened pharmacy.

Maggie caught her lower lip between her teeth and did as he said. She didn't question his order. She had seen what he had done to the innocent driver of this cab he had car jacked. The cabby had probably been lured into stopping because he'd seen Maggie and Delilah, but he'd ended up being pistol-whipped and dumped bloody and unconscious in an alley.

This man called Simon was ruthless. He would stop at nothing.

What on earth was his connection to Del?

"Come with me," he said, shifting Delilah to his shoulder.

Maggie had no choice. She went.

The pharmacy was closed, its door locked, but that made no difference to Simon. He smashed the glass with the butt of his gun, opened the door, pushed Maggie inside and strode in after her. As they moved, she scanned the shelves, looking for something, anything, she could use as a weapon. Would hairspray in the face blind him? Would a bottle of cough syrup shatter over his head? If this place had a silent alarm that would bring the police, could she delay him long enough for help to arrive?

But even if she found a weapon, even if the police came, it wouldn't be any use. Not as long as this monster still had her baby. ''What are you looking for?'' she asked. ''Do you need drugs? Is that why—''

''Shut up,'' he muttered. He stopped in front of the headache remedies, grabbed several bottles and stuffed them in the pockets of his jacket before ushering her back to the stolen cab. Then he shook out four aspirin tablets into his palm and tossed them into his mouth. Swallowing them dry, he told Maggie to drive on.

Aspirin? she thought, feeling a bubble of hysteria rise to her lips. He had broken into a pharmacy because he had a *headache?*

Delilah let out a sudden sob, and Maggie caught her breath. Until now, Delilah had been mercifully subdued, too confused and weary to raise much of a fuss at being handled by this strange man. How would he react if she started crying in earnest?

She eased her foot off the gas. "Please, let me take her. I won't go anywhere, I promise, just let me—"

"Keep driving," he said, over Delilah's building sobs. He muttered a curse, then shifted the baby to his other shoulder, bouncing her up and down until her sobs abated.

His matter-of-fact ease with the baby startled Maggie. How could a monster like this know how to calm a fussy infant? Could there be some core of humanity in him, after all? If she could reach it, maybe there was a chance. She glanced sideways. "Thank you."

"What for?"

"For calming down my baby. You must have done that kind of thing before."

He turned to stare at her. "That's right."

His gaze was so cold, so flat and lifeless, it made her shiver. She must be nuts to hope she could reach him, but she had to try. "Uh, do you have children, Mr. Simon?"

"Yes."

All right, she told herself, taking a steadying breath. This was good. It was almost a normal conversation. "A boy or a girl?" she asked, trying to sound casual despite her racing pulse.

He continued to watch her, his gaze unfathomable. "I have a daughter."

Hope, swift and desperate, sparked in her heart. "Then we have something in common. You wouldn't really want to hurt my baby, would you?"

"Why not?" he asked, his tone disinterested.

Her stomach was in knots. The urge to scream was building again. She swallowed hard. "Think of your own daughter."

He merely looked at her, like a snake sizing up its prey.

She persevered. "You're a parent. How would you feel if someone shot—"

He laughed. The sound was so evil, it made her teeth chatter.

"Don't underestimate my determination, Maggie," he said finally. "It is Maggie, isn't it?"

She clenched her jaw and nodded.

"I know precisely how I would feel if someone shot my daughter." He gave her a smile that wasn't quite sane. "You see, I shot her myself."

Terror unlike anything Maggie had felt in her life knifed through her heart.

Oh, Del, she thought. *You promised it would be all right. Please, please, don't let that be another one of your lies.*

Chapter 14

Exactly one hour and twelve seconds after Simon had walked into the night with everything Del loved most in the world, Maggie's phone began to ring.

The room that was usually cluttered with baby paraphernalia—and only a few hours ago had been filled with candlelight and soft music—held grim-faced men and women intent on their duties. A recorder clicked on. The screen of a computer hooked to the phone line glowed in readiness. The SPEAR agent who had been monitoring the equipment at the surveillance site earlier pressed her headphones to her ears and mumbled something into her mike. Bill nodded and pointed his finger at Del.

Del snatched up the receiver before his partner

had a chance to complete the motion. "Rogers," he said.

Simon didn't waste time with small talk. "Can you give me Jonah?" he asked.

"Yes," Del replied. "He's on his way to New York."

Del was still absorbing the fact that his statement wasn't a lie. One working arm or not, he had been prepared to go down to Washington and take apart SPEAR headquarters brick by brick until he found Jonah. He had been willing to do whatever it took to convince the head of SPEAR to play along with Simon in order to prolong Maggie's life. At least for another hour.

Yet Del hadn't needed to do more than repeat Simon's demands. After the cat-and-mouse game of the past year, Jonah was as ready to end this as anyone. The head of SPEAR had agreed to Simon's request for a face-to-face meeting, even knowing full well that Simon planned to kill him.

Logically, Simon couldn't succeed with his planned assassination. His accomplices were in custody. He would be outmanned and outgunned.

But as long as he had Maggie and Delilah, he held the trump card.

The computer screen flashed a map of the Lower East Side. Bill cupped his hand around his mouth and spoke quietly into his cell phone, dispatching agents to the area until the signal from Simon's phone could be pinpointed. He made a gesture to Del to keep talking.

Even without his partner's instruction, Del had no intention of hanging up yet. "Let me talk to your hostage," he said.

"Agreed," Simon said.

There was a muffled clunk as the phone changed hands. "Del?"

At Maggie's voice, Del's eyes prickled with the tears he had kept at bay. She had always sounded so energetic and full of life. He barely recognized the small, terrified voice as hers. "Maggie, are you all right?"

"Yes, yes I'm okay." There was a cranky sob in the background. "So's Delilah. Oh, Del," she said, her voice cracking. "I'm scared."

"Hang in there, Maggie. You're going to be all right," he said, praying it was true. "I won't let anything happen to either of you."

She was silent. Del didn't know whether it was because she didn't believe him or because Simon snatched the phone away before she had the chance to respond.

As the recording equipment whirred and the computer screen flashed, Simon revealed the rest of his demands in a tone that was as hollow as a tomb. The rendezvous was to take place in thirty minutes in a deserted lot beside the East River. Simon would bring his hostages, and Jonah was to come alone, with one exception. Simon wanted Del to be waiting, unarmed, in plain sight, to handle the trade.

As soon as the connection was terminated, the agent monitoring the tracing equipment shook her head. "Simon's using a cellular and he's in motion. I couldn't get a fix on his position."

Bill strode over to grasp Del's shoulder. "Don't meet Simon unarmed, Del," he said. "You can't do what he says."

Del shook off his hand. "I have to. I brought Maggie into this, I'll get her out. We'll put marksmen around the perimeter. We'll station chase boats on the river."

"But you can barely stay on your feet."

"The medic gave me a shot of amphetamines when she rebandaged my arm. That should see me through."

"Del, don't you understand? Simon doesn't need you there to handle the trade for the hostages. He knows you're the one who shot him. He wants you there because he plans to kill you," Bill said bluntly.

Del slipped his arm out of its sling, gritting his

teeth against the stab of pain as he tested his range of movement. "I know, Bill. He plans to kill us all."

The bright yellow paint on the hood of the taxi gleamed like mustard as the cab passed under the last streetlight. The nearby buildings appeared to have been abandoned long ago, their windows boarded up, their crumbling brick walls covered with spray-painted graffiti. Broken chunks of concrete, all that was left of another structure's foundation, lay in lumps across the ground. Maggie slowed as darkness loomed in front of her.

"Keep going," Simon ordered.

Tightening her grip on the wheel, Maggie steered around the obstacles and into the darkness. Through the window, she caught the rotting, metallic tang of dampness. They must be nearing the East River, she thought. Oh, God. What if this madman intended to make her keep on driving until they went in?

Suddenly, a figure appeared in her headlights. Maggie put on the brakes, her heart thumping painfully.

It was Del. Silhouetted against the night, he looked solid and eerily still. His body was rigid, his feet braced apart. His face could have been carved from pale stone as he stared straight at them.

Simon chuckled. ''Excellent,'' he said. He lifted his gun from Delilah's side briefly to gesture toward a point to Del's left. ''Pull up over there.''

For an instant, Maggie didn't move, letting the sight of Del flow over her like a comforting embrace. He was here. He would help her end this nightmare.

But he was the one who had *involved* her in this nightmare....

''Go on. Do it.''

Maggie drove. Ten yards later, the headlights illuminated a low cement wall. Beyond it was the black swath of the river and the glittering lights of Brooklyn. At Simon's direction, she turned the cab until it pointed back the way they had come. As the lights swung around, Del pivoted to face them.

Simon made her get out first. Keeping the bulk of the cab at his back, he positioned Maggie in front of him and handed her Delilah.

The relief that surged through her at having her daughter in her arms once more was short-lived. Simon wasn't letting her go. He was using them both for a shield.

''Where's Jonah?'' Simon shouted.

''He'll be here,'' Del replied.

Simon hooked his arm around Maggie's neck, pressing her back into his chest. "We had a deal, Rogers."

"Yes, we did. You said thirty minutes. It's only been twenty-nine."

Maggie went up on her tiptoes to ease the pressure on her throat. "Please," she said. "Let us go. You'll get what you wanted—"

"Shut up," Simon said. "You don't know what I want."

"Your argument is with this Jonah person. You don't need me or my baby. Just let us—" Her words were cut off when she felt the muzzle of the gun press into the skin beneath her ear.

"Don't hurt her, Simon," Del said. His voice was as cold as the breeze that blew off the river. "I've done what you asked. Jonah is on his way."

"If he isn't, she has thirty seconds to live."

"He'll be here."

"Twenty-five seconds."

"Don't do it, Simon."

"Fine, I won't. I'll start with the kid," Simon said, tipping the gun to point at Delilah.

"Stop!" Del yelled. He stripped off his windbreaker and tossed it behind him. His shirt followed. Bare to the waist apart from the white bandage on his upper arm, he lifted his hands over his head and took a step forward. "If Jonah doesn't come, then shoot me first."

Maggie hadn't thought she could feel more terror than what was already freezing her veins, but she'd been wrong. Seeing Del offer himself to this madman sent her fear to another level altogether. And she had been wrong to think her tears had dried up. They flowed hot and fast down her cheeks. The pounding of her pulse in her ears grew louder until the breeze from the river turned into a whirlwind—

Suddenly, Maggie realized it wasn't only her pulse she heard—it was the quiet, rhythmic throb of an engine. There was a blur of movement from the darkness of the river. The gusts increased until she could barely draw a breath. She turned Delilah to her breast to shelter her and squinted into the wind.

Like a phantom out of science fiction, a large machine lifted silently over the wall. It hovered there in space, all awkward angles and dull black metal while the air swirled wildly around them. It took a second for Maggie to realize what she was seeing. It was a helicopter.

Del widened his stance to hold himself steady against the push of the rotor backwash. The stealth helicopter had come in low and fast, hugging the surface of the river. Its angular design and nonreflective coating made it invisible to radar, while the night made it invisible to the eye. The special shielding on its engines permitted no more than a whisper of sound to escape. It was the perfect craft to serve as transportation for a reclusive legend like Jonah.

If only it would prove to be equally good as a distraction.

Del flicked his gaze to the rooftops on either side of him. Although they'd had to scramble to find good vantage points in the limited time window allowed, SPEAR agents had placed themselves at strategic positions around the perimeter of the meeting site. The plan wasn't fancy. It was simple and straightforward. There was no need to wait to gather more evidence, no need to wait for a signal. At the first opportunity, they were to take Simon out.

But Simon wasn't making it easy. He refused to be distracted. The spectacular arrival of the helicopter hadn't made him lift his gun away from Maggie. Neither had Del's attempt to offer himself as a target.

The pea-size receiver in Del's ear hissed. "No clear shot. I repeat, no clear shot."

Del tongued the microtransmitter that was taped to his lip. "Don't try for perfect. Just do the job."

"The hostage is in the line of fire."

Despite the cold air that whipped over his skin, Del felt sweat trickle down his temple. While the other SPEAR marksmen were exceptionally skilled, their expertise couldn't come close to Del's. He knew that if he had been on one of those rooftops, he would have been able to find a target. All he needed was one square inch, a dime-size chink in Simon's human shield.

But this wasn't just an exercise or another mission. This wasn't just a job. The human shield was *Maggie*. And goddamn it, she was crying! Del could see the sparkle of her tears even from this distance. Yet her grip on her daughter never wavered. Her fingers moved over Delilah's back in a soothing caress to keep her calm. Even when her own life hung in the balance, her first thought was of her baby.

He felt a primitive scream gather in his throat. This one time, when he needed a cool head more than ever, his vision hazed over with rage. He didn't have his rifle. He didn't have the luxury of setup time. All he had was a gut churning with anxiety, hands that were shaking from fatigue and a pistol concealed behind the bandage on his arm.

"Jonah!" Simon shouted. He put his gun beneath Maggie's ear and watched the hovering helicopter. "Show yourself. That was the deal."

Del tongued his transmitter again. He knew Jonah was monitoring everything from behind the shelter of armor plating. Jonah was too important to SPEAR to take unnecessary risks. But Del wasn't thinking about the organization he had dedicated himself to. Simon had made this personal, and Del wasn't thinking with a hunter's impersonal logic, he was thinking with his heart. "Sir? We need more time."

"All teams, stand by," Jonah said levelly. "I'm setting down. No mistakes this time."

"I'm betting my life on it," Del muttered.

"We all are, Rogers," Jonah said.

Like a huge, ungainly hummingbird, the black helicopter tilted to one side, lifted its nose and cleared the cement wall. Seconds later, its long, narrow skids settled lightly to earth less than twenty yards away from the gleaming yellow taxi and the bearded man with the gun.

Barely daring to breathe, Del kept his attention focused on Simon. From the corner of his eye, he saw the blades of the helicopter gradually slow to a sluggish swirl. Nothing was visible through the darkened windshield, but he knew Jonah was there.

Under other circumstances, Del might have

marveled at the fact that at long last, he was in the presence of the reclusive, mysterious head of SPEAR. Yet that wasn't what went through his mind. The man he had sworn loyalty to eight years ago held the power to save Maggie's life. Why the hell didn't he get on with it?

A door in the side of the helicopter slid open a crack.

Del's ears rang with the slamming of his pulse.

"Hurry up, Jonah," Simon called across the distance between them. "I don't have all night."

The crack widened. From within the darkened interior, a light flashed outward, its beam stabbing toward Simon.

"What's that for?" Simon asked, laughing wildly. "You want to see me, Jonah? Then come here and face me, man-to-man."

Barely discernible behind the light, a figure moved into the helicopter's doorway. There was a second of silence, then Jonah's voice came through Del's receiver in a shocked exhalation. "No. It isn't possible."

"Take a good look, Jonah," Simon said. "I want you to know your executioner." He laughed again. Before the sound had finished echoing from the buildings, he took his gun from Maggie's neck and aimed at the shadowy figure in the doorway.

The instant Simon moved the gun away from Maggie, Del saw his opening. He didn't wait for another heartbeat. All the years of training, all the practice and dedication to his craft came together in one concentrated movement. He plunged his right hand beneath his bandage and wrapped his fingers around the grip of his pistol. Gauze tore away as he freed the weapon and swung it toward Simon.

The bullet caught Simon in the right shoulder. He screamed and dropped his gun, staggering backward toward the river.

"Maggie, get down!" Del yelled, sprinting toward her.

Wide-eyed, her cheek spattered with Simon's blood, Maggie used her free hand to claw at the arm around her throat.

Del sighted his weapon on the run and fired again.

This time, the bullet took off the top of Simon's ear. He loosened his hold on Maggie and slapped his palm to the side of his head, the backs of his knees hitting the riverside wall.

Maggie broke free. Gasping, crying, she stumbled blindly toward Del.

He wrapped his arms around her and took her to the ground in a modified tackle. Keeping Delilah safely tucked between them, he rolled her beneath him to shelter them both with his body.

From the surrounding rooftops came the crackle of rifle fire.

Simon fell. His body rolled off the top of the low wall and disappeared. Over the whisper of the helicopter and the hiss of the wind from its slowly rotating blades, there was the distant sound of a splash.

Del risked lifting his head to look around.

"Simon is down." The jubilant shout from one of the marksmen came through Del's earpiece. "We got him, sir!"

But there was no answering joy from the head of SPEAR. The light that had been trained on Simon winked out. The door of the black helicopter slid shut, securing Jonah within. A heavy silence ticked past. "Find his body," Jonah ordered. His voice over the radio was hoarse. "Now."

Powerful outboard motors roared to life. Instantly, the river was lit by the crisscrossing beams of searchlights.

Over the sound of the chase boats and the chatter in his earpiece, Del heard a baby's indignant wail. He straddled Maggie's hips and pushed himself up on his knees.

Maggie was lying on her back, her eyes

squeezed tightly shut, her cheeks streaming with tears as she continued to gasp for breath. Lying across her mother's chest, Delilah was doing the same.

"Rogers, I need you to—"

But Del didn't listen to the rest of Jonah's order. He yanked out his earpiece, peeled off his transmitter and flung them both aside. He tried to pick up Delilah, but Maggie wasn't letting go of her baby again for anyone. So Del sat up and scooped them both into his arms.

"Oh, Maggie," he breathed, settling her on his lap. "Maggie."

The shaking started in her shoulders. It spread to her arms, then her legs, until soon her entire body was trembling violently. She drew in her breath in big, gulping sobs and doubled over to shelter her baby.

Del felt his cheeks grow wet. He'd seen this kind of reaction to trauma before, and he knew what to expect and how to treat it, yet his training seemed irrelevant in the face of Maggie's emotions. This wonderful, generous, positive, good-natured woman, who had faced and overcome the problems in her life with more courage than anyone he had ever known, was falling apart before his eyes.

He had done this to her, he realized. He had

been the cause of this anguish. He had led Simon to her door and into her world. If he really loved her, he would let her go, get out of her life, allow her to find someone else—

No, he thought, tightening his embrace. He wasn't going to use nobility as an excuse. He wasn't going to hide behind his duty as a way to keep from risking his heart. She showed him what courage was all about. He wasn't ever going to let her go.

"I'm sorry, Maggie," Del said, rocking her in his embrace. He didn't even try to check his tears as they fell on her hair. He had come so close to losing her forever, he was through with pretending. "I'm sorry, I'm so sorry."

Sirens whined in the distance, drawing closer. Motorboats continued to roar from the river, their waves lapping noisily against the shore. Jonah's helicopter leaped into the air with a sudden gust from its rotors, carrying the leader of SPEAR into the concealment of the predawn darkness.

Bill jogged toward Del, his rifle slung over his shoulder. "Del!" he called. "Are you all right?"

The amphetamines had worn off several minutes ago. The wound in his arm had opened up again the instant he had taken his gun from the bandage. He had scraped his bare ribs raw when he'd rolled to the ground with Maggie. Yet compared to the soul-deep agony he would have felt if he'd lost her, the discomfort he was feeling was nothing. He nodded and pressed his cheek to Maggie's head.

"The ambulance is on its way." Bill squatted beside them. He touched his fingertips to her shoulder. "Maggie?"

She cried out and flinched away from his touch.

Del blinked against a wave of self-recrimination. She was too emotionally shattered to listen to anyone now. As much as he wanted to come clean about everything, to pledge his love and promise a future, he had to wait. "I'll ride to the hospital with her."

"She'll be okay in time," Bill said. He handed Del the windbreaker he'd discarded during his confrontation with Simon. "She's a strong woman."

Del felt another round of shivering go through Maggie's small frame. Thank God, it wasn't as violent as the last. He draped his coat over her back.

"You did great, partner," Bill said.

"No, I didn't. I failed."

"What do you mean? Those two shots were phenomenal. There isn't another man alive who could have done it."

"I missed," Del said.

"No, you didn't. You wounded Simon twice."

Del brushed a kiss over Maggie's curls and lifted his head. An echo of the deep, primal rage he had felt when he had pulled that trigger still burned in his belly. He stared at the spot where Simon had gone over the wall into the river.

For eight years, Del's record had been unblemished. He had never taken a life in the course of his profession. Tonight, if not for the shaking in his hands, that record would have changed. "Bill," he said quietly. "I wasn't trying to wound him."

Chapter 15

The mind must come equipped with some kind of protective device, Maggie thought, staring at her bedroom ceiling. When things got too much to handle, it simply shut itself down.

She blinked, her eyelids lowering as if in slow motion. The doctors had given her a shot of something to calm her down. When she had first seen them coming at her with the needle, she had practically clawed her way out of the curtained cubicle in the emergency ward. But Del had listened to her hysterical ramblings and had somehow understood her concern. He had made the hospital staff wait until they could contact Maggie's doctor. Only when Dr. Hendricks had assured Maggie the tranquilizer wouldn't hurt De-

lilah through her milk had she permitted them to
proceed.

The drug had caused her to slip in and out of
sleep, but it hadn't been strong enough to erase
the memory of the previous night's terror. Whenever snippets of those hours would flash through
her brain, her pulse would trip into double time
and she wouldn't be able to catch her breath.

But then she would reach out her hand and
touch Delilah, feel her baby's chest rise and fall
while the warmth of the infant's breath puffed
over her wrist, and the terror would slink back
into the darkness.

She felt her eyelids do another one of those
slow motion blinks as she turned her head on the
pillow. Delilah slept peacefully beside her on the
bed. Del had known Maggie wasn't ready to let
her out of her sight, so he had made barriers out
of rolled blankets and placed the baby safely in
the center. Maggie brushed her fingertips over
Delilah's cheek, then looked past her to the man
who hadn't left her side since she had fallen into
his arms.

Del had brought one of her kitchen chairs into
the bedroom. It was small and uncomfortable, but
it was the only one that would fit into the space
between the bed and the wall. He hadn't said
much—he must have known her mind had shut

down. Instead, he simply sat there and watched over her. From time to time he would rest his hand on her chest to feel her breathing, or brush his fingertips over her cheek, as if he wasn't ready to let her out of his sight....

He was acting the same way with her as she was with Delilah, as if he needed to reassure himself that she was all right, that the nightmare was over.

If her mind hadn't shut down, she almost might think Del was acting like a man in love.

Her lips parted in a sigh that bore the hint of a smile as she once more sank into a dreamless, healing sleep.

The next time Maggie awoke, afternoon sunlight was streaming through the bedroom window and Delilah was crying. She pushed herself up on her elbows quickly and looked around the empty bedroom.

Empty. The bedroom was empty. Where was her baby? Where was Del?

Before the budding panic could take hold, Del walked through the doorway with Delilah in his arms. "I'm sorry for taking her," he said. "I didn't mean to frighten you, but I know you need your sleep."

Maggie sat back against the headboard and

rubbed her face, waiting for her heartbeat to slow to normal.

"I've given her a bath and changed her diaper," Del said. The mattress dipped as he sat beside her. "But as you once told me, there are some things I don't have the equipment for."

Maggie lowered her hands and looked at him.

Had he slept at all during the past forty-eight hours? The skin under his eyes looked puffy and bruised, and the lines around his mouth had deepened into furrows. A day's growth of beard darkened his jaw, and the edge of a bandage peeked out from beneath the short sleeve of his polo shirt.

She couldn't remember seeing him look more wonderful. She wanted to wrap him in her arms and pull him down beside her and reassure herself that he was really here—

No, wait. Her gaze returned to the bandage. Someone had said that he'd been shot. That was a *gunshot* wound under there. The fuzzy lethargy that had enveloped her since dawn was gone. In its place, her mind was rapidly filling with memories and emotions and a million unanswered questions.

Delilah let out an impatient squeal and arched toward her mother.

"She's hungry," Del said, handing the baby to Maggie.

She settled Delilah in the crook of her arm and reached for the hem of her T-shirt. Then she stopped and looked at Del.

He met her gaze levelly. "I'd like to stay. Would you mind?"

"Del—"

"I promised you an explanation. We got interrupted before. That was my fault. I brought that horror into your life, and there is no apology I can make that would come close to expressing the regret I feel." He paused, his nostrils flaring as he took a steadying breath. "All I'm asking is a chance to finish what I have to say this time."

Delilah whimpered restlessly and wetly gummed the front of Maggie's shirt. Still, Maggie hesitated.

"I don't blame you for not trusting me, Maggie," Del said. "But I can't leave you now." He stroked the back of Delilah's head with the edge of his knuckles. "I can't leave either one of you. Please, don't ask me to."

Was that moisture in his eyes due to fatigue? she wondered. Vaguely, she remembered how he had sat with her and watched her, and she remembered what she had thought....

Love. She had thought that he might love her.

But wasn't that how all this started? Didn't her dream of having someone to love, of loving Del, lead to this disaster in the first place? Did she want to give him another chance and set herself up to fall flat on her face yet again? Hadn't she been through enough?

As she looked at the weary, disheveled man who had just bathed and changed her baby, another image superimposed itself in her mind. She saw Del standing alone in the center of that dark, rubble-strewn lot, his chest bare, his arms raised, offering to sacrifice himself in her place.

"I'm sorry," he murmured, shifting as if to stand. "After what I dragged you into, I have no right to expect—"

"Stay, Del," she said, brushing his sleeve with her free hand. "I don't feel like waiting any longer to hear your explanations, either."

He eased down on the edge of the bed and turned to the side to give her a small degree of privacy. "I wish there was an easy way to say this. I've spent the past day trying to figure out the best—"

"Just start at the beginning," she said, lifting her shirt and unfastening one side of her nursing bra. She winced as Delilah, out of patience, latched on with a vengeance. "That's usually the easiest."

He braced his elbows on his thighs and dropped his head into his hands. "I guess you know by now that I've been lying to you practically from the day we met."

She winced again, not from Delilah but from the sharp pang in her heart. Lies. Alan had lied. Until yesterday, she hadn't wanted to believe that Del could do the same. Still, knowing was better than not knowing, even if it meant Del was a criminal, right?

"I don't work for an electronics company," he said. "For the past eight years I've been an operative in a top-secret government agency called SPEAR. That stands for Stealth, Perseverance, Endeavor, Attack and Rescue. We are highly classified. Only a handful of top bureaucrats even know we exist. I have been stationed in New York in a cooperative attempt to trap a terrorist who goes by the name of Simon. The diner you worked in was around the corner from the surveillance site we had set up across from the UN...."

As he talked, Maggie imagined she heard pieces of a puzzle click into place in her head. The small inconsistencies, the mysterious calls on that cell phone, his reticence when it came to talking about his business, the flashes of cold purpose that occasionally hardened his expression, everything she had tried to rationalize and ignore suddenly made perfect sense. Reality was shifting, aligning itself in a new pattern.

Because of Alan, she had thought Del's secrecy had to be due to something personal, like a wife or a family somewhere. She had never guessed in her wildest dreams that it could have been due to…to…

''You're a *spy?*'' she asked.

Del shook his head. ''As an agent, my assignments are varied, but my specialty is sharpshooting.''

She lifted Delilah to her shoulder and rubbed her back, her gaze riveted on the enigmatic man who sat beside her. It turned out her very first impression of Del had been more accurate than she could have guessed. Joanne had called him a cowboy, but Maggie had always felt he was more like…a gunslinger.

So now she knew the truth. Del Rogers, the last nice guy in New York, the man who had stolen her heart with his gentle kindness, was actually a secret agent.

Damn, she really knew how to pick them, didn't she?

The bubble of humor took her off guard. After

what they had been through the night before, she hadn't thought she would ever laugh again.

Yet the more Del said, the better she felt. There were reasonable explanations for everything. And Del was trusting her enough to reveal what few people in the country knew.

She finished burping Delilah and switched her to the other side. She might have found the situation downright bizarre—here she was, calmly breast-feeding a baby while she listened to government secrets—but compared to the events of the past twenty-four hours, this was reassuringly ordinary. ''What happened to that man, the one who—'' She swallowed hard. ''Simon. You shot him, right?''

''He was injured. We haven't found his body.''

''Oh, my God. Do you mean he's still out there somewhere?''

''Given his past ability to elude us, I wouldn't rule out that possibility.''

''Could he come back here? Could he—''

''He won't touch you again,'' Del stated, turning his head to look at her. ''I have two agents watching this building around the clock. And I don't intend to leave you alone.''

Her heart did a sudden leap at the intensity of his gaze. He didn't want to leave her. He had offered his life for hers more than once. He had saved her from the grip of that maniac. He must have feelings for her.

"It's my fault that you became involved, Maggie," he said harshly. "If I had been paying more attention to my surroundings when I came over here after the raid, I would have realized I was being followed. I wish I could go back and change what happened. I'm sorry."

"But you had been shot," she said, glancing at his injured arm. "You were in terrible shape."

"That's no excuse."

"Del, it wasn't you who took me hostage, it was Simon."

"I know that."

"And it turned out okay, didn't it? We all survived."

A muscle in his jaw twitched. "Yes."

"So do you feel that you're obligated to stay here and take care of me because you feel guilty?"

"Damn right, I feel guilty," he said. "But that's not why I plan to stay here. That's not why I was coming over to see you last night in the first place. Maggie, I—" He stopped suddenly, his gaze dropping, as if he'd only now become aware that she was still feeding the baby. The pallor of his face slowly became suffused with a flush.

It was too late to cover herself, Maggie thought. Much too late. She had bared more than her breasts to him the last time they had been together on this bed. She had bared her heart. ''Is this embarrassing you?'' she asked.

''Oh, no, Maggie,'' he said. ''How could something so natural embarrass anyone?'' He reached out, his fingertips gliding over the top of Delilah's head to feather along the side of Maggie's breast.

His touch was tentative, almost reverent, yet it moved Maggie far more than anything he had done before. Even though the fingers that caressed her and her baby so tenderly were accustomed to handling lethal weapons, Maggie felt no misgivings. It seemed...right, sharing this moment of connection with the two people she loved.

Oh, yes. She still loved him. Despite everything he had put her through, she had never stopped.

But what about him?

He shifted closer, moving his hand to the front of her breast. He smiled as Delilah grabbed his thumb and held it there. ''You were made to be a mother, Maggie.''

She looked at the contrast of his hand against her pale skin, her baby's tiny fingers gripping his large thumb, and the sense of connection she felt strengthened. She hadn't believed she could experience anything so incredibly intimate. "Delilah's an easy child to love."

"Even when you were giving birth, you told me that you wanted more," he said.

"Yes, I've always dreamed of a large family."

"A family and forever," he said, his smile fading. "That's what you once said."

She nodded, wondering where this was leading.

"There's something else I've been keeping from you, Maggie."

No. God, no, she thought. Could her earlier suspicions have been right? Was he going to tell her he did have a wife and children somewhere? She could accept his profession, but if he asked her to accept *that,* her heart would surely break.

"And you have the right to know," he continued. "I didn't tell you before because I thought the issue would never come up, but I don't want any more secrets between us."

"Please, Del," she said. "Just tell me."

He hesitated, his fingers tensing on her flesh. Then he looked straight into her eyes and started to speak. "I told you that I once was engaged, and that my fiancée broke off the engagement. I told you it was because I couldn't give her what she wanted. What she wanted was children, Maggie.''

''I don't understand.''

''She wanted a big family, just like you, but I had the mumps when I was twenty-one. As a result, I'm sterile. I can't give any woman children.''

He said it quickly, his tone clinical, as if he were merely reciting the facts, yet Maggie saw the anguish on his face, and her eyes heated with tears. ''Oh, Del.''

''That's it, Maggie. Now you know everything,'' he said, his voice rough.

That was all? she thought. This was the last secret he had been keeping? Relief made her smile. ''But that's not important, Del.''

''It is,'' he insisted. ''You were made to be a mother, Maggie. But I can't be a father.''

''What do you mean? Of course, you can be a father.'' She placed her hand over his and pressed it to her breast. ''You've been a father to Delilah from the minute she was born.''

''Delilah's a special child.'' His gaze darkened with regret. ''But don't you see, Maggie? I've been through this before. I can't give you what you want, either. Someday you'll long to give Delilah brothers and sisters, and—''

''Del, for heaven's sake,'' she interrupted. ''Do you think I'm that selfish?''

He started. ''You're the most generous woman I know.''

''Then why do you think I'd be incapable of loving a child I didn't carry and bear myself?''

''I thought—''

''Del,'' she said firmly. ''Families come in all shapes and sizes. The tie that binds them isn't blood, it's love.''

He stared at her for a long, silent moment before the tension gradually left his muscles and his face moved into a smile. He looked nothing like the man who had confronted a terrorist with a bare chest and a handgun. He looked younger, more relaxed, happier….

And Maggie finally let herself believe there might be a happy ending, after all. Her pulse tripping unevenly, she leaned closer. ''Del? Was there anything else you wanted to tell me?''

He grinned. ''Oh, yeah. There is.''

She waited, hardly daring to breathe.

His gaze flicked downward. ''Delilah's fallen asleep.''

Maggie exhaled hard and followed his gaze. He was right. Delilah's lips were slack, her breathing peaceful and even. She had finished nursing and had indeed fallen asleep.

''Here, let me,'' Del whispered. After one last caress for both of them, he slipped his hands under Delilah and stood up to carry her the short distance to her crib. Maggie had just finished straightening her clothing when he returned and took her hand, urging her to her feet. He eased the bedroom door shut behind them and led her to the living room.

At her first sight of the rest of her apartment, Maggie gasped. The place was filled with flowers. There were violets on the windowsill, showy spears of gladioli in the kitchen and potted mums on the table. ''Del? What's going on?''

Del released her hand and picked up a bouquet of daffodils. ''They're all for you, Maggie.''

''But—''

''A long time ago, I wanted to give you flowers,'' he said. ''I didn't because I was afraid to give you the wrong message.''

She took the daffodils he offered. Warmth as sunny as the color of the blooms spread through her body. ''Is there a message in these?''

''No,'' he said. ''They're just flowers. They're supposed to make you happy.''

''They do. I love flowers.''

''I love you.''

"I always thought they were..." She caught herself. "What did you say?"

Del placed his hands on her shoulders and drew her closer. "I love you, Maggie Rice. I only hope someday you can forgive me for everything I've put you through."

"Oh, Del." She turned her head to brush a kiss over his knuckles. "Of course, I forgive you. I love you."

His hands trembled. "Then marry me."

"Marry you?"

"I can't picture my future without you in it. I want to know I'll go to sleep beside you every night and wake up with you every morning. I want to continue being a father to Delilah. I want a home, a house with a white picket fence, the whole nine yards."

"Oh, Del," she breathed.

"As long as you don't think you'll regret not having more babies..."

"If we want more, we'll adopt," she said quickly.

"You could accept that?"

"Of course! There are thousands of kids just waiting for a home."

"Then we'll have as many as you can handle." He took one of her hands from the bouquet she still held and pressed a warm kiss on her palm. "I promise you a family and forever, Maggie. Will you marry me?"

The words made her eyes mist. She blinked hard. "Yes, I'll marry you, Del."

He enclosed her hand with his. "I'm sorry I wasn't able to get a ring yet. I was able to get the flowers delivered, but I wanted to choose your ring myself and I didn't want to leave you here alone—"

"I don't need a ring," she said, breaking into a smile. "All I need is your love."

"You have it, Maggie. Always. To the depth of my heart and the breadth of my soul."

Her smile grew until her cheeks ached with it. "How did I ever get so lucky?"

"It took almost losing my life to realize that I love you. And it took almost losing you to realize how *much* I love you." His grip tightened. The tenderness in his gaze mixed with a flash of steely determination. "Maggie, when I saw that gun at your throat—"

"It's over, Del," she said quickly. "We're fine."

Raw emotion moistened his eyes as he looked at her for another long moment. Then he pulled her against him so hard she had to gasp for breath. "Damn it, I can't wait any longer. I have to hold you, Maggie. I don't ever want to let go."

It could have been a delayed reaction to the danger they had faced, but Maggie didn't really need an explanation for the sudden shaft of need that rocked her. She loved him. He loved her. That was explanation enough. The flowers fell to the floor at her feet as she grasped his face between her hands and pulled his mouth down on hers.

They didn't use the bed. They didn't use the couch. Instead, they made love—and this time, Maggie *knew* it was love—on a carpet of daffodils.

Epilogue

The car topped the hill, and the countryside spread out before them in a wave of shimmering late August color. Blue sky that was too huge and deep to fathom; rolling, close-cropped pastures behind wire fences; a scattering of white-washed farm buildings that waited expectantly, like parents holding out their arms to a wandering child. Maggie blinked to clear her eyes. "It's beautiful, Del," she said. "Just like you said."

Del slowed, then pulled to the side of the gravel road and shut off the engine. Dust from the tires swept past in a giddy swirl. Crickets chirped from the yellow grass in the ditch. "Yeah, it is, isn't it?" he said softly. "I had forgotten."

Maggie took a deep breath of the Missouri air

and sighed with pleasure. The place where Del had grown up was so different from their new house in Connecticut. Yet while the wide open spaces were nice, she still preferred her own home. She liked the scent of freshly mown lawns and carefully tended flower gardens. "It's still not as beautiful as our place, though."

"No argument there, Maggie." He smiled. "The way you're going, you should buy stock in the local wallpaper and paint store."

"You told me you liked the way I'm decorating."

"You're doing wonders with the place." He quirked one eyebrow. "And I have to admit I'm partial to the color of daffodils."

"I'm going to plant a whole flower bed of them in the fall."

"I'll look forward to the spring. Maybe we should make a tradition out of picking a bunch and spreading them around the bedroom." His smile widened. "Unless we leave them where they are and plant a really tall hedge."

She laughed. "I'm happy with my white picket fence, thank you."

"I still can't believe you talked me into putting up that thing. Bill's been razzing me about it for weeks."

"Well, it's perfect for my fairy-tale cottage."

"It'll help keep Delilah corralled, too. She'll start crawling any day now."

"Well, she *is* a genius."

"That's true. Speaking of which..." He glanced into the back seat. After the excitement of airports and plane travel, the ride in the rented car had had a predictably sleep-inducing effect on their young passengers. Placing his finger against his lips, Del winked and reached for the door handle. "Come outside for a minute," he whispered.

"Why?"

He rounded the hood and had her door open by the time she had unfastened her seat belt. He pulled her out of the car and into his arms. "Because I feel like kissing my wife without an audience," he said, nudging the door shut with his foot.

Laughing, she clasped her hands behind his neck and tilted her face. "No argument there, Del."

With only the crickets and the sky to see them, Del wasn't content with merely a peck. He braced his legs and tightened his embrace, kissing her thoroughly.

Maggie gave herself up gladly to the happiness that spread through her. They had been married for almost three months, yet their passion didn't show any signs of dimming. Just when she thought life couldn't get any better, it did.

"You're smiling," Del said, nipping at her lower lip. "What's going through that gorgeous head of yours?"

"Oh, I was just thinking about how lucky I am."

He moved one hand to cup her bottom and lifted her against him. "Funny, I was just thinking about getting lucky myself."

She laughed and tugged his ear. "Behave yourself, Del. What would the children say?"

"I'll give them a dollar each and send them to their rooms," he murmured, nuzzling her neck. "They'll be millionaires by the time they leave for college."

"Good thing you have a steady job."

"Mmm. There are definite advantages to nine to five."

Maggie fervently agreed. Although Del still had that cursed cell phone, he didn't get called anywhere near as often now that he had taken on his new role as a firearms instructor for SPEAR. By teaching his skills to new recruits, he insured there would be others who could be relied on in a crisis.

Still, no matter how well he trained those recruits, no one could come close to matching his special talent. He was the best, she thought with pride. Her gentle but ruthless cowboy knight, who considered life as precious as she did, was truly one of a kind.

He was also a very wealthy man. Maggie hadn't given a thought to money when she'd agreed to marry him, but it had been a pleasant surprise to discover how successfully Del had invested his earnings over the course of his career. Much to Laszlo's disappointment, she had no intention of going back to work at the diner—being a full-time mother to her expanding family was more than enough to fill her days. And her husband always took care of filling her nights....

After another long, toe-tingling kiss, Del leaned against the fender and turned her around in his arms. He settled his chin on her shoulder as they looked over his parents' farm. "See the house on the far left, over by those pine trees?"

Maggie lifted her hand to shade her eyes. "Yes?"

"That's where my sister lives."

That was the house Del had built for Elizabeth, Maggie realized. She waited, wondering what he would say.

"You once told me I should make some new memories to replace the bad ones," he said.

"Yes, I did. Is it working?"

"Maggie, there isn't any room in my heart for bad memories." He caught her hand and laced his fingers tightly with hers. "Your love has filled it to the brim."

Even after all these months, he could still make her cry, she thought, feeling the moisture in her eyes. She could no longer blame it on hormones. She was hopelessly, gloriously in love with her husband. "Del?"

"Yes?"

"I love you."

"And I love you." He splayed his fingers over her midriff, his thumb drawing a lazy arc under her breast. "What time did we tell my parents we would be there?"

"Del, for heaven's sake," she said, laughing. "We're already late."

But she turned and gave him another kiss anyway.

"Hey, are those real cows, Dad?"

At the voice, Maggie broke off the kiss and looked at the car.

Their new six-year-old redheaded son was peering out the window, his freckles dancing with his smile as he stared at the pasture beyond the fence.

Normally, the adoption process would have taken longer, but Del had made full use of his

SPEAR connections to cut through the red tape. The final papers had been signed just last week, and it couldn't have worked out more perfectly. Delilah had a big brother and Robbie was no longer in the foster care system. He had the family he always wanted, and then some. Armilda was still his grandmother, but he now had another set of official grandparents, along with real aunts, uncles and more cousins than he could shake a superhero cape at.

"Yes, Robbie, they're real cows," Del said. "And if I remember right, there's a pony in the barn that you might be able to ride."

"Oh, hey! Cool! Can we go now?"

"Patience, son. A man needs patience to get what he wants."

"But why are we stopping here?"

"Because I wanted to kiss your mother," Del answered.

Robbie rolled his eyes and groaned. "Aw, geez. You're always doing that."

Del turned to Maggie, love and laughter shining in his amber eyes. "Yes, I am. And it's no secret that I intend to keep doing that for a long, long time."

* * * * *

*Next month in
Intimate Moments, look for*

FAMILIAR STRANGER

*by Sharon Sala,
the explosive conclusion to*

A YEAR OF LOVING DANGEROUSLY!

Turn the page for a sneak preview...

Chapter 1

Jonah rolled from his belly to his back and kicked in his sleep, unconsciously sending his covers to the foot of the bed. Even though the second-story window beside his bed was open, there was little breeze stirring. It was unseasonably warm for the Colorado mountains this time of year, but the sweat on his body wasn't from the heat of the night. It was from the hell in his dream. And even in that dream, he still couldn't control his own warning.

A word slipped from between his lips, too faint to be heard, although it hardly mattered. He'd been alone for so many years he wouldn't have known how to share his thoughts if he'd had the chance.

In the space of one breath, the dream jumped

from the distant past to two weeks ago in New York City, bringing with it the same sense of desperation and leaving Jonah writhing in torment.

From the air, New York City appeared as a vast but inanimate object, with only a small cluster of land and trees they called Central Park embedded within the mass of concrete and steel.

He banked the chopper toward the unwinding ribbon that was the East River, and as he did, his heart began to pound. Only a few more minutes and this hell would come to an end.

Below him was a dark blanket of land peppered with thousands and thousands of lights. Almost there. With the desperation in Del Rogers's voice still ringing in his head, all he could think was, no more. Too many innocents have been caught in this crazy man's revenge to bring me down. Please, God, just let Maggie Rice and her baby still be alive. Let us get them out of all this still breathing and kicking.

Unconsciously, Jonah's hands curled into fists as he relived the descent of the black stealth helicopter he was piloting, all the while knowing that Simon was holding a woman and child between himself and destiny.

A faint breeze came through the open windows, blowing across his nude body, but Jonah was too deeply asleep to appreciate the sensation. The muscles in his legs twitched as he relived landing the chopper.

In the landing lights, the fear on Maggie's face was vivid, overwhelming Jonah with a renewed sense of guilt.

The cowardly son of a bitch, using innocent people just to get to me.

The force of wind from the descending helicopter whipped Maggie's hair and clothes and sent a shower of grit and dust into the air around them. He saw her trying to use her body as a shield for the hysterical baby in her arms, but the man holding her hostage gave her a yank, making sure she still stood between him and the guns aimed in his direction.

As the helicopter landed, Jonah could only imagine what was going through Maggie's mind—all this hell, all the danger to her family— and for a man she didn't even know. He slid open a door in the side of the chopper and flashed a bright light in Simon's face.

In that moment, Jonah's mind shut down. Before his senses could wrap around the truth of what he was seeing, Simon's body jerked. He had been shot by Del Rogers.

After that, everything seemed to be happening in slow motion.

Simon taking another bullet.

SPEAR agents firing from surrounding roof-tops.

The play of emotions moving across on Simon's face—a face that was aged with hate as well as passing years, bearing scars both old and new.

The impact of the bullet as the shot tore through Simon's body.

The desperate lunge Simon made toward the East River in a last-ditch effort to escape.

The way the water parted to let him in.

The knot of dismay in Jonah's belly when he realized that Simon was gone.

Jonah woke with a grunt and sat straight up in bed. It had been two weeks, and he still hadn't gotten over the shock of seeing Simon's face.

He shook his head and then massaged the tension in the back of his neck. As he did, the powerful muscles in his shoulders bunched and rolled. The misery of these nightmare-filled nights was getting to him. He needed to go for a run to work it off.

Every motion was deliberate as he dressed—grabbing a pair of shorts and a clean T-shirt from the top drawer of the dresser, then lacing his running shoes and fastening the holster of a small-caliber handgun at the waistband of his shorts.

Five minutes later he paused at the kitchen table, fingering the single page of a letter he'd received less than twenty-four hours ago. Although the room was too dark to read the words again, he didn't need to read them to remember.

I know who you are. Your time has come. I'll be in touch.

Jonah shuddered. Ghosts. He'd never believed in them until now. He dropped the letter and moved onto the deck. Daybreak was less than an hour away, but he didn't need light by which to see. He stretched a couple of times to ease tense muscles, then stepped off the deck and began to walk toward the trees. Within moments, he'd moved to a jog, and by the time he disappeared into the tree line, he was running, only now there were no demons to outrun. He had a face and a name to go with it and only a short time left before the inevitable confrontation. Only God knew how it would end, and in a way, it almost didn't matter.

Almost.

He wanted this over. All of it. Being Jonah. Hiding secrets. Telling lies. Just over. He wasn't the first man to give up his identity for the good of his country and he wouldn't be the last. But he'd given up more than an identity, and that was what dug at him in the wee hours of the mornings when sleep eluded him.

He'd given up Cara.

SILHOUETTE®

LARGE PRINT TITLES FOR JANUARY - JUNE 2006

SPECIAL EDITION™

January:	THE MILLIONAIRE AND THE MUM	Patricia Kay
February:	THE CATTLEMAN AND THE VIRGIN HEIRESS	Jackie Merritt
March:	WHEN BABY WAS BORN	Jodi O'Donnell
April:	THE WEDDING RING PROMISE	Susan Mallery
May:	FROM HOUSE CALLS TO HUSBAND	Christine Flynn
June:	PRINCE CHARMING, MD	Susan Mallery

Desire™

January:	CINDERELLA TWIN	Barbara McMahon
February:	BILLIONAIRE BACHELORS: STONE	Anne Marie Winston
March:	THE OLDER MAN	Barbara McMahon
April:	BILLIONAIRE BACHELORS: GARRETT	Anne Marie Winston
May:	LOVERS' REUNION	Anne Marie Winston
June:	BILLIONAIRE BACHELORS: GRAY	Anne Marie Winston

Sensation™

January:	THE WAY WE WED	Pat Warren
February:	CINDERELLA'S SECRET AGENT	Ingrid Weaver
March:	FAMILIAR STRANGER	Sharon Sala
April:	WIFE ON DEMAND	Alexandra Sellers
May:	ONE SUMMER'S KNIGHT	Kathleen Creighton
June:	IN A HEARTBEAT	Carla Cassidy